Survival G

An Earlyworks Press Fiction Anthology

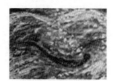

Survival Guides

An Earlyworks Press Fiction Anthology

ISBN 0-9553429-2-9
(ISBN from Jan 07: 978-0-9553429-2-9)

Printed in Latvia by

DARDEDZE HOLOGRĀFIJA

Published by Earlyworks Press
Creative Media Centre
45 Robertson St, Hastings
Sussex, TN34 1HL

www.earlyworkspress.co.uk

Drawing by Nick Richmond © Bella Govan 2006

Editor's Note

Most of these stories are by the winners of the Earlyworks Press Short Story Competition. Siobhan O'Tierney was the £100 first prize winner. I'd like to offer humble thanks to her and to all these writers who submitted such accomplished and fascinating work, and also special thanks to Bella Govan who lent us Nick Richmond's drawing of Mfundo.
Other contributions to the book come from members of the Earlyworks Press online club. Our sincere gratitude to Catherine Edmunds for lending us 'The Diver' for the cover, and to Caroline Davies and Elaine Walker whose works have graced the website from the day we went online, and which now add a touch more magic to an already impressive collection.

Well done everyone – enjoy the book!

Kay Green – August 2006
www.earlyworkspress.co.uk

Contents

Illustrations

Cover and details – *The Diver* by Catherine Edmunds

'Mfundo' drawing by Nick Richmond

My Fantastic Memories

by Siobhan O'Tierney

I wish there'd been more people at Mama's funeral. A few cousins came, my twin brothers and their wives, my sisters, and my father, who was there only because my brothers said they'd kill him otherwise. At least Fr. Casey gave a lovely warm account of Mama's life and how entertaining and generous she could be, and fortunately he never once mentioned Fr Sweeny.

My primary school teacher, Mrs Murtagh, often snapped at me; 'Don't be thinking yourself a big shot on account of your father!'

No fear: 'I've more respect for the slimiest slug in the garden,' Mama used to scream at him, 'You're unworthy to eat my snot!'

But Mrs Murtagh couldn't be told that, so instead I'd imagine Mama's mimicry of her when I got home (providing we'd no visitors). Mama would cross her eyes to exaggerate Mrs. Murtagh's squint and repeat everything I told her in the same hateful voice as my teacher, only sounding like her mouth was full of feathers too and I'd laugh until it hurt. Then Mama would say, 'Ignore her, Deedy, she's just jealous of you, pet of the house. Get used to it. I'm talking from experience. Any daughter of mine is too clever and beautiful for them all.'

I never understood how my siblings could go upstairs straight from school without seeing Mama first. I was also glad - if we'd no visiting cousins then I had Mama to myself. When she had time for me I didn't care about anything else. I was Mama's favourite, the only one who ever listened to her and understood all her suffering. I'd make tea and listen to

9

stories of all the terrible things that had happened to her, while Mama talked and smoked and swallowed a few Librium.

Tony and Stef, my twin brothers, used to play Monopoly obsessively. Sometimes they allowed Ciara and Nina to join in, and I'd beg to join too.

'Scram! You'd ruin the game! You can't even play properly!'

Nina used to promise to teach me the rules when I was older but eventually I stopped believing her. No matter how many birthdays passed I was always the baby who'd never catch up. Ciara was always pinching me, and Tony and Stef ignored me totally. Nina was friendly only when she wanted my help with zips and buttons – she loved dressing up and singing to Marlene Dietrich records. She hoarded all Mama's old clothes and cast-offs from Mama's glamorous cousins. Aged 17, Nina eloped with her French teacher, a married man aged 47. Mama swore she'd never speak to Nina again, and she didn't. None of us saw Nina for another 22 years.

I'm lately discovering how she spent all those years. After three months with Monsieur Cardin on a smallholding in Orkney she left him to travel the world, before eventually settling in Paris, where she claims to have made a living as 'Marlene Dietrich'. Nina is full of surprises. The first we knew of Lily was when she flew back for the funeral. Nina claims to have no idea who her daughter's father is, despite Lily's oriental features. 'Surely the eyes give you *some* clue?' Tony asked. Nina shrugged, 'Not really', like she still hadn't enough of shocking us all.

'I can live here now,' Nina announced after Mama's funeral. She talks about getting her own place but I pray it never happens. I couldn't bear being alone in the house with Papa. I don't want Lily to leave either. I love her curiosity and tell her everything I know about whatever she asks. Lily is neat as a ballerina, with bright blue eyes that are stunning against her gilded skin and jet-black hair. I mind her while Nina sleeps; a week after moving back here she landed the job hosting 'Midnight Moods' on CosmicRadio, 11 pm to 2 am. 5 nights a week

Tony and Stef also left home at 17. 'All I've done for ye! I've given up my whole life for ye! This is the thanks I get! As if I haven't suffered enough already!' I hated them for leaving when they could see how it broke Mama's heart. I also envied them. They moved to a squat in Drumcondra and eventually married the Coyne twins, Mel and Lisa, whose father owned the biggest car-dealership in Dublin. That's how Tony and Stef got into the business, and made it even bigger.

'Guiseppe Mezzetti was highly intelligent, and so were my brothers and myself. All of you got your brains from the Mezzetti's, not that bastard your father Gerry Yates,' Mama told us often. She planned great futures for her children but I'm the only one who went to University. In 1991 I graduated with a first in Law, and then wrote countless letters of application.

'Never mind Deedy. Shur everyone knows that solicitors are trumped up two-faced liars that'd stab you in the back quick as they'd look at you. You're too good for the whole feckin lot of them. If they can't appreciate you, then they don't deserve you!'

Actually, I got one reply from a firm in Kilmacduff, right on the other side of the country. 'I'd die of the loneliness for you Deedy. Don't leave me. You're all I've left. Who'd write my letters if you walked out on me?'

Mama often got cards form cousins, thanking her for her fantastic hospitality. She dictated her replies to me, because, although she was so highly intelligent and wrote her name so beautifully, Mama couldn't write anything else;

11

'Those bitches of nuns tormented me for being left handed so much that I never learned a thing from them. God blast them all. Easy for you with all your education - you'll never suffer the agony of being highly intelligent and totally illiterate. T'would break my heart if anyone ever found out, Deedy. The shame would kill me. Never tell a soul, promise me you won't.' I always shook my head fervently.

One day Mama said, 'Shur, when you think about it, Deedy, Law's only for eejits. You'd be far better off doing a degree in Science, that's where the real brains go.'

Rebellion flickered inside me and promptly died. I was in no hurry to join the Big Bad World. Mama had me so thoroughly convinced of my future in Law, it never occurred to me to consider anything else until she changed her mind.

'Papa won't pay for me,' I objected feebly.

'That bastard *will* pay! Serve him right!'

So I did a B.Sc, and then a H.Dip in Ed. I even got a teaching post, but every evening came home so exhausted I just wanted my bed. After six weeks Mama declared, 'Teaching's only for eejits. Shur your brain's far too big for you to have to be putting up with amadans all day long, Deedy. Insulting your intelligence! You should do an M.Sc.' So I did. I'm still out of work.

Nina's memory is faulty. It must be. Sometimes I think she's winding me up, lying for the fun of it. But I don't argue when she 'recalls' something totally opposite to what I know for a fact. Mama used to say Nina was Papa's favourite; he worshipped the ground she walked on. If anything, I felt sorry for Nina whenever Mama said this, because it meant food had to be taken up to Papa, usually with a request for money. Nina tells me now that she never minded: 'Papa always gave me whatever Mama wanted, and something extra for myself. How d'ye think I saved up enough to elope?'

12

'He's OK really, you know,' she keeps telling me. But Nina's brave, always has been. I've never been comfortable near Papa. I cannot look at him and dread having to take his trays up or collect them. He's too thin and his bony face is always flaky with eczema and wrinkled with anger. His tapping has always filled the house, day and night - even two floors below in our kitchen there's no escaping it. Naked women in contorted postures are Papa's specialty, and his sculptures are in demand all over Europe and America.

Mama was beautiful, she had dark, clear, shining eyes, skin like golden silk, and magnificent black hair which I brushed a hundred times every night before plaiting it. Yet Papa couldn't bear the sight of her. Whenever they happened to meet accidentally on the stairs or somewhere this hatred erupted.

'Frigid bitch!'

'You're an animal! Nothing but an animal!'

'Christ but you were glad to have me once!'

And so on.

Long after I could read, I used to beg Mama to read to me because she made every book so much more exciting. Now I know why; what she couldn't read she improvised gloriously, while I snuggled against her great warmth and softness. My siblings never got snuggled or read to so I always felt blessed for being the last-born.

'Calm down?! What the hell do you mean! Three years after marrying you, you had me tied down with four children! All you ever wanted from me was sex! A bull would have more morals than you, you bastard!'

But according to Nina, our Grandmother did *everything* for my sisters and the twins when they were small, while Mama lazed in bed nursing her 'headaches'. Nina claims her earliest memory is of being in the local park, sitting on a swing until her bottom felt like ice, or walking round the block, her holding one side of an extra-wide pram and Ciara the other, both of them whining to be taken home, while Grandmother coaxed, 'Five more minutes, Darlings. Mama is still sleeping'.

'I was never good enough for her! Never! The jealous barren bitch! She criticized everything I did! How I dressed, how I spoke, how I swept the floor, how I cooked. That ugly bitch with a face like a priest's housekeeper! You should've seen, Deedy, how she used to sneer at me! You know, Deedy, how I make my spaghetti bolognaise, the care I put into it, nothing but the finest of ingredients, isn't that right, Deedy? Could you get finer spaghetti bolognaise anywhere in Ireland! God love me, the time I was so innocent, I gave her some. That jealous bitch spat it out! That God may strike her dead.'

Fr Sweeny was 6' 4 and completely bald, but he smiled easily and always told us *Knock Knock* jokes when he visited. Nina used tell him they were dire but at school the next day she'd repeat them and make everyone laugh. 'Shur he's an out an'out saint, Father Sweeny is, and what's more, Deedy, he's the height of integrity.' Because of him, Mama got involved with fund-raising auctions, which helped make our parish noted as the most generous in Ireland for donations to the Missions. Mama could entertain and cajole a whole hall full of people into bidding far higher than they intended, and was often urged to become a professional auctioneer. 'Shur where'd I find the time? Amn't I worn out rearing my children and looking after my husband?'

Later she'd tell me, 'I only do this for Father Sweeny. But whatever I do for that man, it'll never be enough. Father Sweeny's a saint.' After a huge sigh she'd add; 'Shur, if it wasn't for Father Sweeny my life wouldn't be worth living.'

14

One day I asked how he made her life worth living, and regretted it.

'After the twins I thought another pregnancy would kill me, Deedy. Any man with half a heart would have left me alone but not that bastard your father. I moved to your bedroom and for three years locked the door every night. But then your father went and told the old parish priest, Father Donnelly, that I was denying him his *marital rights*. God help me but I was worn out from being raped every night. That's what it was. Out an' out rape. *You cannot deny your husband his marital rights, Mrs. Yates.* That bastard, Father Donnelly, had the gall to tell me! Marital rights! But your father promised me he'd pull out in time, Deedy, he promised! When I discovered I was expecting you, I swore to God I'd never allow him to touch me again, no matter what feckin priest came to see me. Meantime Father Donnelly retired and we got Father Sweeny and God bless him, but didn't he give Gerry Yates the bum's rush when he went whinging about his feckin marital rights!'

So I can thank Fr Donnelly for my conception.

Nina doesn't know the latest about Fr Sweeny and I'm not telling her. Once I drank ink for a dare at school, and that's the vile taste I get in my throat when I think about him now.

After school, my siblings always went straight to their bedrooms but I'd run to the kitchen to check Mama was OK, because Papa often tried to kill her. Some days Mama's hands would be shaking so much she could hardly hold a cigarette. One time Papa posted her a letter bomb but right away Mama smelt it was dodgy and phoned the Gardai. A bomb disposal expert came, and he was hugely impressed with Mama, because a) she had the best sense of smell he'd ever encountered in all his career, b) she had so much integrity that she agreed to keep the incident top secret. Any other wife

15

would press charges against their husband after such a package, but not Mama. Of course, the bomb disposal expert didn't actually say all that but Mama knew from how he shook her hand as he was leaving that he appreciated the integrity of the woman he was dealing with.

Another time, Mama was driving a cousin into town when an oncoming car ploughed into her. If Mama hadn't been so quick, she and her cousin would have been killed outright! Mama wouldn't waste her breath telling anyone, because nobody on this earth could be up to that bastard, Gerry Yates, so who'd believe her? But she knew by the shifty look of the other driver that he was an out an' out gurrier - precisely the type of tinker that bastard Gerry Yates would hire to kill his wife. She and her cousin spent the afternoon in hospital, and the Doctors couldn't believe how dignified and witty Mama was. 'We expect somebody to be in shock after an accident like that, Mrs. Yates, but you're entertaining us all here!' the senior consultant said, and Mama knew just by looking at him that he was the height of integrity and good breeding.

Nina, surprise, surprise, has another version entirely; Mama was putting on lipstick and checking herself in the mirror when she careened into the oncoming driver, whose speedy foot work saved three lives. Or so Mama's cousin allegedly told Nina years ago, when they met accidentally in a café in Rome. Nina lies.

I've been racking my brains trying to remember all the ways Papa tried to kill Mama. There were dozens - I should remember more. It's not like the effect on my life was insignificant. One time he removed the distributor cap from the car and a mechanic told Mama it was a miracle the car hadn't burst into flames when she turned on the ignition. But God was always on Mama's side. Another time, Papa tried to

16

electrocute her by turning the power back on while she was changing a fuse. And the time she was expecting me, she fell asleep at the kitchen table one evening, and woke up hours later to a terrible smell. The gas oven was turned on full but unlit.

'If you ever find me dead, Deedy, make sure that bastard your father is nailed for it. If you let him get away with it, I'll haunt you, I swear to God I will. He wants me dead and won't rest 'til he succeeds but God help me, not a soul in the world believes me except Father Sweeny, God bless him.'

I've never told anybody any of this, not even Jake. He was a Vet student when I started the B.Sc. and we did the same biology course in first year. One morning, putting my bike into the racks, I realised I had a puncture. Jake happened to be locking his bike in the next rack, and noticing my irritation offered, 'Want help fixing it?' His voice was like a cat purring, and I gratefully said OK. That's how it started. Jake would have been very handsome - I mean - he is very handsome. Sandy-haired, with wonderful cheekbones and lips and teeth – but he has a terrible squint. Remembering Mama's imitations of my old teacher, I knew I could never bring him home. Once in my life, I invited a friend home - afterwards Mama made so much fun of her teeth I could never look at my friend again without guilt.

My brain feels like it's splintering into smithereens. If Nina isn't lying then everything I know is bogus. She rubbishes all my memories as fantasy. She says that all my life, all my thoughts have been preceded, shadowed, or echoed by Mama's. She might be right. It's possible that in a lifetime of thinking, every single thought I've ever had is coupled to Mama's thoughts, a double helix of thinking. But the double helix is sundering and it feels like axe blows to my head. I can't even tell a story straight. Lucky I don't drink - if I started

17

I mightn't stop. Mama's worst ever binge started the day Father Sweeny was finally found guilty of sexually abusing eight altar boys over 14 years.

Nina usually cooked our dinner. But on the days when Mama wasn't worn out from rearing us all I'd come home from school and find her busy making her wonderful Spaghetti Bolognaise. This caused yet another argument with Nina recently. She insists Mama only ever made her Spaghetti Bolognaise once, on the twins tenth birthday. 'Sure it was delicious. But it was a one-off.' According to Nina, everything I recall as regular childhood events happened only once, twice at the very most. 'You're trapped in Mama's parallel universe, Deedy. Everything is a grossly exaggerated or distorted version of reality. Get over it.'

I'd love to know Ciara's memories. She always wanted to be a nun and had pictures of saints all over her bedroom. Mama hated her piety, 'God forbid a daughter of mine would ever be a nun! Nuns are bitches! What good are they! Feckall. Don't be such an eejit, Ciara, for God's sake. Look at you! You can get any man you want!'

My most vivid memory of Ciara happened when I was 12. One morning at assembly the Head Sister announced to the whole school that I'd come first in a poetry competition and everyone clapped. Afterwards, Ciara shoved into me in the corridor, smiling lethally, 'Deedy. *Poetesssss.* I'm jealous.'

I watched her retreating figure in dismay. Don't be! I wanted to cry after her, please Ciara, *you* cannot be jealous of *me!* You have Mama's looks! You can get any man you want!

It broke Mama's heart when Ciara moved to Texas straight after secondary school to work with a pro-life charity. Aged 20, she dedicated herself to God's will in a bizarre way. One morning back in 1995, Mama was listening to the radio

18

and just happened to catch Ciara on a trans-Atlantic phone interview, talking like surrogacy was next to sainthood. Afterwards, after she finally calmed down, Mama swore she'd never speak to Ciara again, and she didn't.

Ciara missed Mama's funeral Mass but turned up at the graveside. Back at the house afterwards she spoke to everyone cordially, even me, although sweat prickled my palms as I offered her a plate of sandwiches. I was ludicrously embarrassed. Ciara sat in the corner of the living room, radiantly beautiful, smiling at anyone who passed but not enough to encourage conversation. Even Tony and Stef were embarrassed. I'd never, ever seen a bigger bump, and she had over two months left. We had to walk around it, almost.

Tony was so shaken he actually called me to talk about it, the night he spent trying to trace Ciara to tell her the news about Mama, and found her website. On www.perfectbabies.org. Ciara describes herself as daughter of a celebrated sculptor, having an IQ of 179 and impeccable morals. She 'gifts' babies to Catholic couples experiencing fertility problems, after extensive vetting. The site included photos of Ciara in white lacy gowns, dreamily handing over white robed babies to ecstatically smiling white couples.

That afternoon, Ciara was expecting her eighth baby but nobody mentioned it. Not Nina, not even Ciara herself. How many heavily pregnant women could sit at the corner of a gathering, blithe as a queen bee, impervious to how her bump is freaking everyone so much they can't even mention it. After an hour or so a black giantess rang the doorbell, asking for Ciara.

'Oh, that's Lucretia, my personal assistant.' Ciara smiled, 'We fly back to Dallas tomorrow.' I couldn't believe they let her on a plane. Seeing her out, Stef, Tony, Nina and I thanked her for coming at such short notice, with the weather being so bad *and everything*. All we managed at the front gates was, 'All the best and….and….and… keep in touch!' I knew it was unlikely we'd ever see her again.

'Shur she's an out an'out gold digger! She hates babies! From the moment her brothers were born you could see in the big black eyes of her how she hated them. And she loathed you, Deedy. God forgive me, I thought, but that child will bring me grief. Even then, I saw it, Deedy. I swear to God. Don't tell me she isn't doing this for money! What kind of mother gives up her newborn baby? Christ Almighty! If anybody had tried taking one of you away from me when you were born! I'd have slashed their throats! Honest to God I would, Deedy! Her own flesh and blood! I've never been so mortified. How can I face Father Sweeny? As if I haven't already suffered enough, God help me!'

All that day, after hearing Ciara's interview, Mama seethed and drank and vowed, 'I'll never speak to her again, Deedy. Never. If she came to the hall door I wouldn't bid her the time of day. She's as callous as that bastard her father before her. Mark my words, she'll never hear my voice again!'

Nina cannot have forgotten Mama's kindness. She surely remembers my eighth birthday. Mama took Nina and me to the summer sales. After searching every department in Clerys, she found dresses for Ciara, Nina and me, sandals for herself and jeans for the twins. My dress was pale pink with a skirt that rose right up when I spun round. When I tried it on in the changing room, Mama agreed to buy it and I begged to keep it on, but she said no, save it for later. Next, in the supermarket, Mama bought every treat I asked for, and lastly we went to a really posh bakery in a side street for lunch, and so I could choose my birthday cake.

Back outside, we'd so much shopping that Mama suggested we get a taxi home, something unheard of. At that

20

very moment a tinker appeared across the street, screaming at her toddler.

Mama's eyes fixed on the tinker. 'Come on, Mama. Let's go,' I pleaded. Nina was urging her too but as I started praying frantically, Mama shouted; 'Leave the child alone! You bully! You don't deserve children if that's how you treat them!'

Abruptly, the tinker stopped and lifted her gaze from her child to Mama.

'Feck off! You bleeding nosey parker! All right for you with all your shopping and your cornflakes and milk and bread and bananas and fig rolls and -'

Her eyes searched our shopping as she screamed at us, her child forgotten, Mama the target of her fury. Mama stood still, stonewalling our pleas to move on. Nina kept pushing her but Mama was big and solid as a pillar. As the tinker kept screaming, Mama kept watching her. Tears burned my eyes. I'd seen Mama lay into people who disrespected her integrity. It was terrifying. But nobody had ever bawled this much at her. My heart was pounding.

'Yous fecken bastards think yous can tell the likes of me what to do! What the hell do any of yous feckers feckin know? Feckall, that's what. What do you know about feckin hunger! What do you know about feckin cold! What do you know about being feckin battered to shite!..........'

The street was empty except for us. I prayed for a Garda, someone, anyone to appear and tell the tinker this was no way to talk to a lady. After an eternity the tinker paused for breath. In that instant Mama spoke, gently as gossamer, 'I'm sorry. You're right. I'd no right to speak to you like that.'

'Wha'?' The tinker was thrown.

'Shur you might as well have all this. There's plenty of food and clothes here. Do you have any other children? Shur we don't need all this at all at all. Do we Deedy? Nina?'

21

Both of us were speechless, and our answers didn't matter anyway. The tinker crossed the road towards us, the child plucked off the ground and covered with a blanket against her chest.

'Put the bags down,' Mama whispered. Bewildered, I did as bidden but Nina had to be told again, sharply.

'I hope that's some help to you in your hardship. May the grace of God be with you always. And here - ' Mama emptied her purse into the tinkers outstretched hand. 'Do you need help to carry it?'

Shaking her head, the tinker nodded towards several older children who had appeared out of nowhere. 'They'll help'.

'Sure now?' Mama was retreating from all our shopping, pulling Nina and me with her. My dress! I wanted to scream, it's my birthday present! Can't I just get my dress out of the bag, please, Mama, *please, please, please*, I'm begging you, let me have my dress! And my birthday cake! But the words glued in my throat as I was pulled down the street. Don't cry. Not in front of Nina, don't cry, don't cry. I kept wiping my sleeve over my face.

'You're nuts,' Nina hissed as we turned the corner. 'What use has a tinker for posh clothes?'

I also wanted to ask that but would never dare. Or maybe I just knew there was no point.

'What do you mean, speaking to me like that? How dare you? Have you ever gone without food in all your life? Or clothes? Ever?! Tell me that? Smartypants! 'Tis fine for you that's never known hunger or cold.' Mama's rising exasperation startled an old couple across the road. 'Pity about you! You with more clothes than the Queen of Sheba!'

At home Nina would have answered back but now she just glowered. Mama drew in a ragged breath. 'Anyway. I've no money left. We'll have to walk home. If it isn't too much

22

hardship for your Ladyship.' She glared at Nina, and then all at once she beamed, 'Shur 'tis only a few miles, and won't the walk do us good on a grand evening like this when all the flowers are blooming and all the birds are singing and we've nothing to weigh us down?'

On the long walk home Mama told us stories until even Nina laughed. Mama told us nothing was more important to her than her sons and daughters and we were the finest, wisest children in the whole wide world. She told us again the story about how Jesus once came down from heaven and told everyone in the world to put all their troubles into one basket. Afterwards, he invited people to step forward and choose someone else's troubles. But everyone snatched their own back. 'For all my suffering with that bastard your father, I wouldn't swap my life with anybody, not for the world, because I'd never change my children. Never! You're everything to me.'

Nina laughed when I reminded her of that story, 'And the only thing that made Mama bearable was the unlikely chance some other poor kid might have an even worse mother.'

When her cousins visited, Mama used to be so busy entertaining them I could have vanished without a trace and she wouldn't have noticed. Loneliness used to really get to me then. I had no friends on our street either. It wasn't that kind of street. I never saw neighbouring children except en route to their private schools. We went to Scoil Nasunta na Gaeilge, the all-Irish school in the city centre, because Papa spoke fluent Irish and wanted his children to be fluent also, which mystified me - he didn't speak to us in any language. On our long, wide, leafy avenue every other house has immaculately tended gardens. A renowned actor lived on our left, on our right the owner of a distillery. In the summer they often had garden parties and I'd watch the guests nibbling, sipping, murmuring and laughing till the sun sank low in the sky. Nobody from our house was ever invited. Just as well, because Mama hated them. 'When I first lived here, Deedy, the loneliness killed me. What I'd have given for a smile from one of them! But all that feckin trumped-up shower of snobs can do is look through you. Not a scrap of integrity between them all. I nearly died from loneliness when I was expecting Nina and cooped up in this house all day long, with nobody but that jealous bitch for company. She thought she'd found a skivvy in me. Which she had of course until I grew wise to her.'

Mama adored her father. 'Guiseppe Mezzetti was the height of integrity. An absolute gentleman. Through no fault of his own he had to flee his country without a penny to his name, God help him. Still and all, by the end of his life he owned his own chip shop.' After finishing school Mama worked in the chip shop, which was where Papa went every night when he was an art student.

    'Oh Deedy, the greatest regret of my life is my children will never know the beautiful person I was before I had them. There was nobody nicer or kinder in the whole world than me. I was the most innocent angel you could imagine before your father married me. That bastard changed me! And that jealous barren bitch of a mother of his!'

None of us were allowed in the back garden, which belonged to the Bitch in the Basement. I used to watch her strolling up and down the long overgrown path throwing sticks for her Irish setter. I was eight years old before I discovered the Bitch in the Basement was my Grandmother. Stef told me so one day, incredulous that I hadn't realised it. 'Cretin! Didn't you know that! She's Papa's mother! She used to live up here with us, but Mama kept fighting with her.'

24

My siblings knew everything, and what they didn't know they could suss out. I only knew what Mama told me, and couldn't suss anything on my own. Despite being surrounded by evidence contrary to almost everything she told me, I was too much in Mama's thrall to ever doubt her. 'That bastard tricked me into marriage. Oh Deedy! I could've had any man I wanted! Todd Lannigan was mad after me, you know.' He and Mama went to school together and he always carried her books. Todd Lannigan lives in Hollywood now and only returns to Ireland to promote his films.

Another surprise Nina told me last week, my grandmother had a title, Lady Rosslea - something else Mama and my siblings never thought to mention. Not that it mattered; Lady Rosslea was long estranged from her son and his family by the time I was born.

'Mama couldn't believe her luck when she discovered the guy dating her had a title. Remember what a snob she was, Deedy? But on their honeymoon in Rome Papa told her he was adopted. It never occurred to him that it could make any difference. Ha! Mama went ape-shit ballistic and then fled to a cousin twenty miles away, hitching there on the back of a hay cart. Remember Fifi? I met her in Amsterdam, and she told me the whole story. She's never forgotten Mama coming up the track to her father's farm in a white sundress and red stilettos. Fifi stayed with us the year we had the Cortina? You *must* remember her.'

I don't remember Fifi - there were too many cousins. I don't even remember a Cortina.

'Mama thought she was marrying into royalty. That's why she married Papa. Remember her obsession with good stock and breeding? Papa couldn't believe her reaction when he told her he was adopted. That's why she always claimed he

25

tricked her into marriage, that if she hadn't been so innocent she'd never have trusted him.'

I never understood what Mama meant, only that she had been cruelly wronged.

'Papa did love her, you know, before they married and for three days after. He told me.'

I don't believe Papa told her any such thing. Nina likes making him out to be better than he is, and making out that she gets on brilliantly with him. I want to say, *Papa doesn't know the word 'love'. He didn't even care when you eloped. So much for being his favourite! All the years you were missing, he never batted an eyelid!* But I don't mention that.

Jake and I used to meet every Wednesday night when Mama was at fund-raising meetings. We always went to a film and, afterwards, Jake would cycle halfway home with me and we'd stop for a cuddle on a bench in Donnybrook. He could wrap his arms right around me and I'd listen to his heartbeat, sturdy and steady as time. Jake was an only child so he had to go home every weekend to help his widowed mother on their farm in Meath. He loved the countryside, it was all he ever talked about, telling me the weekly changes, what birds were arriving or migrating, what crops or wildflowers or fruits were ripening or blossoming or ready for harvesting, and all about his livestock. I loved listening to him. Jake was so passionate about the land I thought he could never love any person as much, which was a kind of relief because I knew I'd never love anyone else like I loved Mama. Sometimes Jake talked about bringing me to Meath. 'When Father Sweeny thinks up a whole weekend of fund-raising events.' I'd laugh wistfully, imagining a weekend in Meath as likely as a lottery win.

My Wednesday nights with Jake sustained me for years. All week I looked forward to seeing him. Once he asked me if I'd ever leave home and I shrugged, thinking I

26

didn't need to explain that I couldn't leave Mama. All through Uni I've had many acquaintances - but I've no knack for intimacy. Apart from Mama, Jake is the only person whose company I've ever been completely at ease and happy in.

A few years ago Papa was invited to give some lectures in London. That morning he appeared in the kitchen doorway. 'I'm going to London for a while. There's accommodation for both of us if you want to come.' He turned and left.

'Bastard! Oh Deedy! Why does he have to take the good out of everything! Wouldn't I be the happiest woman in the world going off to London with my husband if it wasn't him! How dare he speak to me like that! *If you want to come!* Who the hell does he imagine he's talking to? His charlady? I'm the mother of his children!' She then recalled other invitations he'd thrown at her so rudely and disrespectfully all the good was taken from them.

Days later Papa left. With only Mama and me, the house was so peaceful that after a few days I felt like something rigid inside me was yielding. I thought Mama would be happy too, but the whole time Papa was away she cursed him for leaving her behind. 'I should leave him altogether! Then he'd see how he'd cope on his own!'

Papa couldn't even make himself a cup of tea. 'That bitch spoilt him. He never washed a cup in his life. He's a tramp to his bones only I managed to keep him an indoor tramp!' Then she'd wail, 'But where could I go to? What'd I do? I haven't a penny to my name! I can't even write! I'm stuck with that bastard for the rest of my days.'

'Maybe he won't come back?' I tried to cheer her up.

'Never come back? Christ Almighty but he better. I've suffered enough in this world without him running off and making me the laughing stock of the parish!'

'Impossible to please,' Nina says. 'She never wanted Papa but never wanted anyone else to have him either.'

'Who'd have him! He's a tramp to his bones, only Mama managed to keep him an indoor tramp!'

'Jesus, Deedy! Still parroting every word! Haven't heard that in over 20 years! Papa offered to buy her any house she wanted! He can only work in the loft in this house, with all the light from all those massive windows. It's where he's worked all his life. Mama didn't have to live here, but she liked this address too much to leave.'

'What about us? Mama couldn't leave us!'

'Me and Ciara and the twins left years ago. You and her could have gone anywhere then. Why didn't ye?'

It's impossible to tell Nina how much suffering Papa caused Mama. Especially the last few years when he was invited abroad so much, and never brought her anywhere, but just came and went, treating the house like a hotel and Mama and me like chambermaids. She'd have loved to go with him if he ever asked her nicely and if it wasn't such a risk for her to be on her own with him. 'What if I came too?' I suggested once. Mama brightened but only for a moment. 'But shur I'd still have to share a bed with him every night.'

'But why?'

'Don't be imagining I'd let the whole world know we don't share a bed!'

Some years ago Papa became briefly obsessed with Buddhas, and his next few sculptures changed from unnaturally elongated to unnaturally rotund bodies. Mama knew he was doing it just to spite her. Bad enough he never even accompanied her to Mass on a Sunday without making her the laughing stock of the parish by turning into an out an' out heathen. Papa even wanted to go to Afghanistan to see the two

28

giant Buddha's before the Taliban demolished them, but soon realised the journey would be impossible. It was from reading so much about Afghanistan that he became fascinated with Islam. Mama was mortified one day when a journalist quoted Papa exalting the prophet Mohammed in the papers.

After graduating, Jake got a job in his hometown and became so busy we could only meet monthly. I missed him terribly between times, yet somehow imagined our romance continuing forever. One night when we were sitting on our bench, Jake told me he couldn't see me again for two months. I gulped like he'd kicked me in the stomach. Jake laughed, 'Is it that bad?'

I didn't answer. Surely he knew it was that bad, and if he didn't, I wasn't telling him.

'Listen, Deedy,' he caught my hands. 'I was wondering if you'd think about marrying me?'

I couldn't answer. Hadn't he understood I could never leave Mama?

'Thing is, there's a girl working with me now and we get on like a house on fire, and since she lives near me already I'm thinking that maybe I should ask her to marry me. She's a fantastic kisser, I mean she's dead passionate and it's the most incredible - but anyway! If she turns me down, I'd love to marry you. You know that, don't you? You're much better looking than her and all.'

It took me some moments to understand him. Then I stood up, trembling, and got on my bike, pushing away his hands as he tried to stop me. 'Deedy? Hang on Deedy, what is it? Why are you looking at me like that? Have I said something wrong?' I pedalled away furiously, ignoring his calls.

I mourned. I mourned for his arms, his chest, his smell, his mouth, his purring voice describing the flight of a heron, the birth of a lamb, the hawthorn buds. I missed our times at the cinema, our kissing in Donnybrook. I hated him. I cursed Mama silently for the happiness I'd have had with Jake if it wasn't for her. Time is supposed to heal but when each day is the same as the one before it and the one after it, then every morning you wake up with pain as raw as the day it started.

A week later, Father Sweeney was arrested. Thus ended all the fund-raising, and with it Mama's social life. She took to drink and I kept house in a blur of misery, barely heeding Mama's unabated tales of woe. If she noticed my grief she never mentioned it, for which I was glad. But sometimes I wanted to howl with the hurt of it.

Last summer Papa went to London on his most prestigious residency yet and Mama was even more aggrieved than ever before. Her rage intensified when a letter came, containing an invitation, map, itinerary and note; *Will book flight if you want,* in Papa's inky scrawl. It was an invitation to the unveiling of a new Gerry Yates work. Mama glared at the contents before burning them one by one over a lighted ring on the cooker, ranting all the time.

A week later Mama started screaming as the radio announced the news of the four suicide bombers in London. 'Jesus Christ! That's where that bastard your father wanted me to be today. Look Deedy, Listen! That's the station I'd have been in, on that very train! That's the one, the exact same time and all! I knew he was out to kill me! He'll stop at nothing! That's what all the so-called interest in Muslims was about! Plotting with them! What did I always tell you?'

I listened speechless, baffled and bewildered, as Mama recalled every detail from the map and itinerary she'd burned so swiftly. She understood Papa's devilish conspiracy in its every twisted detail. 'That feckin bastard!' She screamed at the radio.

'Mama, it's just a coincidence. You can't really believe Papa's got anything to do with that.'

'*Coincidence!* Christ almighty Deedy Yates! You're supposed to be intelligent! You with all your feckin degrees! *'Just a coincidence'*? Nothing's ever a *coincidence*! D'ye hear me? Nothing! Coincidences don't happen with bastards the likes of Gerry Yates! Are you such an ignoramus that you've learned nothing your whole life!'

'You mean he's colluding with terrorists to kill dozens of people just to get at you?' I wanted to slam my head on the table, or Mama's.

'I knew he was up to something! But who could I tell? Who in the world believes me?' Her eyes were wild. 'God help me! Nobody on this cursed earth believes me except - !'

I froze, dreading the name Father Sweeny. But she stopped herself in time. His name would never be mentioned again.

Papa returned days later. I don't know if he was anywhere near any of the bombs. Mama followed him up the stairs straight after he came in the door. Their screaming started immediately. I went to my bedroom and turned my radio on full blast. I wondered who I could call for help, and eventually phoned Stef. It took ages for him to come to the phone in his Malahide showroom. You'd think he was clinching the deal of the century and every second talking to me was a second lost. 'So they're fighting. That's all they ever did! What d'ye want me to do about it?'

'But this is much, much worse fighting than ever before!' I used to envy Tony and Stef's impassiveness to Mamma and Papa's rows but right then I hated Stef.

31

'Do yourself a favour and forget about them. Move out.'

She thinks he plotted with the London suicide bombers to kill her! I wanted to scream at him but I knew he'd think I was the mad one. I considered ringing Tony, but he'd be even less help, and I had no idea where in the world my sisters were.

The fighting continued, right through the evening and into the night. I'd have given my left arm for Mama's and Papa's screaming to stop. Their fury at one another was inhuman. About midnight I heard Mama scream so loudly it ripped into me like a knife. Then there was silence. I stared at the ceiling, holding my breath, bracing myself for the next outburst. I waited, and waited. *Go up and see what's happened,* I urged myself, but my bones felt like cold porridge. *Go up and see what's happened. Go up and see what's happened.* I stayed on my bed, clutching my duvet round me.

I heard Papa on the stairs. For seconds after he opened my door we stared at each other, and then he coughed. 'Your mother's just jumped through a window. She left this for you.' He walked over to my bed and handed me a torn A4 page.

My dear children,
    My life is no longer bearable without Father Sweeny and with that bastard your father. May the grace of God be with all of you always, your loving Mama.

I looked at him, 'Where is she?'

'Back garden. I'm going to look for her now.' He stopped at the door and looked back at me, 'Coming?'

I shook my head.

'Call an ambulance then, and the Gardai.'

I promised Mama a hundred, a thousand times, that I would never, ever, under any circumstances whatsoever, tell anybody that she was illiterate. The Gardai, the coroner, Tony and Stef, Nina and Ciara, all read Mama's note, and reread it, time and time again. 'Is this Mrs Yates writing?' a Garda asked Tony when he arrived after midnight, and he nodded.

Repeatedly, Papa told everybody who came to our house how he tried to stop Mama jumping but she was too strong for him, she always had been.

She fell through an oak on the way down, before cracking her skull on the coalbunker. She took her own life. That's the verdict. Everyone must know it's a lie. The waiting for her to haunt me is horrible. I want to tell Lily all about what a beautiful person her grandmother once was, only there's too much else I don't want to tell.

Time Runs Away With Mfundo

by Bella Govan

"Mfundo, be a good boy, hmm?"

I do not reply.

Surely Mamma *knows* that it is *never* my intention to do anything less than my best.

"Please obey my instructions about the dump today, Mfundo."

Mamma reaches out, lays her hand on the top of my head in the way that I like very much.

"Too many diseases lie in wait for you children there. And as for the book, please don't let time run away with you, Mfundo."

My heart jumps.

How does Mamma know about the book?

My eyes stray to where I've hidden it.

Behind the tin shovel next to the sweeping brush; *my* things for *my* chores: Mamma has no reason to look there.

No, nothing of that book can be seen, nothing whatsoever.

To tell of things that are yet to come, that Mamma has these powers is well known.

Does Mamma also have sight of secrets that have already happened?

How else could Mamma know that yesterday I'd gone to the dump, too late to find any empty beer bottles to sell back to the bottle store, and that in a very bad mood, I had kicked out at an old cardboard box, watching it tumble down the side of the dump, then nearly at the bottom, had seen something falling out of it.

I slither down the slope to have a look, and there it is - a storybook written in Xhosa.

34

In the public library in the town, you can find many storybooks in English, much in Afrikaans - but a storybook written in Xhosa is still an unusual thing.

It is well known that reading is something of a pastime with me - also that reading *anything* in Xhosa is a very special thing to me, even the new street sign in the town, despite the fact that when left is the only junction, this sign directs you to the right. Zola says that when learning English he was taught the words 'open' and 'close' at the very same moment in time. Thus Zola will sometimes say 'close' when he means 'open' and vice versa, as in "We must listen to those who encourage us to close our minds." Thus the mystery of the street sign that says 'right' instead of 'left' is solved – the person in charge of signs must have learned the Xhosa words for 'right' and 'left' at the very same moment in time.

"Mfundo – have you heard one word of what I've just said to you."

"Of course, Mamma. 'Sweep and tidy the house today, Mfundo. Do the kitchen very nicely. I do not wish to come home to start cooking the evening meal in a place that isn't as neat and tidy as you can make it.'"

"But Mamma, you must *know* that I will do *all* that needs to be done."

Again, in the way that I like very much, Mamma lays her hand upon my head. "It was not my intention to hurt your feelings, Mfundo."

From our doorway I watch Mamma set off for her work in the town, waiting for her to reach the street below, when the colours of Mamma's headwrap will appear through the gaps in the straggly grey-green bushes growing between the church and the bottle store. Next, I watch for sight of Mamma passing by the early morning taxivans. I hold my breath when I see her hesitate there. With the sun already fierce in the sky, the three-mile walk into the town will seem like a mountain to climb. Very seldom does Mamma ride in those taxivans, but whenever I see her stop and enter one, no matter how much my friends and I play during the rest of the day, a dread hangs over all our games.

Now I breathe a sigh of relief as I see Mammy walking on past the last of the taxivans.

But today I am not going to be playing with anyone at all.

Today I am going to read a storybook in Xhosa.

I close the door of our house tight shut, winding the twine tied to the nail in the door tightly to the other nail at the edge of doorframe. Now I pull the curtain on the kitchen window closed; same for living room and bedroom, so that anybody walking by our house will think that no one is at home.

Now, with only a few little chores to do, which will take next to no time at all, the whole day lies in front of me.

I pick up the storybook from behind the shovel, bring it to the kitchen table.

For a long time I look at the picture on the cover of this book.: Rondavels, kraals, cows, birds, all the grasses of the veldt.

I'm a township boy, the world of this book is not one that is well known to me.

For a long time I look and dream of the lives of the people on the cover of the book: some handsome young warriors, several very honourable-looking big men; happy looking women and children - and old people with white hair.

This storybook picture must have been painted a long time ago, before the coming of the skinny disease. Many people in our township get this disease. Many white people in the rich countries also have this disease. Rich white people in Europe and the United States have invented powerful medicines to halt the sickness, but also for the sake of profit,

36

charging much money for their medicines, far beyond the means of the people of the township. Zola tells me there is soon to be a rebellion over such as this. Zola tells me many things, most recently saying that global warming must soon come to mean more than the melting of the earth's icecaps – it must come to mean the melting of the hardened hearts of the wealthy and powerful. Compared to the majority, these people are few in number. To the powerful, this has always been a well-known fact. Zola says that now that the majority of the people are becoming wiser in the ways of the world, people will soon, each and together, know how to break the levers of power from the grasp of the greedy.

When the township people with the skinny disease can no longer work, they grow quiet and fearful. On the one hand they become resigned to the death that they know will soon come, but they remain anxious till the end over what will become of those they leave behind: children, wives, husbands, brothers, sisters, elderly parents.

Smiling there in one corner of the storybook picture is a herdboy who, I will tell you, I myself resemble very much, although it would be true to say that he is possibly just a little bit more handsome.

I open the book to the first page.

Short every-day words are quite easy to decipher. To figure out the more complicated words that I have often heard spoken but never seen written down, takes a little longer. Then there are those words which I have only very occasionally heard spoken, have never myself used. But sometimes from the sense of the words around them I can guess their meanings.

But there are many words, I admit, whose meanings I cannot guess at all.

Yet I do not mind this, because it pleases me to know that there are so many Xhosa words out there in the future only waiting for me to discover them.

I admit to you that my reading of that storybook went rather slowly.

I must tell you, though, that this was not only because of difficulty with words, but because some of the thoughts written down there thrilled my heart - and these I repeated to myself several times.

'Nizisule iinyembezi kulo mehlo alilayo kungabi sabaho sijwili nasikhalo. '

'Wipe your tears from your eyes and there shall be no crying.'

Ubuntu - Umntu ngumntu ngabantu.

The world is one - it cannot be otherwise.

Under the burden of the noonday sun, the corrugated roof of our house begins to creak and sweat gathers at the back of my knees, dampens the underarms of my shirt.

But it matters not - I, Mfundo, am inside the world of brave warriors, of clever shamans who know how to cure many illnesses, of wise elders who know how to right many wrongs.

Unfortunately, in that storybook there was one very wicked family who had much wealth, yet, each of them and together, they behaved very badly indeed. I did not like them at all. Although this family was very clever in the ways of the world, they did not possess true human wisdom. They did not even understand the most basic of such truths: that monstrousness breeds monstrousness. Unless they changed their ways, this family, each of them and together, were destined to exist for their short time on this earth disrespected by humanity, then to die without honour.

A loud banging at our door startles me right out of the world of the book.

38

Do not ask me where the time has gone - but a glance through the top of the window above the curtain tells me by the shadows on the wall of the next-door house that hours have flown by.

Fear of thieves out to rob my mother and I of the little we possess was very strong in my heart.

I sit very still in my chair, making not a sound.

Only if the robber stands on tiptoe and looks through the window above the top of the curtain will he discover me sitting here.

Just when I think the intruder must have given up, there's another fearsome banging on the door, much louder than before.

Now someone is even *kicking* the door – but I have wound the twine very tight and it holds firm.

What if the robber has knife, or a machete – a gun even?

No matter how thunderous heartbeats may sound to you, the fact of the matter is that *no one* can hear the beating of a person's heart from behind a closed door - nor the sound of drops of perspiration falling onto the page of a book.

Fearful though I was, nevertheless, I must also tell you how much I was preparing myself in my mind to fight them off. Oh yes, I, Mfundo, will fiercely *oppose* any robbers who *dare* to try to open that door!

Making not a sound, I tiptoe over to where the tin shovel and sweeping brush are propped against the wall beside the door.

Swiftly I grab them up – and now I am at the ready!

You will understand, therefore, that I was both very relieved and much *annoyed,* to hear the voices of Themba, Thandile and Nosipho coming from the other side of the door.

"Mfundo *is* in there, *believe* me!" declares Themba.

Themba and I are in Grade Four together. He is my best friend.

In a very firm voice, Thandile, Themba's sister, is now telling her brother, "Mfundo *cannot* be in there - otherwise he would have *opened the door!*"

"You are *wrong*, Thandile!" argues Themba, "*You* do not know Mfundo as *I* do. Mfundo's got his head stuck in that storybook he found at the dump yesterday, I *know* it – he's forgotten all about real people."

When Themba's father has work, Themba is in charge of his younger sisters, Thandile and Nosipho.

However, Themba's position of being *in charge* is not so simple, because, Thandile, although a girl and a whole year younger than Themba, *never* does what he says.

Thandile can be very charming. She has a very beautiful smile. And she is always polite to grownups.

But make no mistake, Thandile *cannot* be told what to do.

I myself do not even try.

The careless taxivan driver had been driving at great speed on worn tyres and one of the tyres had burst. The taxivan driver didn't know that stepping hard on the brake was not the correct thing to do: this made the taxivan go into an unstoppable skid, whereby the taxivan span right across the roadway and slammed head on into a tree.

The driver was instantly crushed to death. Another taxivan driver stopped and tried to help, pulling Themba's mother out of the wreck, carrying her to his taxivan, driving fast to the clinic in town where the nurse may, or may not, have been able to help. But Themba's mother died in the back of the taxivan, never regaining consciousness.

That is why Themba is always in charge of his sisters when his father has work.

40

Even though my Papa can seldom come home from the goldmines, it is well known that Mamma does not share her blanket with any other man. It is as a sister that Mamma comforts Themba's father, stopping his tears, calming him down, when she holds his hands in her own, saying to him in her own special way, "Forgive no iniquities - but forge new worlds from your pain."

"*Mfundo*," comes Nosipho's gruff little voice. "I *hungry!* Want *milk! Mfundo!* I want milk n*ow! Open!*"

Nosipho, like her big sister Thandile, also has a very big mind of her own.

This is not to say that Nosipho isn't also quite a heartstealer at times.

But now Nosipho begins to bawl, "*Wah, wah, wah! Waaant milk! Wah, wah wah! Waant miilllk!*"

"*Behave yourself,* Nosipho!" shouts Themba. "You must *wait* until Papa comes home and *brings* us milk."

"*Wa, hawa, hawa! Want miilk! I huungry!*"

Then comes Thandile's very angry voice, "Mfundo, if you're in there - *you'd better open up this very minute, I tell you!*"

I replace the tin shovel and sweeping brush. I slam the storybook shut. I unwind the twine from the nail and yank open the door.

I hold the cup of milk for Nosipho to drink. She drinks *very* noisily – then almost before she's finished drinking the milk, she's falling asleep in my arms.

I carry Nosipho to the big armchair in the living room. Although very old and battered, it is a very comfortable chair indeed. Within minutes Nosipho is snoring loudly.

Themba, Thandile and I, can't help giggling over such very loud snoring coming from such a little person.

Now Thandile is asking me "Mfundo, where's that giant jigsaw puzzle your Papa brought for you at Christmas? Let me do it today."

"Mfundo, have you got any wire to make toys with?" asks Themba. "Yesterday I watched Zola make a toy wire bicycle with *two moving wheels*. I think I now know how to do this for myself."

"Well, if *you're* going to make a *bicycle*," I said, definitely interested, "then I'm going to make a model *bus*. With *four* moving wheels."

From under my bed I drag out the cardboard box in which we keep our tools, plus all the little things that one day may be useful.

I empty the box onto the bedroom floor. We extract several wire clothes hangers, a small coil of new telephone line wire, the hammer with the broken shaft and the pair of rusty pliers.

Themba and I take our materials into the living room.

I step into the kitchen, bringing back two knives, two spoons, two forks, against which we can bend the wire in the manner we require.

Since there is only one hammer, one pair of pliers, and since the knives, spoons and forks are good for certain kinds of shaping only, Themba goes outside to get some stones which we can also use to bend and shape the wire in necessary ways. Not all the stones prove suitable, so Themba has to make quite a few trips outside, because Themba is as determined as I that our work will be as perfect as we can make it.

Perhaps my work, and Themba's, could even be as good as the wire models the big men try to sell to the tourists on the train which stops late at night at the water tank a few miles from our township.

42

Thandile has taken the jigsaw puzzle from its place on the shelf in the kitchen and is studying the picture.

"It is *so* big," I tell her, "that it does not even fit on the kitchen table. I myself have completed it *three* times already. This is how I do it. From the bins outside the bottle store, I bring home a cardboard box. Half a cardboard box fits the kitchen table exactly. I then start with one side of the puzzle, and when I complete this, I take this piece of the picture on the cardboard *off* the table, put it on the kitchen floor. Then I put the other piece of cardboard on the kitchen table, and work on the other side of the puzzle. When I finish, I then put this half of the puzzle on the floor beside the first half, except the whole puzzle does not quite *fit* on the kitchen floor, so some of the picture extends into the living room. There is also a bit of a *gap* between the two halves of the jigsaw puzzle. This, however, is only to be expected."

"*No!*" says Thandile, "I wish to see the completed picture *all at once - and without any gaps! I* shall complete the entire puzzle on the *living* room floor. Come, help me move the furniture."

Themba and myself push the few pieces of furniture to the corners of the room, including the armchair in which Nosipho still sleeps deeply.

Themba picks up our tools and materials from the living room floor and he and I return to the bedroom, pulling the curtain that divides the bedroom from the living room closed. However, for some reason, Thandile decides to pull this curtain open again, closing the one that divides the kitchen from the living room instead. Often, I do not understand the minds of girls. Perhaps Thandile wishes me to notice, without the distractions of thinking about any food that might be in the kitchen, how cleverly and quickly she can put that very big puzzle together. Of course, she may also wish to observe, equally without distraction, how skilfully I will work in order to make this bus with four wheels.

Themba and I watch as Thandile empties the jigsaw pieces onto the middle of the living room floor.

I notice that Thandile's way of solving the puzzle is not to concentrate on images of this or that, but to lay out *all* the straight edged pieces on the floor first. Now she's working inwards from what, I admit, are very clear guiding borders.

But it is a *very* complex jigsaw puzzle, and I can't help but notice that Thandile too cannot avoid some of the difficulties that I myself have had with that picture.

Once, I had a plan to go in the night to the water tank with Zola.

I waited until I was sure Mamma was sound asleep.

But even as she sleeps Mamma's powers to detect people's secret thoughts do not entirely leave her. Just as I unwind the twine from the nail, step silently outside, Mamma calls softly to me from the bedroom, "Be a good boy, Mfundo, go back to bed, hmmm? No wire to be found anywhere this week. Zola has nothing to sell tonight."

Zola has friends who curse badly and say that all the greedy, lying, careless people of the world should be relieved of the burden of their existence.

But Zola himself says the business of existence belongs to forces of creation; the business of humankind is to see to the fair sharing of our labour over the fruits of the earth. Zola says that he and those of his friends who believe this to be true will not neglect the very special work required to make this truth become reality. *Ubuntu; Umntu ngumntu ngabantu.*

It stands to reason that my bus will be much more intricate to make, and thus require the finer telephone wire. However, Themba's bicycle, which he will make with the much thicker coat hanger wire, will be much larger to scale than my bus.

44

You will already have worked out that the front door of our house opens onto the kitchen; that you then go through the kitchen to the living room, through the curtain to the bedroom.

Unfortunately, during his stone gathering tasks Themba did not stop to wipe his feet on the old sack that Mamma has placed outside the front door for the wiping feet before entering the house. Therefore, into all the rooms of our house came quite a lot of red dust, little clumps of earth, dried grass and bits of old spiders' webs, a fact of the matter that we did not notice until much later.

Except for Nosipho's snores, for some time there was hardly any noise in the house at all. Themba, Thandile and myself working at our tasks quite contently.

Then Nosipho wakened.

Now Nosipho comes several times to myself, Themba and Thandile, *"But let me play with you! I want to play too!"*

When Nosipho goes to Thandile for the fourth time, unfortunately Nosipho accidentally steps all over the top half of Thandile's jigsaw puzzle, knocking nearly the whole top border into very annoying disarray.

But even Thandile had to later admit that it would have been next to impossible for Nosipho *not* to step on the puzzle, since the plain fact of the matter was that the outline of that puzzle covered almost the entire living room floor. This was bound to happen very quickly, of course if your method is to start with all the outside edges first,

Nevertheless, I think you will agree that Thandile's annoyance was very understandable. Thandile gave Nosipho just a little push, shouting at her, *"Behave yourself! Go away, Nosipho! Stop bothering me!"*

Nosipho then comes into the bedroom to complain to myself and Themba. "Thandile, she not nice to me - not *nice!* You *tell* her, Mfundo!"

45

Then Nosipho spies the two newly made wire wheels for the toy bicycle and the three wheels that I had already made for the model bus. Letting out an excited whoop, Nosipho grabs up all the wheels - quite unacceptably bending them out of shape as she does so.

Themba and myself later admitted that for a child as young as Nosipho, grabbing these newly made wheels was probably next to impossible *not* to do, since those wheels were almost perfectly formed, and in the case of the wheels for my bus, very bright and shiny.

Nevertheless, is not my own and Themba's annoyance also very understandable?

We grabbed the toy wheels back off Nosipho, giving her not a very big shove, yelling at her, *"Behave yourself!* Go *away, Nosipho.* Stop *bothering* us!"

It is at this point that Nosipho finally gets the message. In a very big huff, she crawls under the curtain and disappears into the kitchen.

There, Nosipho must have spied the half full bottle of milk. Before she'd even had a chance to drink much more of it, the bottle must have inadvertently slipped from Nosipho little hands. You'd think that even a plastic bottle half full of milk hitting the kitchen floor would have made a very distinguishable noise - but surprisingly we heard not a thing.

It is an inescapable fact, however, that spilt milk went all over the kitchen floor, mixing in here and there with the red dust, little clumps of earth, dried grass and bits of old spiders' webs.

It is true that In the township, there are many thieves and drunkards. But it is also true that there are many more people who believe that we must all be as generous with each other as our possessions allow. Therefore, only the week before, our neighbour had given to us as a present a packet of very tasty chocolate biscuits. Nosipho must have found this

46

packet of biscuits. She then must have walked around the kitchen expertly nibbling the chocolate cream from the centres of the biscuits remaining in the pack. Since Mamma and I had taken only one each as our Saturday evening treat, Nosipho had obviously enjoyed the chocolate cream centres of a considerable number of biscuits.

That Nosipho must have dropped less interesting bits of half chewed biscuit anywhere and everywhere is also a deducible fact.

I expect it took Nosipho some time before she finally managed to open the kitchen cupboard, because that cupboard door, being lopsided, has to be shifted slightly before it will open. But once opened, Nosipho would have discovered what must have seemed to her a treasure trove of things to play with. Because another deducible fact of the matter is that every single item in that cupboard ended spread all over the kitchen floor.

To me it seemed strange that the three tin mugs and the three tin plates had been placed *under* the kitchen table - until Thandile said that for someone the size of Nosipho, a table is like a little house with a good roof - and so, of course, it is the most obvious place in which to pretend to live.

With the tin plates and the tin mugs, then with the frying pan, the saucepan, the knife, fork, spoon, two tins of sardines and the handful of mealie meal still left in the bag, Nosipho must have played very quietly for quite some time – at any rate, we heard not a thing.

Nosipho must then have climbed up onto the chair, got herself onto the table, reached up to the kitchen shelf for the three eggs nestling inside the half carton without its lid.

Since there was no raw egg on the kitchen table itself, Nosipho must have climbed back down again with the eggs more or less intact. Perhaps Nosipho tried to play with the eggs as if they were those little imitation rugby balls you can sometimes spot in the window of the General Store, hiding behind the likes of barbed wire, spades, broom handles, shears, batteries, exhaust pipes, etcetera. If so, I suspect Nosipho must have been quite amazed at how the eggshells which, on the one hand seemed so impenetrable, on the other hand broke with such shocking ease when she tried bouncing them on the kitchen floor.

Nosipho must have then gone on to make what she must have thought were very interesting sorts of patterns all over the kitchen floor, mixing in the raw egg with the spilt milk, the mealie meal, the red dust, the little clumps of earth, dried bits of grass and old bits of spiders' webs.

Thandile says, no, I am *wrong* in this - that Nosipho had less interest in making particular patterns, than in finding out how things as different as egg yolk, milk, red dust, little clumps of earth, dried grass, egg shells, mealie meal and bits of old spiders' webs feel to the touch. Thandile also claims that Nosipho must have experimented both with how such things feel separately and how they feel when *mixed.*

Whether it is I, or Thandile, who is correct in this, is not known.

What is known is that Nosipho made extensive use of all the materials she had to hand, which resulted in the fact that there was hardly an inch of the kitchen floor left unpatterned.

Lastly, Nosipho must have found the nice bright sugar and tea tins with the tightly shut lids.

Now, as far as Nosipho was concerned, up until that very moment in time, tight lids were us bigger children's business, since only people from about aged seven upwards could undo those lids - or so it had been thought.

We hear Nosipho shout to Thandile. *"I clever! Look! I clever! "*

48

"BEHAVE YOURSELF!" Thandile yells at Nosipho, not even looking in her direction. "Go *AWAY*, Nosipho! Stop *BOTHERING* me!"

Nosipho runs to complain about Thandile to Themba and I, *"But I clever - I clever!* Mfundo you *tell* her!"

Unfortunately, just at that point I was for the third time trying to do the very tricky bit of connecting a very well formed, I thought, but necessarily very small steering wheel to the shaft and main chassis of my four-wheeled bus.

Themba was just then also having trouble with the handlebars of his bicycle.

Problems such as these, I think you will admit, require extensive concentration.

I admit that Themba and I, without even so much as looking in her direction, shout at Nosipho even louder than before. *"BEHAVE YOURSELF!* Go *AWAY* Nosipho! Stop *BOTHERING* us!"

Nosipho got the message, crawling back under the kitchen curtain.

There was quiet for a while.

Then came this very loud clanging noise when Nosipho must've flung the now empty sugar and tea tins on the kitchen floor.

"NOSIPHO, WHAT IS ALL THAT NOISE?" yells Thandile.

"NOSIPHO, WHAT MISCHIEF ARE YOU GETTING UP TO NOW?" yells Themba.

I will admit that the noise of the clanging tins suddenly sparked such worrying thoughts in my mind that I myself yell, *"But the kitchen must be all clean, neat and tidy for Mamma coming home! Nosipho, if you have made a mess in the kitchen, I SHALL BE MOST ANNOYED WITH YOU!"*

Themba, Thandile and I jump up from our tasks. Thandile yanks back the kitchen curtain – and we see for the first time all that has happened to it.

It is in this very same moment that we also see Mamma holding Nosipho in her arms, and giving Nosipho all the hugs she wants.

But, over Nosipho's delighted little head, Mamma is surveying the state of our house.

When I see all that Mamma is seeing, my heart sinks, as if deep into the packed earth of the kitchen floor.

Mamma's voice is low and weary. "It is *I* who am most annoyed with you older children, each of you and together, because it would appear that not one of you has given much thought to little Nosipho today.

"But it is with you, Mfundo, that I am most disappointed.

"You seem to have forgotten all about your responsibilities to this household today, choosing to spend your time doing precisely as you pleased.

"Mfundo, yet again you have let time run away with you."

Mamma's words sting me very sharply.

I also see by that other look on Mamma's face that this must have been a day when Mamma had been asked to wash the madam's dirty underwear, a task, Mamma says no stranger should require of another, a task all healthy people should do for themselves.

Although there are now washing machines in the houses of many rich Madams, some households decree that all undergarments, on which inevitably there will be traces of bodily fluids, and in the case of women the stains of menstrual blood, that no undergarments are to contaminate the washing machine. The servants must wash such soiled undergarments separately by hand.

50

Oh yes, when I, Mfundo, grow up, oh yes, with all my friends, we will make the government pass laws forbidding that poor women like Mamma be told that they must wash the rich people's dirty underwear, a task that all healthy people should do for themselves.

Oh yes, and when I, Mfundo grow up, with all my friends, we will make the government pass laws forbidding that poor men must risk their very lives to go down into the dark bowels of the earth to bring them gold.

Oh yes, we will see to it that all the badly behaved, careless, greedy people can no longer cause so many others on this earth to work so hard for so little reward.

Themba's father once asked Mamma if it was better that many of the new Madams were no longer white women, but women of our own country, Mamma's black sisters. "Forgive no iniquities - forge new worlds from your pain," was Mamma's reply.

Try as I might, I cannot prevent these traitorous tears from plopping onto my cheeks.

I, Mfundo, a boy in Grade Four, weeping. What a disgrace!

I can see nothing, but I can hear Themba say softly, "I will tell no one, Mfundo, that I saw you weep."

Then in what was, for Thandile, a quiet voice I hear her declare, "Mrs. Mabhida, It is myself, Themba and Nosipho who are more to blame. It is Mfundo who gave Nosipho his milk today - look how we've repaid him Further, we brought nothing into this household today, Mrs. Mabhida, not even one empty beer bottle from the dump.

It shocks me even further when Thandile comes and puts her arm around my shoulder. "But do not worry, Mfundo: many hands make light work. In no time at all, we shall have everything in its proper place – and all shall be very clean, neat and tidy. Nosipho, pick up all those bits of biscuit, then you can start putting the jigsaw pieces back in the box. Themba, fetch some water. Mfundo, put the furniture back in place. Themba and Mfundo will then sweep and wash the floors, Mrs. Mabhida. *C'mon, let's hop to it!"*

Nosipho, Themba and I, we hop to it.

Thandile gives Mamma one of her beautiful smiles, says very charmingly, "Mrs. Mabhida, sit yourself down in the big armchair and have a nice rest. I will soon make you a nice cup of tea..." Thandile's voice trailing off as she sees the empty milk bottle, the empty sugar tin, the empty tea tin.

But as you may have guessed, nothing stops Thandile.

Thandile is now on her hands and knees, following the half sodden squiggly lines of sugar and tea through the spilt milk, egg yolk, mealie meal, red dust, little clumps of grass, egg shells and bits of old spiders' webs. She manages to salvage a few grains of sugar here, a speck or two of tealeaf there. But there is nothing that can be done about the milk, all of which has soaked into the hard packed earthen floor.

Mamma sits in the big armchair, looking very stern.

As the mess begins to clear and I can see that, in some respects at least, the situation is not as entirely irretrievable as I'd believed, my dread begins to subside just a little

Then Themba, looking in Mamma's direction, gives me a nudge.

Mamma is still looking very stern. But as she watches us children doing our serious best to put the house in order, make everything as clean, neat and tidy as ever we possibly could, every now and then Mamma's shoulders betray her with a shake of silent laughter.

Nosipho runs to Mamma, with some bits of not very noticeably chewed biscuit on a clean saucer, "For you! *Nice!"*

Thandile calls from the kitchen. "Mrs. Mabhida, your tea is nearly ready - and you'll be *very* pleasantly surprised at

52

my very good idea! In place of milk, I'm putting in little drops of margarine!"

Mamma calls quickly to Thandile, "*No, no - do not worry*! I often take tea without milk, Thandile!"

Too late.

Thandile is already handing Mamma a cup of with an oily sheen on top of very weak looking tea.

Mamma sips politely at her tea. "Very nice Thandile. Thank you."

Mamma puts down her cup, looks at me and says, "Come here, Mfundo."

I drop the tin shovel, run to stand in front of Mamma.

Mamma reaches out and lays her hand on the top of my head in the way that I like very much. When Mamma does this, it makes me smile inside, just as Nosipho smiles outside when my mother gives her all the hugs she needs.

"Time may steal you away now and then, Mfundo, but your heart is golden and I am every day more and more content that I can see the man in the boy."

Mamma turns to Themba, Thandile and Nosipho. "Mfundo, it pleases me also that you know well how to choose your friends."

It surprises me at how quick Thandile is to answer. "Mrs. Mabhida, It is also *I* who would always choose Mfundo. Mfundo, although a boy, never tries to boss me about. Nor does Mfundo ever say that this book, this puzzle, this milk is mine and mine alone.

"Also, when Mfundo smiles, he is not such bad looking boy."

Right there and then It occurs to me that Thandile, although a girl, could one day, after Themba, become, as a matter of fact, one of the very best of my friends.

Picture Perfect Love

by Douglas Bruton

A garbled message was relayed over the loudspeakers. Everywhere people stopped to listen, as if the message might be for them. The singsong voice echoed back from the metal-framed, glass-paned ceiling – the words ran into each other so that there was tune but no lyric. A pigeon with misshapen pink feet and stiff cloth wings folded across its back, stabbed mechanically at a discarded cigarette end with the stub of its beak. Somewhere metal clashed with metal, again and again. An impudent horn sounded and a shrill whistle shrieked.

He moved against the sudden flow, wading through crowds of people streaming towards platform 21. Suitcases swung out of his path and around him or roared past dragged on thunderous wheels. A sticky-fingered child collided with his knees and was then pulled away, back into the swell surging past him. He tossed an apology over his shoulder; it sank like a stone – without ripple or trace.

Although the short curtain of the photo booth was drawn shut he could see that it was empty. He ducked inside. Even though the pleated blue curtain only reached as low as his chest, it was like stepping into a bubble of calm. The hustle and bustle of the station was effectively shut out. He sat down facing a dark glass window somewhere behind which the camera was positioned. The seat shifted unevenly underneath him. He paused to catch his breath.

The instructions were printed below the glass panel. There were half a dozen simple line illustrations to help clarify each of the operational steps. He first had to adjust the seat until his eyes were in line with two points marked on the glass. He stood up and twisted the chair like a giant loose screw. The chair wobbled less and less unsteadily the lower it shrank. He sat down and checked his eyeline against the two red triangular pointers. He adjusted the seat twice more before it was right. He could choose to have an orange curtain drawn behind him, or a blue one. Alternatively he could opt for the plain white wall of the booth. The wall was scratched with someone's name under which someone else had added a familiar obscenity in black marker; the orange curtain was stained and torn, so he decided that the blue curtain would do. He jerked it across and sat down again without noticing that it hung squint behind him. He then had to select the type of photograph he wanted.

Turning to the left he could see beyond the curtain the disembodied legs and feet of those who passed, could see the bags that they carried or the cases that followed in their footsteps like obedient pets. It was a strange view of the world where a person might be judged on the shine of their shoes, the thickness of their ankles or the trundle of their suitcase.

He selected the passport-sized strip of four separate poses. He counted out the right number of coins and fed them one after the other into the slot of the machine. When the correct amount had been entered he clicked the dial to the right. Then he sat back to wait for the red warning light that signalled a photo was about to be taken.

In a flash, or more precisely four, it was over. He stepped out of the booth to find the station changed, almost empty where before it had been crowded and full. At his feet another club-footed pigeon jabbed at dropped tickets. It might have been the same pigeon as before. He couldn't tell. The announcer sang another wordless jingle and somewhere a dog barked. The photo machine hummed and whirred as though it was a new-fed beast.

'Three Minutes' it said on the front of the machine and a bright red arrow pointed to a hole through which his image, processed and printed, would be regurgitated. He

55

checked his watch against the station clock and was surprised to find them in agreement. He leaned back against the booth and felt its rumble and gargle as though they were part of him.

Suddenly there was an urgent throaty choking sound and a strip of photographs was coughed up – sooner than he had expected. A red light blinked on and off. He withdrew the strip, being careful to handle it by the edges as though it was a thing easily broken. The strip was still wet, as he had known it would be. He waved it back and forth in the air to aid the drying process, before inspecting the results. Behind him the machine continued to gurgle and whine.

When he looked at the pictures it took him a moment to register that they were not him, that he had the wrong photographs. The same blue curtain was pulled across the background, though not so crookedly; but it was the face that stared back at him that was not his own. It was a girl, a fair-haired girl in a red unbuttoned coat. In one picture she smiled up at him as if she knew him. In the next she winked at him as though they shared a private joke. In the third she held a hand in front of her mouth and laughed. In the last she blew across the flat of her raised palm, blew a pantomime kiss out of the picture at him.

He looked across the almost empty concourse, looked to right and left in search of a flash of red. He took a step forward, craning to see if she was in the shop next to the photo booth. The pigeon at his feet, startled by the suddenness of his lunge, flapped away, the scowling red in its eye turned on him. The yellow light was on, the glass door ajar, but the shop was empty. She was not there.

Behind him the choking noise from the machine sounded again and this time his pictures were spat out. The mechanical red eye winked up at him and then went out. Somewhere inside a cog turned and a metal lever fell with a final dull clunk; the photo booth fell silent.

56

At first he did not venture far from the photo machine in his search of the station, kept the booth in sight in case she returned. He looked along the platforms where trains were expected. Red lights flipped to green. A station employee in a peaked cap inspected his fob watch, nodded to himself and then slipped it back into the small pocket of his overstuffed waistcoat. A train pulled in. The air vibrated with the distorted cracked voice of the station announcer heralding its arrival. Passengers filed past, flashing the stubs of their tickets at the bloat-faced inspector. The station concourse was suddenly busy again. But still she was not there.

He moved further off, his strip of pictures flapping in one hand, hers in the other. He circled the station twice, returning each time to the empty photo booth. She was not curled up in any of the waiting rooms, not sharing a coffee with a girlfriend in any of the cafés, not seeking information or travel advice at any of the queues for tickets. She was not hidden in the flower shop, not waiting for service at the money exchange counter, not lost in the aisles of books and magazines at the newsagent's. He looked for her on empty platforms and crowded ones; he peered into departing taxis and waiting cars; he watched the coming and going of several coaches. She was not anywhere. Twice around the station, he was forced to admit that she was gone.

He waited until both sets of photos were dry, folded both strips carefully in two, slipped them into his jacket pocket and left the station.

'Who's this?' said Mark.

He looked up from the book he was reading. Mark was examining the photos of the red-coated girl. He silently cursed himself for having left them where Mark could find them, pretended not to have heard the question and returned to his book.

57

He studied the page as if he was reading; in truth his eyes scanned the same line over and over without deciphering any meaning in what the words said. All the time he was aware that Mark was still there, still peering at the face of the girl he'd never met.

'She's gorgeous,' said Mark. 'Who is she?'

'No one,' he said, without this time looking up.

Mark had found the strip of photos on the desk where he had emptied his pockets the day before. A jumble of loose change, used bus tickets and crumpled shop receipts was piled into a small heap next to which his photos and hers had been laid side by side. He didn't really know why he had kept hers. He should have thrown them away, but he hadn't.

'She have a name at least?' said Mark.

'It's not what you think,' he said.

'Well, I don't think she's your sister,' jeered Mark. He pointed to the last picture on the strip, the one where she blew an airy kiss across the lifted palm of her hand out at the viewer.

'She's not anything,' he said.

'Oh dear, do I sense a lover's quarrel?' said Mark.

He shut the book, got to his feet and snatched the photos away from Mark.

'Hey, don't worry. I won't tell a soul,' said Mark. He backed out of the room, his arms raised in mock submission.

'There is nothing to tell!' he protested.

'Our little secret then,' whispered Mark.

'You ok?' said Susannah.

He reached past her and lifted a glass from the kitchen cupboard behind her head.

'What?' he said.

Susannah had not dressed yet, though it was already afternoon. She leaned back against the sink. One sock-covered foot rested on top of the other so that the crook of one knee jutted out in front of her. She nursed a cup of tea in the closed bowl of her two hands.

'Only, Mark said you might be a bit low. Girl trouble or something,' she said. She held the cup close to her face and breathed in the hot steam from her tea.

'Don't believe what Mark tells you. I am fine.' He turned the cold tap on and let it run a while.

'And your girlfriend?' she said. She looked at him over the rim of her raised cup, looked to see how he would react to her question.

He dipped his glass under the jet of clear water streaming from the tap and then turned it off. He drank from the glass, drained it in a single draught and wiped the back of his hand across his mouth. He made no reply to her.

'Sorry, I don't know her name. Mark didn't say. Is she new, then?' said Susannah.

'There is no girl.' He rinsed the glass clean and stood it upside down on the draining surface.

'Mark told us about the photographs,' she said.

He knew he should have thrown them away, dropped them in a bin before leaving the station concourse instead of bringing them back to the flat with him.

'Mark said you had both had photos taken at the same photo booth,' said Susannah.

'Mark shouldn't have told you anything.'

She reached one hand out to him, rested it reassuringly on his forearm. He felt the warmth of her touch through his shirt.

'He said she looked really nice. Fair-haired. Pretty.' And after a short pause she withdrew her hand again and returned it to the hot cup. 'Who is she?' she said.

'She's just a girl,' he said, caught off guard.

'She must have a name?'

He knew she must. It didn't make sense to have a stranger's pictures in his room, even though that was the truth.

'Jennifer,' he said. It was out before he could stop it.

'Jennifer?' said Susannah.

'Yeh, Jennifer,' he said again. And then, 'Jen for short.'

Susannah blew across the surface of her tea before lifting it to her mouth. He watched the purse of her lips, just like the silent kiss that Jennifer blew at him out of the photograph on his desk.

'What's she do then, this Jen?' said Susannah.

'Oh, office work, secretarial stuff, you know.'

He wasn't prepared for Susannah's questions and said the first thing that came into his head.

'Where'd you meet?' she pressed.

'At the station,' he said. That much at least had something of the truth in it, though technically they hadn't really met.

'At the station? When was this?' said Susannah.

'Look, what's with the twenty questions?'

'Sorry, just showing a little interest,' said Susannah.

It was a mistake bringing the four photographs away from the station. It was a mistake leaving them on his desk where Mark could find them. It was a mistake giving Susannah a name to hang all kinds of speculation on. He hadn't intended any of this.

Back in his own room he looked over the strip of pictures again, four of them, one on top of the other. He searched them, one at a time, examined them closely looking for clues as to who she might be. 'Jennifer,' he said to himself.

'Jen for short.' It seemed to fit. She was pretty, just as Mark had told Susannah she was - a luminous prettiness that would turn men's heads. Her fair hair fell in untidy corkscrew rings about her shoulders; like twisted ribbons of pale gold, he thought. Her blue eyes stared at the camera from out of an elfin face; stared at *him* now. She looked nineteen, maybe twenty. In the first picture her smile was everything. It was not simply an arrangement of her lips or a product of the upturned corners of her mouth. It was in her eyes too. There were tiny creases at the corners of her eyes, like a small bird's footprints in fresh snow, and her eyes sparkled. It was a whole smile that she offered up to him.

In the second picture she winked out at him. Her smile had widened so that the white of her teeth just showed. There was mischief in her child's face, a kind of impish wickedness that would be easily forgiven. He wondered what she was thinking, what joke was cartwheeling through her thoughts. Was it all part of a game they played together? He couldn't help returning her smile. At her neck the fingers of her left hand were caught in a thin silver chain that she wore. He noticed that her nails were painted a pillar-box red to match her red plastic coat with its wide collar and its large shiny buttons.

The third photograph on the strip showed her with her hand cupped across her mouth, trying but failing to hold back the laughter that was there. Laughter is never silent and he tried to imagine what it would be like to hear Jennifer laugh. Her head leaned forward slightly, as though she was rocking back and forth on the uneven seat; her face was placed a little lower in the frame. Her hair fell in ragged coils across her cheeks. He wanted to brush them back in place. She was a little out of focus against the sharp creases of the blue curtained backdrop, her features blurred and softened by the quick movement of her hand.

In the final picture the image was crisp again. Now she held one palm level with the point of her chin, the fingers of her hand turned towards him. Just above the upturned palm her lips formed a pert pout, blowing across her hand the lightest of blown kisses. That kiss was his now, whoever it might have been directed at before.

He tacked the strip of photographs to the pin-board in his room. Let them think what they want, he thought.

'So, Jennifer?' said Mark when they met in the kitchen.

'Jen,' he said.

'Yes, Jen... Well?' Mark marked the page of the book he had been reading, set it to one side and gave him his complete attention. 'Well?' he said again. He expected to be told everything.

As he helped himself to coffee and slid two slices of brown bread into the automatic toaster, he could feel Mark watching him. He was worried that he would see the lie.

'Well what?' he said, pretending that the stirring of his coffee demanded his total concentration. The clink of his spoon against the edge of the cup was the only sound as Mark waited for him to say more.

'Tell me all about her,' said Mark.

'Nothing to tell,' he said. It was true, he thought. There was nothing to tell. He leaned over the toaster, as if inspecting the inner workings of the machine. He could see where the thin filaments of metal already burned a fiery orange, could feel the heat on his face. There was a faint burning smell, too, from the charring of an accumulation of breadcrumbs inside.

'I've seen her photographs, remember? She's really something. There must be stuff to tell. Why so secretive?' Mark narrowed his eyes, feigning suspicion.

'No secret, really,' he said.

Mark lifted the coffee pot, tested its weight and then topped up his cup. It came out thick and dark. He did not take milk, but sloppily shovelled in two heaped teaspoons of sugar and, without stirring it, sipped noisily at the sweetened black liquid.

'Susannah says she's a bimbo secretary or something?'

He bristled at the sneer that lay under Mark's words. It was what he liked least about his flatmate, the barely disguised intellectual snobbery. He felt immediately defensive.

'She's not a bimbo,' he said. 'She's working as a secretary to pay her way through college.' Another lie. It came easier this time.

'Oh right,' said Mark.

'A year out, that's all,' he added

'Oh, I see. So she's clever then?'

'Smart as paint,' he boasted.

A spring in the toaster was suddenly released and two slices of toasted bread were lifted clear of the cooling elements.

'So if she's so smart, what's she doing with you then?' He caught his distorted reflection in the surface of the coffee pot. His hair stuck out in all directions and his face was buckled into a grotesque mask. He tried to smooth his hair flat with the press of his hands. What *was* she doing with him, he wondered.

'We just hit it off,' he said.

'Hit it off?'

He scraped the butter to the furthest corners of each slice of toast and watched it melt and soak into the bread. 'Seems we have things in common,' he said. He cut each slice of toast into two neat triangles.

'What things?'

'You know,' he said, 'things.'

'You're not giving much away. Tell me how you met,' said Mark.

'None of your business,' he said, worried now that the lie might at any moment suddenly collapse about him.

'Susannah says you met at the station?'

Yes, he had said that. He'd said that because it was almost the truth. He tried to recall what else he'd told Susannah. He had to be careful; he had to think ahead.

'We collided with each other,' he began. 'Her suitcase connected with my knees. It was bloody sore. She dropped her handbag and I helped her pick up the spilled contents. She'd just arrived here.' He wasn't sure from where; he'd have to think about that. 'We went for a coffee. We talked for hours without realising that time was passing.'

'What'd she say?'

'Oh, I don't remember the things she said. We just talked, that's all. You know what it's like.'

'When was this and why haven't we heard about her?' said Mark.

He hadn't thought this through. When could all this have happened? Why had he kept it a secret from them? He didn't have the answers.

'I don't have to tell you everything,' he said.

'Yes, but this is big news,' said Mark. 'Where you keeping her?'

'As far away from you as I can,' he said.

'Sorry,' she said.

'No, my fault,' he said, though really it was nobody's fault, just an accident. 'Let me help you,' he said. He bent to pick up her handbag from the dirty marble floor of the station concourse. It was a patent red leather shoulder bag that matched her shiny red coat and her red shoes. He dusted off the bag and passed it to her.

64

'Thanks,' she said, 'you don't have to...'

'It's no trouble, really.'

He collected together the spilled contents of her bag and held them out for her to take.

'Thanks,' she said again.

He was close enough that he could smell her perfume, close enough that he could see the colours in her hair – like old straw with just a memory of summer combed through it, he thought. He could see that her suitcase was heavy for her.

'You got a train to catch?' He would offer to help her.

'No, just arrived. Someone's picking me up, only they're late,' she said.

'Boyfriend?'

'Sister.'

'Listen,' he said, 'why don't I take you for a coffee? At least until she comes – your sister.' It was easy to be brave in a dream, he thought.

'It's me should be taking you for coffee,' she said.

'Ok, you take me, then.'

He lifted her suitcase and led the way to one of the smaller coffee shops. It was almost empty when they got there. An old woman wearing a glassy-eyed fox fur around her neck sat at one table. She smiled up at them as they entered. It was obvious that she mistook them for a couple. It pleased him that she did.

They retreated to the undisturbed quiet of a corner table. He placed the case so that it was out of the way against one wall. He cleared the dirty cups and plates to another table.

'I'm Jen, by the way,' she said.

'Jen?'

'Short for Jennifer.'

'Jen,' he said, as if it was a new word he had learned.

She drank her coffee with milk and no sugar. It was something that they had in common right away. They sat facing each other, a little uncertain at first, a little tongue-tied. He wasn't sure what should happen next. He'd told Mark that they had talked for hours, talked without noticing the passing of time. But now he was here with her, with Jen, he didn't know what they talked about.

'So, what are you doing here?' she said.

'Sorry?'

'At the station. Why are you here?'

'Oh, why am I here?'

He hadn't really thought about why he had come into the station. The simple answer was that he was there to meet her. That was why he was there, to meet Jen.

'That's sweet, but how did you know I'd be here?'

'Serendipity,' he said.

Mark wouldn't buy it but Susannah might.

'I just happened here by chance and there you were,' he said. And there she was.

'Well. I'm glad you did happen by; I hate to imagine whose knees I would have bashed with my suitcase if you hadn't been there.'

She had a sense of humour. He knew that already. Sitting opposite him in the small station café she laughed at her own joke. She lifted her hand to her mouth as he had seen her do before. The picture was blurred for a moment. She laughed like in the photograph, only this time it was different; this time he could hear her laugh, could feel the infectious tug of it.

The old woman with the fox fur boa nodded across at him. She was laughing too.

The station announcer's voice crackled over the tannoy speakers; it filtered into the café as muffled laughter.

He looked down at his coffee and he laughed.

66

'Perfect,' he said.

'What?' said Jen.

'Nothing, I was just wondering where you are travelling from?' he said.

There was a pause, a break in the conversation. She didn't know what to say. He could see that.

'You must have come from somewhere,' he said.

'Of course,' she said.

He tried to think. She smiled at him, like in the first frame on the photostrip. She waited for him to sort out the problem, confident that he would.

'You've come here to work,' he said, speaking his thoughts out loud.

'That's right. My sister has found me a job.'

'In an office,' he said.

'Secretarial work, just for a year until my college course starts.'

'And then there's the question of your college course,' he said.

'Maybe none of that really matters,' she said.

'Maybe they don't need to know,' he said.

The woman in the fox fur boa got up from her seat. She fastened the buttons of her coat, hooked a black leather handbag over one arm, lifted a train ticket from the table and made her way to the door. She passed by their table. He looked up. She winked at him. 'What matters are the moments you have together,' she said – only her voice sounded exactly like Jen's. The old woman pushed her way out of the café and disappeared.

When he turned back to Jen, she was disappearing too, one palm raised to her chin and the perfect 'o' of her lips blowing him a kiss out of his dream.

'Do you want to go for a drink sometime – you and Jen?' said Mark.

'Yeh, that'd be great,' he said. 'I'll have to check with her first.'

'Any night would suit me,' said Mark.

'Right,' he said.

He made notes in pencil in an old book, kept them ordered like in a diary. He recorded their first meeting in detail including what the old woman had said, the woman with the fox fur wrapped about her neck.

He invented dates that they had, places they visited together. They went for long walks in public gardens, walked hand in hand for hours stopping to swap kisses on empty paths. She exchanged her red coat for a blue one he saw in a shop window and he bought her gloves to match – or said that he did. They sat in almost empty film theatres watching films he had already seen, or shared a coffee at a busy town centre café. One Saturday they went to an exhibition together, paintings by someone *she* liked, but *he* didn't.

He met her sister once. They shared a flat, just the two of them. Her sister's name was Claire. He met her only briefly; she was just leaving as he arrived. Jen had told her all about him and she was pleased at last to be seeing him – was beginning to think he was nothing more than a dream Jen was having over and over again.

Each day he added more information about Jen in his book: her birthday and horoscope sign; her favourite novel (one he had also read and enjoyed); the names of songs she loved to dance to; the titles of films she had cried over. He didn't see her every day. Some days he just phoned her.

Mark heard him on the phone one day. He was only on for a few minutes, unable to prolong the pretended conversation beyond that. He said he'd call her again later.

'So, did you ask her?' said Mark.

'Ask her what?'

'Out for a drink. Susannah'll come. It'll be just the four of us. We promise not to embarrass you – at least not intentionally.'

'Sorry, forgot to mention it,' he said. The lies came more easily now.

'Well, ask her,' said Mark.

He invented commitments for her: Extra classes she was studying as preparation for her college course, emergencies at work that necessitated her working late some evenings, unexpected visits from her family. Some nights she suffered headaches that sent her to bed early.

'I get the impression she's avoiding us,' said Mark.

He shrugged his shoulders.

'Either that, or you don't want her to meet us,' said Susannah.

'Maybe, she's not so perfect, after all.'

'What do you think, Mark? Maybe an exaggerated stutter? Or a pronounced lisp?'

'Or when she laughs, it sounds like a cow giving birth,' said Mark.

'Or maybe she wobbles from side to side when she walks.'

'Dragging a club foot behind her in the dirt.'

'Or,' said Susannah, 'she's taller than you. That's it, isn't it? She's a good six inches taller than you so that when you stand together her chin rests on your head.'

'And when you hug, it's her hips you hold close to your heart,' said Mark.

They were both laughing now.

'I bet she has to bend her knees so that you can kiss, or do you have to stand on a chair?'

'And when you walk down the street together, does she wear flat shoes and walk in the gutter to even things up a bit?'

He wished they would stop.

'That's it, isn't it?' said Mark.

'Actually, we're going through a rough patch at the moment,' he said. It just came out, an escape plan of sorts.

They fell immediately silent, their laughter stilled in an instant.

'Yes, things are not going so well just now. I'd appreciate it if you would...' He left the request unfinished and walked from the room. Behind him he heard Mark swear at himself under his breath.

It had to end. He knew that. It was foolish to have kept it going so long. He didn't know why he had done that.

They met at the station café again, the one they had first met in. They occupied the same table in the corner. He bought them coffee. There was a sort of symmetry in their meeting, except that this time they had the place to themselves.

'So what's the emergency?' she said. She looked at him just as she had that first time – just as she always did. She was wearing her red coat once more. It was as though they had wound back time and were starting over again.

'We have to talk,' he said.

'Sounds serious,' she said. She leaned across the table towards him. Her hair fell across her cheek in ragged twisted ribbons. This time he reached out and brushed them back into place.

The sound of the station announcer filtered into the café. He could not make out what it said. Somewhere beyond

70

the glass window lights flicked from green to red and another train screeched to a halt. A ticket inspector tucked his watch and chain into his waistcoat pocket and prepared for the onrush of passengers.

'I know this isn't real, any of this,' he said.

'It never really is,' she said.

'I know it is all just an invention.'

She winked at him. 'Don't worry,' she said. 'It always is. Like a game we play.'

'Or like a madness that overtakes us,' he said.

'If you like.'

He could not look at her. He knew she was trying not to laugh, could picture her hand raised to her mouth, the bird's footprints deepening around her eyes.

'I never expected this,' he said.

'Love comes when you least expect it.'

'Love?' he said, as if he had not known that this was what it was.

She could not hold it back any longer; she laughed – not like a cow in painful labour – but like water bubbling over pebbles. A part of him wanted to laugh too; a part of him wanted to cry.

'But how can that be? You're not even...'

'Love is in the one who loves, not in the one who is loved,' she said.

He repeated what she said. It sounded familiar, like something he had read somewhere, like a line from a book.

'And now...?'

'I think we both know what happens now.'

He unpinned her photographs from his pin-board.

'You can keep those,' she said. 'Something to remember me by.'

In the last picture she was still blowing a palmed kiss out to him. For a moment he could feel her breath on his cheek. He tucked the strip of photographs into the pages of his notebook and closed the book shut.

The Man Who Loved Landscape

by Cathy Whitfield

James McCloud loved landscape and I loved James McCloud. Oh, not in *that* way! I'm as normal as the next man, if you can call any man normal. No, I loved James McCloud in a quite different way, though I didn't know how until many years later.

We were both loners I suppose, me from a certain awkwardness with other people, him from a self sufficiency I profoundly envied. But, whatever the reason, we were both drawn to the mountain park, that vast tract of wilderness with its empty valleys and high cloud-wreathed peaks. It was a place where you could be alone without awkwardness, where you could walk for miles, or days, and not see another soul, a place that drew you back time after time. I took to spending my weekends there, tramping the tracks that led to the interior, camping beside shadowed lakes, climbing up to the high snowfields. When I returned from these expeditions I'd usually had the loneliness beaten out of me, and a longing to be with other people would take me to one of the many inns that surround the park - watering-holes for the rangers, walkers, trekkers and climbers who're drawn to the hills and crags and wild empty spaces. It was in one of these places that I first saw James McCloud, in a group by the fire who were poring over an old map.

I've always loved maps and in winter when the weather was poor I'd take up my own maps of the park and read them as another man might read a novel. I'd trace the routes and follow the contours, giving shape to the places I hadn't been, and memory to the places I had, seeing them in my mind's eye – a hollow beneath a cliff perhaps, sere with winter-bleached grasses and cloud blurring the sky-line.

73

Perhaps all who walk the wilds feel the same fascination, and the crowd around the fire was large and noisy enough for me to join their outer fringes without being noticed.

The scraps of conversation were familiar, of course. *That track... this ridge ...* Most had a story to tell of this place or that, of this occasion or the other; the usual sort of thing; of weather closing in, the wrong ridge descended, a long walk back or a night spent in the open. I heard tell of days of wind and rain, of clear winter sunshine, of fog blinding the sky, and snowfields as hard as ice beneath the moonlight. But one man had nothing to say. He alone remained silent, his face lightening in recognition, or darkening with memory, like a slope swept by wind-blown breaks of sunlight. And all the time he touched the map with faintly trembling fingers, tracing the soft swell of the moors as a man might trace a woman's breasts.

I stopped listening to the bragging tales, and stood at the fringe of the group, as was my practice, silent, as was my nature, and watched James McCloud. He noticed eventually and looked up, his fingers stilling for a moment, a brief lift of recognition flickering across the sunlit coruscation of his expression.

You too? he seemed to ask.

We didn't speak. Naturally. We never did speak until that night in October, the night that was to change me. But after that evening in the inn by the fire I began to listen for his name, to collect stories about him and weave them into a legend. He hadn't spoken that evening, but on other occasions he could apparently be persuaded to talk, but when he did the things he told weren't the usual stories. Instead he'd speak of older times, of ghosts and spirits and strange lonely creatures; stories that were remembered and repeated, that glinted in your memory like the surface of a lake stirred by fish ascending from great depths. Sometimes, trudging down a

74

track, heading for the high peaks, I'd repeat the stories out loud to myself, until I'd caught the timbre of a voice I imagined, and the lilt of an ancient tongue speaking the names of the places that had trembled beneath his fingers. *Hill of the stag, the yellow slope, corrie with the wing of snow.* Phrases that would roll over the tongue like cold clear water with the tang of peat at the back of it.

But for all the tales and stories, true or imagined, I came no closer to the man himself until I met the girl. Oh, yes, there was a girl. Isn't there always? Julie was her name, and I wanted her almost as much as I wanted to be alone. I was as normal as other men in that regard. And so, it turned out, was James McCloud.

I'd seen her occasionally, noticed her immediately. Her presence was enough to lure me to the outer margins of whatever group she was in. I didn't speak, of course, but I watched and listened. I began to nod in recognition and, after a moment of puzzlement, she'd nod back.

You too? I'd ask her without words. But I didn't get an answer until one night in June, when the nod was followed by a smile, a chance drifting away of her companion, a shift along the bar and the end of my pint. Diffidently, I offered her a drink. She accepted and indicated a vacant table in the corner of the room. Heart racing, I thought of so many clever things to say that they knotted themselves together at the back of my dry throat. But it didn't matter because she wasn't interested in me at all. She just wanted to talk about James McCloud, and over a drink or three the reasons came spilling out.

They'd met by chance at the end of the season, midweek, both expecting to find a particular camp-place deserted. Instead they'd found each other. But it was the end of a trek and the tug of other people was strong, so they'd made the most of things. A shared campsite had led to a

75

shared meal, a shared half-bottle of whisky leading, in its turn, to another sharing.

'But it was *strange*, you know,' she said. 'It was like I reminded him of someone. No, that's not right. It was as if I made him think of a *place*. Somewhere he was trying to find.'

Then she laughed as if she'd said something foolish, and began to talk of other things, but I'd stopped listening. All I could see was those trembling fingers tracing out a route; the hollow of her neck reminding him of a corrie he knew; the ridge of her spine recognised and named, the angle of her elbow recalling a bend in a particular river. A place, she said; a map to be explored, its contours followed. And then forgotten.

After that, when I saw her, she'd nod, but nothing more, a faint flush and a turning away telling me she regretted saying anything at all. And then she disappeared from the park. I never saw her again.

Perhaps because of the girl, I paid more attention thereafter to the tales about James McCloud, though I didn't see him for months. But others did and they began to speak of a strange dichotomy in the man. If anyone met him as he walked into the park he would, like most walkers, stop to talk and exchange plans and weather forecasts. But he seemed distracted, they said, excited even, with some compulsion tugging at him that was beyond the usual pull of the unexplored.

'A woman,' one suggested. But I was sure it wasn't that. I barely knew the man, and yet I seemed to know him as well as myself. Better, even. No, it was something more compelling than a woman. Yet, whatever it was, it seemed to be something he didn't find, for those who met James McCloud on his return from those trips spoke of a different man entirely; a morose uncommunicative man who'd lost his knack for language, a man disappointed by something, or someone. And yet a man relieved by his own disappointment, as if what he searched for was also to be feared. This I understood too, for I was at the age when you search for something you've no name for, something you fear will hold disappointment in the finding. Or the not finding.

I've always found autumn a troubling season; a time when fires are banked down and sap sinks, when days contract in the cold that seeps from the North. A time of last chances. That was what took me deep into the park that October weekend, in days that were blue and calm, with the low light golden on the bracken and picking out the yellow flags of the birches that still held their leaves, though the pines had already turned winter-black and inward-looking. In two weeks it would be Samhain, the old end of the year and, as always in the park, the sense of ancient times was strong. With each step I felt I travelled into the past James McCloud would speak of sometimes; a past peopled by the lonely spirits of wood and water and wind. So, as I walked, I thought of James McCloud and when, at nightfall, I came across the man himself, it seemed more than coincidence.

He nodded, recognising me, and would, I think, have passed on, but he was returning to civilisation and his longing for company warred with his longing for solitude. I nodded in return, tongue-tied as ever in his presence. Perhaps this too accounted for what happened; the prospect of my silence and yet a listening ear. The long night was drawing in, and the place we met an ideal campsite - a dry meadow sheltered by a stand of stunted alders.

We spoke of little things to begin with; of journeys, routes and way-marks, of herds of deer seen in the distance, a pair of eagles soaring over a ridge, a crag where ravens bred. I asked no questions and offered no opinions, fearful of breaking our nascent brotherhood, and eventually, as our fire burned down to ash, he began truly to talk – a different sort of sharing.

I've never forgotten what he told me that night; how one day he'd headed for a particular peak, thinking to descend a spur that ran away to the south, but long before he'd done so the cloud had fallen and, in spite of his years of experience, he'd lost his way and found himself descending in the wrong direction. There was a trackless slope, a stream that flowed from beneath a black cliff-face, a river gathering other waters to itself and coiling cold and silver in the pale green meadows of a valley. A single rowan clung to the rocks above a bend in the river.

'It's a valley,' he said. 'A day's walk from here, right in the heart of the upland, between the two peaks.'

I was confused, for the place of which he spoke was a high plateau of sere grasses and rocky outcrops, of wind and emptiness. I knew of no such valley, but his certainty made me reach for my map and a torch.

'You won't find it there,' he said, taking the torch from my hand and switching it off. 'How could you? It's a place I'd never seen before, a place I couldn't find on the map, and yet it was utterly familiar. It seemed as if I'd known it all my life, grown up there, grown old there, and never left it. Have you ever come back from a long journey to a place you know and felt it claim you? Been aware of every slope and slant of it as if it was another person? As if it was *yourself*?'

He said nothing more for a long time. The fire burned down and the cold of the October night was bitter and yet we both remained by the glowing ashes, listening to the quiet of a night that was not truly silent; to the mournful piping of a curlew, the purl of water between rocks, the alders creaking in the wind.

'I don't know how long I stayed,' he continued. 'Moments, perhaps. Or it could have been days. It let me go

78

in the end, or I let myself go. On the way back I met a girl. I forget her name. It doesn't matter. All that mattered was that she was something other than what I'd seen, experienced ... been. And yet I couldn't forget it. In the darkness, all I could see, and feel, was that place. The spurs, the slopes, the bend in the river. I've searched for it since, so many times, and never found it. Yet it's there, waiting for me. Calling me back. Listen! It's calling me now ...'

I listened, hearing nothing at first but when I did the hairs rose on my arms. It was the sound of rock and water and the dry rustle of grasses; of wind in trees, wind that has swept through a vast forest - not the patchwork woodlands of the park, but the greater, denser forests that lie far to the north, empty, mysterious and treacherous. It was the sound of wind on rock, on ridges that scar the clouds, in black chimneys of cliffs that reach up into mist and down into shadow. It was the sound of grasslands; of steppe and tundra where only the cries of geese break the endless whine of the wind. And yet the sound was not only the wind, for at its core was a wordless cry of uttermost wilderness; profoundly lonely, impossibly ancient, and yet startlingly familiar. It was the voice of a man, or something other than a man, who loved landscape more than he loved people.

In the morning I woke to find him gone, with no more evidence of his presence than a depression in the grass and a still warm smoor of ash. I never saw James McCloud again. No-one knew what happened to him, for they never found his body. An enquiry concluded that he'd made one further trip back to the mountains, about two weeks after I'd seen him. The weather had been bad, rain turning to snow. There are many ways for a lone man to die in the mountains in winter. People nodded sagely and the case was closed.

But not forgotten. He's still there. I'm certain of it. The man who'd loved landscape had been claimed by the thing he most desired, had become the place he'd so longed to find. He'd searched for something in the wilderness and found, perhaps, only himself, or a semblance of himself. A fetch. There are such things in the world, in the empty places, and we give them names in whatever tongue we speak; dryad, sidhe, uraisg, the big grey man. We give them a shape too - our own - though they have neither shape nor form. Only a voice. Only a folding of the land by mist or moonlight. A creation of the self's searching heart.

I stopped going to the mountains. Time overtook me. Or life. That's what I told myself. There was a motorcycle accident, a long period of convalescence, a physiotherapist whose name, co-incidentally, turned out to be Julie. We married, and later, for life is rarely straightforward, divorced. I'd found the thing or person I'd been searching for, but the fear of disappointment proved to be its own terror. He lay between us, James McCloud, his hand on her cheek, her breast, tracing out the contours of a place that didn't exist.

It's autumn now, October, a few days from Halloween, the name they give Samhain these days. The night of the dead. Children of the more old-fashioned sort carve turnip lanterns to frighten away the spirits. But they can't hold back the night. Or the voice on the wind - a voice that is oddly familiar. I hear it as an echo in my own ears.

I have a few days off and the forecast is good. I get out my old maps and trace the contours of a high plateau where no valley is to be found. I imagine the shape of it; the curve, the ridge, the valley falling away to silver, and one rowan clinging to a rock. It's a place shaped by my own longings, a place that calls to me with my own voice. I trace the contours, and feel my fingers tremble.

The Fifth Circle

by Don Nixon

"I hope you won`t be offended but have you considered counselling, Mr. Blake?"

The motherly looking woman in the Personnel Department was embarrassed as she pushed a leaflet across the desk. She had seen the look in my eyes as she gave me the redundancy papers to sign and the way I had difficulty in controlling the pen. She meant well and I suppose I was still in shock after the interview with Bennet. I brushed the offer aside angrily and looking back, perhaps it was a mistake. I know Eva thought so.

I was hurt and bitter. Since the old chairman had headhunted me at Oxford, I had lived and breathed the job but my mentor and protector had long gone. Now, smooth networking creeps like Gerald Madison, who could talk the current management babble, were the rising stars.

Eva blamed my collapse on the drugs. It was true I had been snorting more lines than the others on the trading floor as the pressures mounted when we started shadowing the euro, but I could handle the deadlines. I enjoyed the adrenalin rush when mayhem hit the screens in the last few minutes of trading. That gave me a bigger buzz than the cocaine. No, it was Gerald who knifed me. He had spread the rumours and hinted that I was becoming too much of a liability, taking too many chances. He was the one who had triggered my breakdown after Italy. Eva saw it as drug-related paranoia but then she could never see beyond Gerald`s easy charm.

I admit I had been foolish in Rome but it had all been quietly hushed up. The Italian house had badly wanted our business and luckily they had a working arrangement with the

81

local police. My name was kept out of the case and I even got to keep the crack I had just scored when the comic opera cops broke up the party.

I was totally unprepared for my reception in London. After securing the firm a good foothold in the Italian commodities market, I was expecting the fatted calf or at least a hefty bonus but Gerald had been busy. I should have noticed he was getting too close to the new head of section. Bennet was a tight-arsed little prat who had been brought over from Accounts and he had never liked me. The interview was short. I was given the choice of a face-saving redundancy or the sack.

"You were fortunate the Italian police decided not to prosecute."

Bennet spoke slowly, carefully enunciating each syllable. He had worked hard to iron out the Cockney vowels and glottal stops in his nasal voice and as he rose in the firm`s hierarchy, the pace of his delivery became more and more hearse-like. He paused and his carefully produced consonants sharpened.

"Even one so talented as you, Blake, cannot continue with this growing addiction to illegal substances without bringing our name into disrepute. We were fortunate this time but our image is threatened by your behaviour."

I could have told the little creep that at least half the department was high most days by the close of trading but I sat there silent in shock. I was out.

How I hated Gerald Madison! Thanks to him, I had lost my job and then my girlfriend. Eva finally walked out when I discharged myself from the rehabilitation unit she had persuaded me to try. After a week of the hell of cold turkey and the other smackheads, I had had enough. The only thing I now wanted was to see Gerald humiliated as I had been and then totally destroyed.

With my lump sum I bought the cottage I sometimes used for holidays in the Lake District. It was in an isolated spot in the mountains above Lake Buttermere. There, with my computer for company I brooded on the treachery of my former junior and friend. Only Eva knew where I was. I had emailed her when I arrived but there was no reply. I guessed she was in Europe scouting locations for a new TV series or perhaps she had decided to write me out of her life for good. I was on my own.

I soon found out however that I was not alone Out there in cyberspace were other bruised egos, who like me, found the anonymity of the chat rooms a relief from their frustrations and shattered egos. Some took refuge in the porn that oozed around the net but my frustration wasn`t sexual. Since the redundancy, my libido had vanished completely and I certainly hadn`t missed Eva as a partner in bed. Perhaps the drug scene was a form of compensation.

Now I just wanted to talk to guys who had been knifed by so-called friends and the chat rooms were full of them. I spent hours in front of the screen reading and responding to the fantasies of revenge with which we regaled ourselves. The buzz was heightened as I started snorting more coke and sometimes I dropped acid as well. It was all too easily available in the pubs in the Northern Lakes and cheaper than in London. I soon had an arrangement going with a dealer down in the nearby village and once he realized I was a regular and always paid up front, he offered to deliver to the cottage on his motor bike. After I had been at the cottage a month, the dealer was the only human being I spoke to and our transactions were brief. I never invited him in. My world was now governed by my modem. Like some modern day Alice, I went through the looking glass of my computer screen to what had become for me reality.

Gerald would have dismissed us as a bunch of "saddos". "Get a life" had been one of his favourite expressions. Sometimes, someone in a chat room would write that we were well out of the rat race but who was he kidding? I missed the trading floor. The coke was no substitute for that adrenalin rush when the screens went mad.

That Friday afternoon after the pusher had left I sat flicking in and out of chat rooms. I was bored. I'd heard most of the stuff before and it seemed to be taking longer than usual for the crack to have an effect. I'd opened one of the new packets the dealer had brought and I began to wonder if he was starting to rip me off. He'd assured me it was pure Columbian and very strong but there was no hit. I got up and did another line. This time I felt the burn in my nostrils. At that moment the picture on the screen dissolved into a whirling kaleidoscope of colours. A stab of pain crunched the back of my eyeballs and as suddenly was gone. The screen slowly began to stabilize.

A blast of trumpets sounded, almost shattering the loudspeakers at either side of the screen. I recognized the music. It was from the Verdi Requiem. The massed choir shrieked in terror.

"Dies Irae, Dies Illa."

It was the Day of Judgment section - the Day of Wrath when sinners trembled to know their fate. I had heard it at the Opera House in Rome. It was exciting and I had ordered the CD. The sound gradually faded and the screen went blank. I blinked and managed to get my eyes back into focus.

Pinpoints of light flickered and gradually a picture began to emerge. An elderly man dressed in a flowing white Roman toga appeared in the centre of the screen. He stood beneath an arch. Inscribed above the arch were the Italian words - "Lasciate ogni speranza voi ch'entrata."

84

I translated slowly. "Leave all hope, you who enter." I'd heard the quotation but for the moment couldn`t place it. The trumpets sounded once more. I winced as the sound seemed to engulf me. I realised I must have pressed a wrong key combination which had taken me from the chat room into one of the interactive computer games that some of the nerds I talked with liked to create. I'd played some of these games before but this one seemed different from the usual space wars and monsters. I shrugged. It was a way of passing the time.

A speech bubble formed above the old man`s head.

"I am Virgilio, your guide to the Inferno."

The screen became filled with flames. In the fires naked bodies were writhing and being sucked down into a funnel-shaped vortex. Galleries ran around its sides from which peered grotesque figures like mediaeval gargoyles. The trumpets blared again and once more the voices shrieked - "Dies Irae, Dies Illa."

The picture gradually faded with the sound and Virgilio returned. A new bubble formed.

"Who is to be punished ?"

I felt a surge of excitement at the thought of Gerald being tormented by the devilish creatures in the vortex. Virgilio seemed to nod as though reading my mind and an empty box appeared at the bottom of the screen. "Type in your answer," came the instruction.

"Gerald Madison."

My fingers trembled as I hit the keys. Once again the trumpets sounded and flames flickered momentarily across the screen as the vortex reappeared and the gargoyles cavorted. As they disappeared, the screen filled with a close-up of the Roman`s face. The speech bubble now emerged cartoon-like from his mouth.

"Please complete the following."

A questionnaire dropped down the screen. I scanned the list of questions. My answers were all focused on Gerald. I entered his address, telephone number, the make of his car and his personalized registration. I gritted my teeth as I typed in his occupation as Chief Commodities Broker, the position he had stolen from me. Finally, I was asked to describe Gerald`s offence. I recalled my interview with Bennet and angrily pounded the keyboard.

"He got me sacked and took my job."

The fury I had felt at the time returned and for a moment I was unable to continue. I got up and walked around the room. I did another line of coke. My hands were shaking and some of the powder spilled and scattered down the front of my T shirt. I lifted the fabric to my mouth and licked the white flakes. I ran the tip of my tongue round my lips and felt the sting of the crack. I willed myself to relax and returned to my desk. Virgilio was waiting.

"You must now choose the degree of punishment you wish to be inflicted on Gerald Madison."

A diagram of the galleries in the vortex appeared by Virgilio`s side and he pointed to them as he explained.

"These are five of the circles in the Inferno. The level of punishment increases as you descend. The upper circles are for relatively minor transgressions whereas in the lower there is no limit to the pain that may be inflicted. Make your choice of circle."

I did not hesitate.

"The fifth."

The little Roman seemed to smile.

"That is a serious decision. It signifies termination. Are you sure?"

"YES." I typed in capitals.

The smile was replaced by a frown. "I have not the authority to make a decision on the fifth circle. I will need to

86

refer the matter to Signor Alighieri. Only he can deal with termination. But I must warn you that this is a very serious matter and there will be conditions. If he agrees to your request, you will be contracted to perform a service of similar magnitude for him."

I imagined Gerald in the flames of the vortex and laughed. Virgilio`s face appeared in close-up and his expression was serious.

"Think very carefully. Once you agree there is no going back. Signor Alighieri is the capo di capo. He is inflexible in his requirement that all contracts are honoured. Do you agree to the conditions?"

I did not hesitate. Fuelled by the cocaine, I was floating. All I could think of was Gerald. I was consumed by my desire for revenge. In one part of my mind I knew it was all a game, a fantasy created by a "saddo" from one of the chat rooms, but for that moment it was real. I wanted him to burn.

"I agree," I typed.

Virgilio disappeared and once more the galleries of the Inferno appeared. Now the flames flared more brightly and the screen became filled with the conflagration. The Verdi trumpets rang out again. The surge of sound and the pounding rhythms reverberated through the room and as the choir made its entry, the words of the Requiem drilled into my skull.

"Dies irae, dies illa!"
I heard my voice as if from outside myself screaming the words. Spasms of sharp pain shot down my arms and I retched as I felt a blockage in my throat. I gagged and felt as though a fist had hammered my throat. I was choking. The screen exploded in a kaleidoscope of swirling colours. I closed my eyes.

When I opened them Virgilio had returned and the music had stopped. He was smiling.

"It is authorized."

He pointed to the arch above him. The inscription had gone and scrolling across the crossbeam, a message in blood red italics appeared.

"Welcome to the Inferno. The contract is made. Within 24 hours your subject will be consigned to the Fifth Circle. Soon after, Signor Alighieri will be in touch and you will receive your instructions. A CD Rom is the usual method for company communication."

The little figure of Virgilio seemed to bow and he disappeared through the archway. Again the trumpets blared out and the constriction in my throat eased. My breathing became easier and as the music faded, I felt as if I was being drawn down, spiralling into the great funnel of the vortex. But now there were no devils, no tormented bodies only a soft velvety blackness which enveloped me.

I woke early the following morning slumped over the keyboard. I opened the computer and saw an e-mail had arrived. To my surprise it was from Eva. I brought it up to full screen.

"Hi there !

I suppose you`re still up in the wilds licking your wounds in that draughty cottage. Whatever possessed you to buy it; it's a real pneumonia trap? I got back yesterday and found your e-mail. I don't suppose you listen to the news up there so you won't have heard about Gerald Madison. I tried to phone you earlier but I guess your modem was on. I know you blamed him for it all, but what's happened is awful. It was on the early morning news. He crashed his car on the way home last night. I've just rung his secretary and got the details. He hit a fallen tree. Apparently he couldn't get out and the car was on fire. He's so badly burned that the police have asked her to identify him as it's too grim for his wife to see. I can't understand it. You know what a careful driver Gerald was and he'd never drink while driving."

I got up and went to the window. I felt excited. I had wanted Gerald to writhe in flames and so he had as Virgilian had promised. But the Fifth Circle ? I shook my head. That had been a drug fantasy; it was just a coincidence. But I was glad he was dead. I felt no pity. He deserved it, the conniving bastard. I stared out of the window, watching the road down the valley. I must keep calm I told myself. I noticed a motor bike rounding the first of the hairpin bends far below. I concentrated on it until it disappeared from view.

I read the e-mail again visualizing the horror of the burning car and Gerald trapped inside. I still could feel no pity. I was glad and at the same time felt slightly ashamed. Perhaps the firm might take me back; they had nobody now with real experience in that sector. Should I play hard to get? It was all a coincidence; I refused to think about it. It was the drugs playing me tricks last night. It was a warning. I must cut down on the crack. I heard a motor bike outside. Was I so confused that I was losing track of days? It wasn't time for the dealer to be back so soon. I walked to the rider in the yard.

He was taking off his helmet. It wasn't my pusher. Long glossy curls fell to his neck. With his regular rather girlish features, he might have been the model for the Donatello `David`.

He smiled and held out a package. I suddenly felt chilled and caught my breath. I steadied myself against the doorpost and the Verdi trumpets rang out from the computer, reverberating round the yard and pounding in my brain.

"Dies Irae. Dies Illa."

I found I was screaming the words but there was no sound of my voice. It was trapped inside my skull.

He stepped forward into a shaft of sunlight and his black leatherclad figure seemed suddenly sinister and threatening.

"Mr. Blake?"

89

He gazed up at me from under long black eyelashes. The pose was almost flirtatious but there was the same calculation I had seen in the eyes of the golden tanned youths hanging round the Spanish Steps in Rome. The 'fallen angels' my friends had called them. I staggered back and closed my eyes trying to blot out the image of the twisting bodies as they dropped into the Inferno. I felt his hand on my arm, the grip firm. I tried to shake him off. He was pulling me down. The circles of the abyss seemed to spin before me. I forced myself to breathe deeply and opened my eyes. He was smiling like Raphael's Lucifer as he placed the package in my hand.

"Your CD, signor."

To Every Pot A Lid

by Siobhan O'Tierney

Ellen kept feeling odd moments of peace. Maybe tonight she would *not* relive umpteen incidents of her marriage but perhaps even sleep until morning without recalling even one. She had no idea where this solace was coming from. Was she finally becoming reconciled to living alone? No! She hated it. Indeed, the inexplicable sense that she was no longer alone was what she found so cheering. But of course she was utterly alone, no less now than on the day Geoff first scarpered. Yet lately the house seemed less bleak, so that Ellen felt a curious tranquility, as if some kindly presence had moved in to watch over her. Crazy! She knew fine well that ghosts, poltergeists and spirits did not exist, never had, and never could.

On another side of town a young couple lay sprawled.

'Where could he be?' Ratz whispered.

'No idea' Jaqi laughed.

'Aren't you worried?' he kissed her ear-lobe.

'Why should I be?'

'Well, for instance - your old man's disappeared.'

'Oooh. How *sad.*'

Jaqi's remorse vanished in giggles as Ratz tongued her navel.

They never mentioned Maurice again. Jaqi hadn't time. She was 25 and talented and beautiful. Maurice was forty-five and morose. They'd met at a book-signing; Maurice had written a tome on Celtic ghosts. Jaqi, recently graduated, thought there was something extraordinary about his mournful eyes. Back then she was writing the most provocative, astute, grittiest first novel ever and was very attracted to any kind of misfit, the more misfitted the better. Also, Maurice looked scrawny and Jaqi loved cooking. She asked him sideways if he'd like to haunt her. A smile momentarily illuminated his whole face and Jaqi got the heady but erroneous notion that she could endlessly repeat the transformation. So she invited Maurice to dinner and later - much, much, later the same night, she proposed to him.

Ellen awoke feeling unusually refreshed. Even her bedroom seemed less offensive, the garish pink that young woman had painted it looked a shade softer. Ellen had hated this ugly terraced red-brick on first sight, but the couple wanted a quick sale so the house was a bargain. Every room needed redecorating to a moderate colour and the departing couple had left more junk than she had the energy to deal with. The cellar was choc-a-bloc with stuff; she hadn't ventured there since the day she moved in. Ellen had glimpsed the husband only once - surely twice his wife's age. His apparent melancholy stirred her sympathy, until she remembered Geoff with his youngster and then Ellen allowed herself a vengeful smile - men who courted women half their age *deserved* to be miserable.

It took a couple of years for Jaqi to finally realise that his first incredible smile had been pure fluke. Nothing cheered Maurice. He practically lived in the cellar, his 'study'. Nor was he tempted by all her cooking but remained spectrally thin, eating barely enough to keep him alive - if that wasn't overstating his mode of existence. In a reckless effort to cure his despondency she insisted they sell the house he'd lived in all his life. By now Jaqi had discovered an aptitude for the kind of erotica much prized by the *Purple Silk* label and abandoned social realism, and she could afford a more spacious house by the coast. Jaqi had never meant to be callous; she *had* been fond of Maurice. It couldn't be her fault that he remained so tenaciously glum. Not even living by the sea could cheer him. His fault if she stopped caring. A month after moving into the bright new house he went for the paper one morning and never returned. But by then Jaqi had already met Ratz, a promising fiddler with a hugely promising rock band.

Friends kept advising Ellen how much she still had to offer, she looked at least a decade less than her age, Geoff's exodus should be seen as a beginning not an end, she should find herself, take up new interests, she'd surely find someone new - there was plenty of fish out there. Ellen listened and nodded, thinking they were mad. What *were* they on about - find *herself?* Find *someone new?* Plenty of *fish!* Geoff was all she wanted. She couldn't stop remembering him, his laugh, his voice, his body, his eyebrows, how he tightened his tie, the way he............Stop! *Nobody* could replace him. Even Geoff had suggested she might find someone new, which had made Ellen livid. *He* couldn't keep *his* word but no way, ever, would *she* break *her* wedding vows. Ellen believed Geoff still suffered qualms about leaving her - no way would she ever withdraw that hook. She'd *never* consider another man. Never. Never. Never.

Maurice slept rough and watched the house for several days before slipping into the cellar one morning. Luckily the locks were unchanged and Ellen's routines were constant. Every Sunday she lunched with her sister Mary, a madam by the sound of her voice on the ansafone. Maurice wondered why Ellen bothered with it, only Mary ever called. Otherwise it was silent. Jaqi's ansafone used to be constantly recording her friends riotous voices. Thankfully, now his house was silent again, even when Ellen was home she made little noise.

Some friends and colleagues advised Ellen; 'I'd never hang around waiting', 'I'd never let my husband back if he did that,' etc. etc. etc. which promptly turned her right off them. Easy words for those who've never been tested. Her sister, Mary, was the worst. She knew better than anyone how Ellen had suffered years of brooding while Geoff abhorred children; you'd no guarantee how a child would turn out, he'd rather play Russian roulette. Why spoil their perfect marriage?

Surely she didn't want to forfeit that! Ellen would have forfeited her legs for a baby but she blinked away her screaming hormones. Then when she was 45 Geoff left her for a 25-year old air hostess, bearer of his twin sons. 'Not just turning the knife in you but making it spin,' Mary liked to pronounce. Like Ellen needed telling.

Seconds after the front door clicked shut Maurice ran upstairs. From a window he watched her go down the street. He liked her walk, not swaying like Jaqi's but steady - almost solemn. He'd yet to see her face properly. He hadn't seen a photo anywhere and he certainly wouldn't snoop. That wasn't his plan. Not that he actually had one.

Definitely, her new house was haunted, but Ellen didn't and couldn't dare tell anyone. She knew exactly what would happen; after furtive sniggering her friends and colleagues would discretely recommend some alternative therapies. But it was worse than that, immeasurably worse - not only had Ellen to deal with the overturning of a lifelong extreme skepticism about supernatural beings, but after finally admitting to herself the undeniable evidence that her house was indeed haunted, Ellen was also trying to make sense to herself of the fact that she liked the ghost who was haunting her.

No, she knew nobody who might even remotely understand the comfort in knowing that you're not *quite* so alone any more.

Maurice found himself sweeping up before he knew what he was doing. Stop!!! He must *not* leave a trace. He almost scattered the toast crumbs back onto the floor. After one small black coffee he returned gladly to the cellar. Maurice had an immense capacity for stillness, (Jaqi who habitually misunderstood, misconstrued, misinterpreted and misread everything about him had called it laziness) and he could day-dream for hours. In good moods his mother used to call him a saint, but more often she was angry, or despairing of

94

him ever finding a *real* job, leaving home, getting married - then she called him dumb. He had disappointed her more and more with every passing year of his youth, by his complete failure to acquire any interest in material concerns. Then cancer struck and she was glad of it. Maurice nursed her devotedly for six years. Her last words were a wish that he would get married. At least Jaqi had satisfied that. His mother hadn't stipulated *staying* married.

His books were still in the cellar, and his old camp bed and blankets. Jaqi hadn't even packed them! Neither had he of course, but Maurice didn't dwell on that. To admit that he had purposely left everything behind implied some intent to return, which was inadmissible. With great caution, he would stay here a long time. Beyond that, Maurice couldn't bear to think.

Her ghost became bolder. It happened very gradually, one evening the floor looked swept. Days later Ellen saw that her breakfast dishes had been tidied to one side of the table. She stared at them for some time, first in fear then in wonder. Searches through her bedroom, bathroom and living room showed nothing else had been touched. She could hardly call the Police to say someone had broken in to her house to tidy up. Several evenings later her dishes had been placed in the sink. Ellen smiled. So it continued. She imagined some old butler; maybe he'd been killed while washing up and could never find peace now till the dishes were done. Who could object to such a ghost? She shuddered now at memories of Geoff's slovenliness. He used to snack at all hours, leaving smears, crumbs, stains and spills all over the kitchen. Which she cleaned up without complaint, otherwise Geoff grew petulant at anything remotely resembling a 'nagging' and would sulk for hours. Now she laughed aloud, she'd never again have to clean up his mess! How wonderful to picture that young air-hostess wiping up after Geoff at this very moment.

95

Ellen was the third and by far the best woman he had ever lived with. She surely had no idea of his existence. If she noticed any food missing she was doing nothing about it and the amount of electricity he used must be negligible. He could do as he pleased, sleep, read, write or day-dream as long as he liked with no fear of a sudden demand to know what he was doing *now*. He had never known such peace, and in return did more and more housework. Now every evening Ellen found her floor swept, dishes done, table spotless.

One morning, shortly after she'd left for work, the phone rang. Maurice braced himself for another bulletin from Mary. Instead a man spoke, *Ellen, Geoff here. Could we meet? For dinner perhaps? Please call me at work, darling.*

Sharp pains stabbed Maurice in the chest. Geoff? Who's he? What did he want with Ellen? Why was he calling her darling? Cheek! There were no men in Ellen's life, Maurice had been certain of that. Like him, she was a person of great quietude, and didn't need other people. Maurice's mother often urged him to go out with girls. What was wrong with him? He wasn't *you know* was he? Crimson with shame he'd look away, unable to tell her that he never fancied *anyone*, neither male nor female. He lacked whatever it was that impelled people to seek out partners. All his life he'd waited for lust, libido, desire, passion to hit him, overwhelm him - it never happened. It had been a relief to find he could do it with Jaqi but he'd never *longed* for it.

Until the message came from Geoff. Who the hell is *Geoff?* He sounded like a total prat. Didn't the guy know Ellen already had someone? How dare he interfere! Maurice was so stricken by a sudden longing for Ellen that even breathing hurt. He wanted Ellen here, right now, in his arms, he wanted to hold her and hug her and have her. Was this desire? He glared at the ansafone. Am I jealous? But in literature jealousy seemed exciting - not like the acid Maurice could feel burning up inside him. Ellen, he heard himself whisper Ellen, Ellen,

Ellen. How beautiful her name was, so full of sympathy and longing and loveliness. Maurice snatched the tape from the ansaphone, burned it in the sink and then spent hours in a frenzy of cleaning.

That evening Ellen's cooker, fridge and microwave sparkled so much she stroked them in amazement. How splendidly clean her kitchen was. Though her every nerve and limb grieved for that ...... swine, Ellen liked this gleaming kitchen immensely. If Geoff was ever to consider returning then new ground rules were essential. Dream on! As if he would come back - eighteen months gone and never a word. Eighteen months! Yet she was surviving. More than that? No! Absolutely not! Make no mistake - her heart was still broken, she was still desperately lonely for Geoff. But extra hours at work had paid off in a recent promotion, and at home she could read to her hearts content. Geoff used to complain if she spent too long with her head in a book. If only her bed wasn't so cold and lonely at night.

Maurice paced his cellar, bewildered by a vortex of feelings previously unknown to him. Sitting still was impossible. His thoughts, which usually came to him in calm steady sequences, were now whirling violently as fear, anger, longing and wanting consumed him. As he listened to Ellen moving about upstairs and it took all his will not to run up to her and hold her to him like he'd never let go.

Hours after he heard her go to bed Maurice was still pacing as Geoff's message replayed torturously in his head. Finally, at 2.36, he could not bear it a moment longer and crept lightly as a cat up to the kitchen, through the hall and up the stairs, into Ellen's room. Maurice kneeled by her bed and stroked her hair with the gentlest of touches and Ellen didn't stir from her sleep. In the moonlight she looked pale and beautiful as an angel. With infinite care Maurice slowly raised the duvet and climbed in beside her. Still sleeping, she turned towards him and then - his breathing stopped a full minute -

97

she reached her hand around his chest. Finally he exhaled and drew breath again, and then edged nearer still to her. It was incredible that she didn't wake, that the pounding of his heart, so loud he could feel it in his scalp, in his eardrums, in his throat and stomach and loins, didn't waken her.

Maurice waited a long time, willing his heart to settle, waiting for her hand to withdraw from his chest so he could slip back out of her bed without waking her. But after awhile – he had no idea how long, she moved closer to him, and stretched her arm more tightly around him. The pounding of his heart was impossibly loud – surely she'd waken? Ellen murmured some noises, too faint for him to catch, and her face tilted towards his. After the longest time - or it might only have been seconds or moments - he brushed his lips against hers lightly as a falling leaf. Ellen's lips parted and pressed his in return. Maurice could not stop himself now. He started kissing her fervently.

Maurice tore himself from her warmth and crept back down to the cellar, terrified of pushing his luck. He'd had an astonishing flight of bliss, as wordless as it was miraculous. He couldn't tell how awake Ellen had been and was too terrified to ask, but she had responded to his kisses with a hunger that blew his mind. Had he committed a crime? Surely, surely not? Ellen had given herself to him so completely he was horrified at the thought that he might have taken advantage of her. It didn't bear thinking. He'd just had the best experience of his entire life, and was reeling from bliss to frantic worrying that he'd breached some law or ethics.

Ellen woke up in a heady daze. Had it been a dream? But no dream had ever been so tender, so real, so... *astonishing*. Was she going mad? It had happened, hadn't it? Or was it the figment of raging hormones? *But how?* She was alone, entirely alone and hadn't dreamed of Geoff in months (anyway it was never *that* good with him). Ellen checked the hall door and every window, nothing was touched, and nobody had broken in.

Maurice willed and willed himself to stay in the cellar, but by 3am he couldn't bear the longing and went up to Ellen.

At work they wondered at Ellen's new sparkle; nudge, nudge wink, wink, who is it? Nobody! She protested every time. One lunch break she furtively bought a magazine on the paranormal. Inside she read a story which was incredible, ludicrous, and insane. Weeks ago she'd have ridiculed and scorned it. Now Ellen read *My Phantom Lover* avidly. Everything had been turned topsy-turvy. Geoff, who never wanted babies had fathered twins. Geoff, who always slated men who succumbed to mid-life crises and left their wives for bimbos, had done just that. She who'd never believed in ghosts was now living with one quite happily. And now! She who'd never really known passion couldn't wait for the small hours of every morning. Her ghost was extending his territory? All the better.

Geoff called Ellen at work. She heard herself tell him that she'd rather not meet him - that actually, she was happier solo and furthermore, now that she was used to living alone she found her life was wonderfully fulfilled. "By whom," he snarled. "Just a feeling I get, that's all," Ellen smiled, putting the phone down.

Really and truly though, at the back of her mind Ellen suspected she'd have to confront her ghost one day and find out more about him. But for now she liked him just the way he was.

The Plot

by Mark Frankel

Dekker glanced at the threatening sky. That shade of pink meant a dust storm was on its way.

He parked the excavator and headed for home. The wind had become fierce and he struggled to reach the shelter of the storm porch. Once inside, he re-pressurized before hanging up the bulky surface suit and sliding open the door.

The house was a typical Mars cabin - basic duplex with living and leisure space at ground level under the dome - sleeping quarters and washing facilities below. Some of the larger family dwellings went down five levels. Mahler had three all to himself.

It was four days before the wind dropped and he was able to get back to work. That evening his screen displayed a dinner invitation from his neighbour. He flew over as soon as he had showered and changed.

Mahler was a lean, scholarly-looking man with straight white hair reaching down to his shoulders. Dekker looked longingly around the spacious living area that would one day be his. It was at least twice the circumference of his own cabin and he knew the two lower levels were the same size. He had often explored the house when Mahler was away at the sulphur springs. They had exchanged security codes so that each could monitor the other's property in his absence.

Mahler lived well. He was something of an electronics genius and the room was packed with gadgets. In contrast to the sparse furnishings in Dekker's home, he had surrounded himself with the best of everything.

Tonight they were going to enjoy a meal prepared by the Savoy Hotel chef in London, England. Mahler kept a selection of such delicacies in his cold-store.

"Try this," he said, handing Dekker a glass of amber-coloured liquid. "It's a Tokay wine – supposed to be the perfect companion for tonight's meal."

Dekker sipped cautiously. "Good," he said and took a long swallow before putting his glass down. The Tokay was too sweet for his taste but Mahler was something of a wine connoisseur and he had no wish to upset him. He glanced at the EarthLink screen on the far wall. A series of small explosions had suddenly disturbed the silence. Fireworks illuminated the night sky over New York.

"What are they celebrating?"

"Fourth of July." Mahler lifted something off one of the low tables. "What do you think of this?"

Dekker handled it curiously. It looked like an animal horn, curved and about a foot long. The surface was smooth and beautifully polished. Flecks of colour - green, red and yellow - appeared as they caught the light. It was surprisingly heavy. He knew Mahler was clever with his hands and made sculptures out of rocks but he hadn't seen anything like this before.

"What is it?" he said.

"Cow horn."

"But it's solid; cow horns are hollow."

"Not these."

"But aren't they usually black?"

"That's what I always thought – until I tried the buffer. Happened to be looking at a pile of them recently and realised it was the only part of my animals that wasn't useful. What do you think?"

"Pretty," said Dekker, handing it back.

Mahler slapped his knee and chuckled. "Got orders for five hundred – at a hundred dollars each," he said, triumphantly. "Some of the smart boutiques in London are snapping them up."

101

Dekker shook his head admiringly. You had to hand it to Mahler. Whatever he touched seemed to turn to money. "What's the market news?"

Mahler obligingly switched channels. "Marble up fifty – wool a hundred and fifty. Looks like we're both doing all right."

Dekker had grown up on a sheep farm on Earth. When his foster parents, Tom and Sarah Marshall, were alive they had always treated him as one of their own children and even promised him a share in the farm when they died. He was grateful and often did the work of two men without complaint – but he knew the children resented his presence.

When the will was read out, he found that he had been left a sum of money - but nothing else. He was convinced the three Marshall children had somehow turned their parents against him. The knowledge that his parents had abandoned him had always rankled and he was subject to mood swings that occasionally erupted into violence. He had nearly killed one of the brothers before leaving with a burning sense of injustice.

Twenty years ago, the government was still offering free passage and grants for colonists on the inner planets and he had seized the opportunity. He stared thoughtfully at the screen. Since the decline of sheep farming on Earth, wool prices seemed to rise at an unprecedented rate.

"Thought any more about retirement?" he said.

Mahler laughed and stood up. "All in good time. Let's eat."

The food was delicious but Dekker was relieved when they finished the Tokay wine and switched to red. Afterwards they watched a documentary about the new space station on Europa.

102

When it was time to leave, Mahler pointed to a large box by the door.

"That's for you. Watch your back; it's heavy."

"What is it?"

"Cow horns. You've got a buffer, haven't you?"

Dekker nodded.

"Well - something to do in your spare time. Watch out for the points, though. They're pretty sharp. You need to smooth them down before you handle them. I'll give you fifty dollars for each one that's up to standard."

The scream of the drill split the stillness of the Martian air. The planet's harsh, red soil was fashionable for terraces back on Earth where it was compressed, polished to a high sheen and marketed under the name of Mars Marble. People seemed to like the idea of walking on the surface of a different planet without actually having to leave their own.

Every six months a freighter arrived with supplies from Earth and departed loaded with Martian produce. The next ship was due in two months. Dekker was behind schedule. Dust storms had been particularly troublesome lately.

When he had come to Mars, the farming concessions had long gone. He had hoped he might find water on his plot – but no longer. The earth tremors that had caused the subterranean rivers to flow into the huge Elysium crater must have drained every drop of liquid for miles around.

There were vast areas of water-ice on the planet, of course, and the conversion engineers had already started work on an irrigation network – but it would take time. Dekker hoped his mining days would have ended long before it was completed.

In the distance, the dusty wind ruffled the government hemp fields marking the edge of his land and the beginning of Mahler's farm, one of several around the Elysium sea.

Sunlight glinted off the yellow water and Dekker gazed enviously at the scattered cattle on his neighbour's pastures. Even from this distance he could see they were heavy with wool. Hybrid trees were gradually replacing the carbon dioxide with oxygen while seeding stations generated nitrogen. The animals were native to the planet but seemed to be thriving on the enriched atmosphere.

Scientists claimed that the next phase - converting Phobos into an artificial sun - would complete the hydrological cycle; raising the surface temperature on Mars and turning the planet into a tropical paradise.

The population of Mars was mainly male. Some came to get away from family life; others to escape from life itself.

Mars was known as the planet of lonely men but Dekker actually preferred his own company. His neighbour, on the other hand, had a son that he kept in touch with.

During his forty years on Mars, Mahler had prospered through his own hard work and initiative. Now the virus that had decimated Earth's sheep farms had substantially increased the value of his. But he took no pleasure from this and his sympathies were with the farmers who had lost their livelihood – unlike Dekker. Not knowing the miner's background, he had wondered at the vehemence of his delight when the news had reached them.

Mahler planned to retire and return to Earth soon and had promised to sell his farm to his neighbour.

Phobos had been rising in the west when Dekker had left his house that morning and it was disappearing below the eastern horizon now. That meant he had worked an eight-hour shift. Descending the ramp to the shower room, he stripped and

104

stood in front of the mirrored wall. The reflection showed a large, heavily muscled man with some grey starting to show in his thick black hair and heavy beard. Years of scowling had joined his eyebrows together so that they ran in a straight line, dividing the top third of his face from the rest. The hot steam room eased out the tiredness and sharpened his hunger. Two of Mahler's cows had been badly injured in a fight some months before and had to be slaughtered. He had given Dekker one of the carcasses.

The meat had little flavour; but it made a welcome change from his normal diet.

The gift had puzzled him. Mahler was not a mean man but neither was he in the habit of giving anything away. Dekker, suspecting an ulterior motive, was on his guard for the next few weeks.

Afterwards, he spent the rest of the evening copying out some verses. The cabin was littered with books and the walls covered with examples of his painstaking calligraphy. The first time Mahler had visited, he had been astonished to discover this unexpected side to Dekker's character.

Several months passed before he saw his neighbour again. The weather had improved and by working long hours, Dekker had been able to meet his quota. Mahler had invited him over to see the Earth Ice Hockey final.

It was after the game that Dekker's world fell apart. Pictures of a smiling family appeared on the screen; a man in his fifties who bore a strong resemblance to Mahler and a young man and woman.

"Sorry - forgot to download them," Mahler said casually.

"Who are they?"

"That's my son, Paul. The young fellow's my grandson Roddie with his wife Suzie. She's expecting a baby." He chuckled. "Looks like I'm going to be a great grandfather."

The young man on the screen suddenly waved. "Looking forward to seeing you, Grandad," he said, before the pictures faded.

"What did he mean?" said Dekker, a surge of excitement colouring his face.

"They're coming out for a visit on the next ship. Thinking of settling here. Their farm's had it; the virus wiped out most of my son's flock. Nothing to keep them there, now."

"What will they do?" A cold knot of fear had tightened in Dekker's stomach.

Mahler was carefully topping up their glasses. "They want to take over my farm."

"What about our agreement?"

"Been meaning to talk to you about that; suppose I should have said something sooner..."

Dekker abruptly stood up, towering over the smaller man. "We had a deal - you said the farm would be mine when you retired."

"Circumstances have changed, Dekker. This is family. I know it's a disappointment for you but family comes first. You must realise that."

"But it's not fair; you can't treat me as if I was dirt."

Mahler's face was suddenly hard. "I'm sorry – but that's the way it is."

Dekker sat up all night until the blood had stopped pounding in his head and he could think clearly. No - he wasn't prepared to accept it. The only thing that had kept him going this last year had been the prospect of owning the farm.

He went through to his work room and picked up one of the cow horns, testing the point against his thumb. Mahler was right. It was sharp – very sharp.

A few days later it was on the news screen. Mahler's body had been found out on the pasture. It appeared that he had been attacked by one of his own cows and his surface suit ripped. He had frozen to death.

It was a week before the call came from the mayor's office. Examination of Mahler's papers had confirmed Dekker's claim on the farm. When he had visited his neighbour's farm that night, it hadn't taken him long to copy Mahler's signature onto the agreement. The registration documents were awaiting his signature and bank details.

It proved difficult to find a quick buyer for the quarry, however, and Dekker was forced to sell it back to Land Registry for a modest price. You had to be resident for thirty years before you were allowed to own a second plot.

He awaited the next ship from Earth with some trepidation but instead of the dead man's family it brought a team of nuclear engineers. They were ready to begin work on converting Phobos. Within a few weeks, mining ships were landing on Mars' main satellite.

Dekker had made discreet enquiries about his previous home on Earth and discovered that the Marshalls' financial situation was grim. They had been trying to sell the farm for some time but the market was overloaded. Through an agent, he offered a derisory sum which was promptly accepted. He would have to travel to Earth and was looking forward to seeing the expressions on the faces of his erstwhile family when he revealed himself as the purchaser.

His second luxury was signing up for EarthLink. Switching channels one day, he found himself halfway through a report of the effect on industry if the Phobos conversion turned Mars sub-tropical. Wool-cattle were mentioned and his blood chilled as he caught the word 'doomed'.

It had never occurred to him that the dramatic change of climate might affect farmers like himself. Now, he monitored every news bulletin, anxiously watching the steady progress of the work on Phobos. The talk was no longer about industry; it was about holiday resorts and hotels.

Among his messages one day was the proposal for a leisure complex to be built on his old mining plot. The idea of hundreds of strangers invading his privacy appalled him. He flew into town early the following morning and in due course received official notification that his arguments had been rejected. He had no right of privacy. The project had been approved. Several restless nights later the obvious solution occurred to him and he slept easily for the first time in weeks.

The Leisureland offices occupied the top floor of a gleaming black glass and steel tower. The building hadn't been there last time he visited town. Clearly, a lot of new money was flowing into Mars. The bearded Dekker was welcomed effusively by the manager, a smooth-cheeked, smartly-dressed man in his late forties.

A huge map of Mars dominated one of the walls of the luxuriously-fitted office, its individual plots clearly numbered.

"Well, as you can appreciate, Mr Dekker, we're certainly in the market for land purchase. Mars is going to be one of the hottest projects we've ever handled – if you'll forgive the pun." He walked towards the map. "Perhaps you'd like to indicate your plot."

Dekker eagerly pointed to a spot with a green marker in it. "That used to be my old quarry - number fifty-five - the one you're planning to develop."

108

The manager let out a long, low whistle. "Wow! Hope you got a good price for it; it's worth billions now."

"My farm's the double-sized spread right next to it," Dekker said, triumphantly, shifting his thick finger along.

"By the Elysium sea?"

"That's right."

The manager shook his head. "Afraid that's volcanic - extrusive igneous rock, according to the geologists. Unstable land as far as we're concerned. The smallest hotels planned are a hundred storeys high. We're talking five million tonnes of bauxite. Wouldn't take the weight." He shook his head sympathetically as he saw the stricken look on Dekker's face.

A month later, Dekker alighted at London Spaceport. It was the first time he had been back to Earth since he had left, twenty years before, and was surprised at the increased security. He was met by two uniformed police and escorted through to a small room on one of the lower levels. A police inspector was sitting at a table.

"Name?" he said when Dekker was seated opposite him.

"Karl Dekker."

"Permanent residence?"

He gave his Mars address.

"Reason for visit?"

"I'm buying a farm."

"You're planning to stay, then?"

"No - I'm just here to sign the papers."

There was a knock at the door and a head appeared. "Mr Mahler's here, sir."

Dekker stiffened.

A fair-haired man entered the room. Dekker recognised Paul Mahler. He got to his feet. "What's going on?"

"I understand you were the last one to see my father alive?"

"Who says so?"

"Please sit down, sir," said one of the officers. "We'd just like you to look at a document."

Mahler seated himself in a corner of the room while another officer entered and stood with his back against the closed door.

Dekker sank uneasily into the chair and examined the paper slid in front of him. It was the purchase agreement for Mahler's farm.

"Do you recognise this?"

"Of course. That's my signature on it – underneath Mahler's."

"At Mr Paul Mahler's request, we had this document examined by a graphologist. It appears that the Mahler signature is a forgery?"

"That's ridiculous."

"A computer has confirmed that both signatures are by the same person."

Dekker jumped to his feet. "What is this – some kind of frame-up? I refuse to answer any more questions until my lawyer is present."

"Of course. You may contact her shortly. We just have one more thing to show you first, though."

The inspector pushed a button and a screen rose from the table. Pictures of the farm appeared, in the sharp, green tint of night-vision. He saw himself pulling the head of one of the cattle down and forcing a horn into a dark shape on the ground.

Dekker leapt to his feet and sent the table flying as he tried to reach the door.

A stun-gun knocked the wind out of him and he sank to the floor. Restraints were clipped over his wrists and ankles and he was hauled back into a chair. Paul Mahler had got to his feet.

"You didn't know that my father had installed security monitors all over the farm, including inside the house, Mr Dekker. I had the equipment removed and sent to me before you moved in. We've just finished examining the recent disks and have pictures of all your visits – including the one where you forged my father's signature."

There was a long silence.

"You may contact your lawyer, now," said the police inspector.

A Loss of Memory

by Wendy Dunn

Slowly stirring in that state between sleep and wake my eyes
focussed on blue velvet curtains. How my head thumped.
What was I doing lying fully clothed on this double bed? As
my eyes became accustomed to the gloom I realised with a
sense of panic that I hadn't the faintest idea where I was. The
panic was accompanied by a wave of nausea. I rushed to the
washstand and retched for what seemed forever. When the
feeling passed I sat back on the counterpane to take stock.. It
was then that it hit me. Not only did I not recognise the room
but also I didn't know who I was, nor had I the faintest idea of
what I was doing here.

I took a small towel and moistened it with water from
the bowl. This I placed against my forehead and found that it
provided some relief. The questions were flying through my
brain: What? When? Where? This was no good; I would have
to get a grip on myself and calm down if I was going to sort
this out. There had to be some clues around the place.

What about my clothes? I was wearing a thin grey
ankle-length coat bespattered with dried mud. A search of the
pockets produced nothing but a small lace handkerchief. Just a
minute, there was an initial in the corner. A ring of flowers
surrounded the letter R. Had I embroidered them? And what
did R stand for? I was wearing black patent ankle boots; no
clue there, nor in my high-necked white lace blouse, my long
black skirt or my calico petticoats. Lying on the bed were a
small black hat and a reticule. Inside the reticule was a comb,
some rouge, face powder, a purse containing thirty pounds and
a photograph. Thirty pounds was a huge sum, how had I come
by that? The photograph was of a man of about thirty, with a
dark moustache, large brown eyes and dark curling hair. His

112

features were regular and he was handsome in a theatrical sort of way. He wore a high-necked, stiff collar and an expensive looking suit. The back of the photo solved the letter R mystery. It read "To my darling Rose, Forever Bobby." So I was probably Rose, but who was Bobby? I glanced down at the narrow gold band on the third finger of my left hand. It looked very much as though he was my husband, but I had no recollection of meeting him let alone marrying him. Where was he now?

Outside I could hear the sounds of milk being delivered and the smell of bacon wafted up from below. Drawing back the curtains I turned my attention to the room. It was obvious that it was a hotel room for on the bureau was a brochure detailing the hotel services. It said that the hotel was called the Cavendish and was situated in the Tottenham Court Road. It also said that breakfast was served from seven thirty in the main dining room. A glance at the travelling clock on the bureau showed that it was seven fifteen. Realising that I was hungry I decided to take a chance on being a guest here. A trip to the dining room might satisfy more than my hunger. Looking in the wardrobe I found just one dress hanging there. I brushed my hair and making hasty work of my toilette donned the dress. It was obviously mine as it fitted so well. I paused only to note that there was no evidence of Bobby in the room, not even a pair of cufflinks. Summoning my courage I descended to the foyer of the hotel.

On the reception desk were copies of the morning papers. I picked one up and saw that today was Tuesday the fourth of October 1912. I entered the dining room and the waiter greeted me.

"Good morning Mrs Granville would you like your usual table?" He must have noticed my hesitation: "Sir not joining you this morning?" he added as he led me to a table.

113

Several of the guests inclined their heads as I passed. It appeared that Mrs Granville was not unknown to them. I didn't feel like a Mrs Granville. I didn't feel like a Mrs anybody. I managed to eat some toast and some bacon and on the way back to my room enquired if there was any mail for me. There wasn't, and I was just about to enter the lift when I heard someone calling.

"Mrs Granville?"

Turning, I saw a police constable clad in a wet shiny cape, crossing the lobby towards me. Praise the lord, he was smiling! "I just called by to see how you are, ma'am, it must have shaken you up badly," he said.

I asked him if he would join me in the card room, which fortunately was deserted apart from one elderly gentleman who was having a snooze. The constable, looked a little surprised, but removing his helmet followed me, pleased no doubt to be in out of the rain. I explained to him that I didn't know how I had been shaken up, in fact I couldn't remember anything, and just how very worrying this was. He listened intently making sympathetic noises at the appropriate moments.

"My dear lady, I will help you all that I can."

He then explained that this part of the Tottenham Court Road was on his beat and that he called into the Granville kitchens regularly each evening for a mug of cocoa. Apparently last evening as he was approaching the hotel he had seen me run out into the street in what he described as extreme haste, right into the path of an oncoming hansom cab. He said that the driver had done all he could to avoid me but that I had been thrown into the gutter. He and the driver had picked me up and were of the opinion that physically I seemed none the worse for wear. I had apologised for not looking where I was going, told them not to worry and said that all was well. He said he thought that I had been crying and he had

114

helped me into the hotel where both he and Mrs. Spiller, the manageress had assisted me to my room. I said that I would be fine when I'd had a little lie down. Mrs Spiller put a 'Do Not Disturb' sign on my door and they left me, assuming that my husband would be back shortly.

"And that's as much as I know Ma'am," he concluded.

The constable kindly offered to fetch Mrs. Spiller to see if she knew anything of my husband's whereabouts or could throw any light on my circumstances. Mrs Spiller was a motherly looking soul whose only concession to style was a large tortoiseshell comb pressed firmly into her upswept hair. When she heard about my loss of memory she seemed genuinely concerned at my predicament and had I not been one of her paying guests I feel sure she would have hugged me to her more than ample bosom. Her sympathy was most welcome and I would not have been averse to a hug.

She told me that my husband and myself had been staying at the Cavendish on and off for over a year now. Apparently my husband regularly had a couple of days business in the city and when he came to town brought me so that I would not be lonely. She told me that we were booked in until tomorrow night and were due to check out on Thursday morning. Our bill had been paid in advance and in the register my husband had put our home address as simply Bristol.

She told me that she and I had often had little chats in the past and that during one of these I had told her that my family lived in Cornwall. Mrs Spiller and the constable thought that my husband would probably be back by tonight or at the latest tomorrow and that the best thing I could do was sit tight. In the meantime Mrs Spiller would send for a doctor to discuss my loss of memory and to give me, as she put it, the once over. The constable said that when his round was complete he would check at the police station to ensure that there had been no accidents.

115

Towards midday the doctor arrived muttering something about a busy surgery. My breakfast was making me feel extremely nauseous but I managed to fight the feeling off. He examined me and then explained that it was difficult to predict how long my memory loss would last. It could be days, weeks or even months but would probably start to return slowly during the next few days. The good news, he said, was that the baby was fine. He must have seen my shock.

"Of course you don't remember being pregnant." He patted my hand and gave Mrs Spiller some arnica for my bruises. I could see that he wanted to ask for his fee – people in my predicament might disappear overnight. In a daze I pulled some money from my reticule and he quickly gave me change, volunteering that if my husband had not identified my own doctor by tomorrow that he would be happy to call again.

We hadn't booked for lunch, and Mrs Spiller, kindly soul that she was, invited me to join her for a bite. I accepted her hospitality and during a fish pie lunch she told me what a wonderfully attentive man my husband was and so handsome, and that if I returned to our room she was sure he wouldn't be long in returning. I could think of no other option so I took her advice.

During what seemed an interminably long afternoon I paced the floor trying to work things out. Why hadn't he been here last night? Where was he now? Why didn't I feel married? Where were his clothes? My thoughts were interrupted by the kindly constable who had called to tell me that no accidents had been reported. I was pleased that this was the case but would have settled for a minor accident if it could solve my unanswered questions. I slept little that night, as would most women, anticipating the arrival of a husband they couldn't remember.

The next day, Wednesday, dawned fine, but the weather did nothing to change my mood of anxiety. Finding

116

again that there were no messages I told Mrs Spiller that I could not sit around all day waiting for something to happen. She promised that if my husband returned whilst I was out she would tell him what had happened and get him to wait for me. I stepped out into the watery sunshine drawing my thin coat around me. I found myself hailing a hansom.

"Where to, miss?"

"Paddington Station."

Why did I want to go to Paddington Station? For some inexplicable reason the words had sprung to my lips and I felt compelled to go there.

I paid off the cabby and entered the station. The crowds streamed from the trains all intent on their own personal business. What was mine? I studied the various boards detailing arrival and departure times. Standing at platform three with steam hissing from its funnel and its chocolate and cream carriages almost full was the train to Penzance. People were boarding. It went to Bristol and then on to Cornwall, but what was the use if I didn't have an address in either of these places. Despondently I decided to return to the Cavendish, and was passing the news-stand when I heard a young cockney voice call the name Rose. I checked to see if he was looking at me and he was. The young lad was about sixteen with a mop of auburn hair, a freckled snub nose and a really cheeky grin.

"Rose, wot yer doing 'ere? I knew you 'ad a few days orf but didn't fink you was going away. Lucky blighter. Ave yer 'ad a good time? Bin 'ome to Cornwall I bet. Alright fer some." As he paused for breath I managed to say, "Do I know you?"

"It's no good coming yer airs and graces with me, Rose, it's Jimmy, remember?"

His face lost its grin as he could see that I didn't. "Wots the matter luv?" As he spoke he took hold of my arm,

117

steering me towards the buffet whilst telling me that I looked as though I could do with a cup of 'char.' Over a cup of tea I explained to Jimmy that I had lost my memory and would be very grateful for any information about myself that he could supply.

Jimmy explained that he called at Paddington Station daily to collect the newspapers for the hospital. The hospital was St Mary's in Paddington and he said that I had worked there for the last two years. My name was Rose Johns. I had come to work as a parlour maid for matron but for the last year had been nursing, which, according to Jimmy, I had always wanted to do. I had left the hospital on Monday morning for a three-day holiday. Jimmy said that when I had made him a cup of tea first thing I had been very secretive about where I was going and had seemed very excited.

"That's all I know, Rose, watcha gonna do now? I'm sure that if we go to the orspital they can fix yer memory."

I told him that I thought I had better accompany him to try and find out more.

"That means you'll 'ave ter see Matron." Jimmy sounded nervous.

"Is she so awful then?"

"She's a bit of a dragon but she always 'ad a soft spot fer you Rose. You'll be alright."

As we walked to the hospital, Jimmy pushing his barrow of newspapers, my mind was in turmoil.

Twenty minutes later I found myself sitting in matron's office. As I waited the questions raced through my mind. How could I be Rose Johns who worked at the hospital, and also be Rose Granville who stayed at the Cavendish with a husband from Bristol? I looked around me. The room certainly looked familiar. I knew that I had been here before.

Matron swept into the room. She was a very tiny lady but made up for that with a large amount of presence, which

118

was assisted by a heavily starched uniform. A small lace cap was anchored firmly to her head with an abundance of pins. She motioned me to remain seated and sat down herself. She shuffled some papers on her desk and glanced at the timepiece pinned to her chest.

"Well, Rose what's this I hear about your loss of memory?"

I found her tone offensive but realised I would get nowhere by showing my annoyance. I decided that I probably needed to tell her some of what I knew, but at this point decided that I would omit any reference to Bobby. Some sixth sense told me that this would be wise. When I had finished my tale she said that now she would tell me what she knew.

"I gather you have been a foolish girl, Rose. Last Monday evening at a fairly late hour I received an unexpected visit from Dr. Robert Godwin." She paused for me to say something and when I didn't went on,

"You know Dr. Godwin?"

When I still looked puzzled and shook my head I think she realised that my loss of memory was genuine.

"Before long you will no doubt remember, Rose, that some two years ago you wrote to me from Cornwall asking for work. I wouldn't normally have taken you on as you had no qualifications but you had worked in your local doctor's surgery and there was something about your letter that I liked. You worked very hard Rose and I was proud of you. During the last year you proved yourself an able and competent nurse, but now what are we going to do with you?"

I made no reply and she continued; "When Dr Godwin came to see me he explained that he felt ashamed because he had led you to believe that his intentions towards you were serious. He said that he had become very fond of you and that he had been seeing you for the best part of a year. You know, Rose, that this is a teaching hospital with a fine reputation to

119

maintain. Dr. Godwin came to us from Canada for a year of post-qualifying experience. He left the hospital yesterday morning to return to his wife and two small children in Canada."

As I could not remember Dr. Godwin I felt no overwhelming heartache - more a sense of injustice that he could do this to me. Slowly I drew the photograph of Bobby from my bag and passed it to matron.

"Is that Dr. Godwin?"

She took the photograph, looked at it for a moment then turned it over and read the message on the back. She heaved a big sigh and with a wry smile nodded assent. I wondered if I should tell her about the baby. Had Bobby known? If so had he told her? Until now I had been worried and confused but the clues had all pointed to my being a married lady with a wealthy husband in secure circumstances. In the space of minutes I had learned that unless Bobby had married me bigamously I was to become an unmarried mother with few if any prospects. What was matron saying?

"You must try and put this whole thing behind you, Rose. None of the nurses or staff must know and I will expect you back to work first thing tomorrow morning."

I asked her if she had an address in Canada for Dr. Godwin. She told me, no.

I knew that the hospital must have but I also knew there was no way they were going to give it to me. I blurted out, "Did he tell you that I was pregnant?"

Matron looked shocked and paused for a moment before replying, "In that case my dear you must go home to your family tomorrow morning."

She asked me if I had any money and I told her I did. She said that Dr Godwin had told her that he had given me some money. So that was where the thirty pounds had come from. She said that the hospital would post my wages to my

120

home in St Austell and that she would be writing to my parents. I told her that I didn't know my home address. She pulled a card from a file and copied my address on it. When I read it aloud it sounded vaguely familiar.

"It is terribly important Rose that nobody in the hospital knows about you and Dr Godwin. You must go to your room and pack your belongings now. It would be better if you didn't stay here tonight. Do you have somewhere you can go?"

My mind flashed back to the Cavendish. Mr and Mrs Granville had one more night paid for. I told her that I had. She led me via the back stairs from her flat to my room and we returned the same way some fifteen minutes later having packed all I appeared to possess in a battered looking suitcase.

I walked with my head held as high as I could manage down the drive to the entrance of the hospital. Only two people saw me leave, Matron who watched from her window and Jimmy who called to me. I walked quickly on pretending I hadn't heard him. I didn't wish him to see the tears of shame and anger.

I left my case in the left luggage at Paddington Station. Throwing caution to the winds I took another cab back to the Cavendish. I don't know what I told Mrs Spiller but she seemed satisfied with my explanation. After dinner that evening I lay on my bed trying to recall my home and what had happened on that last evening I had spent with Bobby. Pictures of my parents waving me off to London on the train kept appearing before my eyes but no Bobby. Again I slept fitfully.

Sitting on the train to Penzance I glanced at the newspaper which the man opposite me was reading. Thursday October 6th. I let my head rest against the back of the seat and closed my eyes. A mist was swirling around but through it I was back

121

in the room at the Cavendish. Bobby was with me. He was explaining that he had to go home to Canada but that he would return and see me some day. As he talked he was placing some money in my reticule. I could hear myself begging him not to go and clinging to him. He was holding me at arms length and I was sobbing hysterically. He said he was going to get a drink at the hotel bar and would be back shortly. I stood at the window wondering how these few days that were going to be so perfect were going so horribly wrong. Never mind, when he came back I would tell him about the baby - his baby - and everything would be as it had been. I glanced down and saw Bobby crossing the road hailing a cab as he went. I threw on my coat and rushed out of the hotel trying to stop him going. I heard myself scream; I was lying in the gutter - a policeman was picking me up - then everything swirled into oblivion.

The man opposite folded his newspaper and made some remark about the weather. I pretended not to hear. It had been so very wonderful being Mrs. Granville. I pulled the gold band from my third finger, slipped it into my pocket, wiped the tears from my face and blew my nose.

I knew that although my parents loved me very much and would stand by me, my mother would tell me that I had made my bed and that I must lie on it. She was right. Rose Johns, it's down to you now my girl.

The Sentinel

by Pam Eaves

How long had he been crouching here? The night seemed
endless as Bibbi worried about the children. Were they warm
enough to sleep in the cave? They must be rested enough to
move on before daylight. Little Anna had looked exhausted
and Milka must have been worn out after that laborious climb
through the rough undergrowth, sobbing and frightened. Even
Radi had gone quiet. Bibbi felt dog tired himself, but the cold
seeping up his skinny, teenage frame from the frosty ground
kept him alert. Shivering in his thin jacket, he tried moving
cautiously but his legs were stiff and cramped and he lurched
sideways, his numb foot turning on a stone. A twig cracked as
he nearly fell and, heart thudding, he listened, but there was no
other sound on the still, cold air. Holding his breath he relaxed
a little then exhaled in relief as the silence continued. Who
knew where the enemy were until they burst from cover, guns
blazing, malevolent faces full of hate. He shuddered at the
memory of death in the afternoon sunshine, the smell of
burning, shouts and screams.

What had happened to Mama? That pig had taken her
away. Bibbi's eyes filled in sorrow and shame. He should have
done something, made an effort even though she'd said if they
came that he was to run with the others, run as far and as fast
as they could. Not to worry about her, just get Milka and the
children away. He'd done as she said but he should have
helped her. Papa would have known what to do. Papa would
have saved her. Hot tears coursed down his cheeks. Mama,
Mama, where are you?

A small, nocturnal animal rustled in the undergrowth
and Bibbi tensed again, but the small furry creature scuttled
away. All right for him. He wasn't being hunted. Wishing he

123

had the courage to stand up straight so he could see all round, Bibbi knew he was a coward. Papa would stand up and not worry if his huge frame was outlined against the dark sky. He wouldn't be crouching here afraid but would be a proper lookout, see them creeping up the hillside, not skulk behind a bush. Ah, but Papa always had a gun. Bibbi wished he had a gun, then he could protect the others properly. What could he do if they came? He'd be just as helpless as when Mama...

"Bibbi." Milka's soft whisper made him jump.

"Milka. Get back in the cave. If they come I'll shout to warn you so you can get the little ones away. Go on, get back." Hissing angrily at his sister, Bibbi pretended a courage he did not feel.

"They're asleep. I thought I'd keep you company for a bit."

"It's too dangerous. If they came, you..." His voice broke as he remembered Mama again. "You know what they do to women, young girls." Bibbi blushed in the dark. They never spoke of such things at home.

"I'm not frightened. I know you'll look after me." Milka's fourteen-year-old confidence strengthened and shamed him.

"That's why I'm ordering you to get back in the cave with the little ones. I can guard you from here, but you must keep them quiet." Bibbi whispered harshly, authoritatively. "Suppose Radi woke up and came looking for us, calling. He'd be heard for miles."

"Alright. I'll go back, but I keep thinking of Slivitch's face. He used to be Papa's friend, but when he came today... Why did Mama go with him?"

"She thought she'd be nice to him, have a chat so we could get away. You know how he always complained when Radi was naughty. She was probably afraid he would hit Radi

124

or something." The whispered explanation sounded lame but Milka seemed to accept it.

"Perhaps she'll come tomorrow. She knows where we play. She'll probably bring Papa with her. He'll take care of us." Comforted, Milka turned and crept back to the cave.

Bibbi shuddered as he saw again the puddle of blood under the thick, silver-streaked hair. Papa wouldn't be coming. He'd tell Milka later, when they were safe. Can't have her weeping and wailing and setting the little ones off. It was up to him now to get them away.

Papa would have laughed, sneered...

"You? What can you do Bibbi? That name suits you. Mama's little bibbi. Radi's more of a man than you and he's only seven."

What would he do if Slivitch and his gang came? Bibbi trembled as he remembered the lascivious glances the burly neighbour had cast on Milka; the barely concealed innuendoes just before the men had left the village. Such rejoicing when they all went. The women laughing, hugging each other. Papa had said grimly they'd be back, but the others didn't believe him, opened bottles of wine, and toasted their new life in the village without fear. Then they came back with guns. If only he had Papa's gun. Not that he could aim straight. Papa had tried to teach him, but the bang was so loud. He hated it. If only he'd concentrated.

A burst of gunfire from the valley frightened him and Bibbi's heart started thudding again.

"Are they coming?" Radi was jumping up and down with excitement behind him.

"Shut up," Bibbi hissed. "The whole village'll hear you." He pushed his younger brother. "Get back in the cave with Milka and Anna. Someone's got to look after the women while I keep watch."

"I'll kill them with this when they come," boasted Radi in a hoarse whisper, picking up a thick branch and waving it about.

"Fat lot of use that'll be against guns. Better to keep quiet and hide until they've gone. That's the only way we'll get out of this." Bibbi started a whispered argument with Radi out of habit, then checked himself and ordered fiercely, "Get back with the others. I'm relying on you to look after them."

Radi sullenly moved away, muttering, "Papa wouldn't hide. He'd fight."

And look where that got him Bibbi thought as he peered round the bush down the hill. All quiet again. Perhaps they were all down there eating and drinking. Where are we going to find food? Already little Anna had cried with hunger when they reached the cave. Perhaps there's a farmhouse the other side of this hill. We've never been over the top. Papa said this was the best way to come if we had to leave, but then he was coming with us. He would have known what to do.

A pink streak appeared down in the valley. Dawn? No, too early. And too red. Bibbi had no watch, but the nights were long in the winter. They could only have been up here a few hours. They're burning more houses. His eyes filled again. Poor Mama. All the beautiful things she collected and polished so lovingly. Poor Mama. She'd tried not to cry when Radi broke that vase Papa had bought her, tried not to be angry with Radi, but Bibbi knew how upset she was. She loved her home. Evil bastards. Bibbi shook with anger. He'd kill them for destroying everything.

A loud sneeze startled him and Bibbi tensed. Someone's coming.

"This way Slivitch. The cave's up here." A hoarse shout with no attempt at concealment cut through the still air. The man was almost on top of him while he'd been daydreaming again. Bibbi was furious with himself.

126

"You sure it's where they'd go? There's wine down in the village. If you've dragged me up here on a wild goose chase, I'll..."

Bibbi crouched undecided. Shall I shout warning now? Slivitch is some way behind. If they were together Milka might get the kids away, but there might be more of them, a whole gang spread out. He shook with fear and indecision.

"You want the little partridge, don't you? She'll be juicier than her mother and she always brings the kids up here to play. I've watched them. You can go first with her. That's if you can make it up the hill you fat ox, but I want my turn after." Reeling drunkenly, the speaker was nearly at Bibbi's hiding place as he choked on raucous laughter, then swore as he tripped and fell.

Filthy pig. Beside himself with rage, and forgetting all caution, Bibbi grabbed the branch Radi had dropped, swung it with all his strength and cracked it into the man's face as he tried to rise. Blood oozed black as he fell forward and Bibbi struck again at the back of his head, then again and again until he lay, spread-eagled and unmoving on the ground. Breathing heavily Bibbi turned towards Slivitch ready to attack again but the man was further down the hill, some distance away.

"Goran? Where are you Goran? Wait for me. I don't know my way up here. Slivitch halted his noisy progress and looked around, then crashed clumsily on up through the frosty undergrowth. He stopped again to get his breath and saw Bibbi's silhouette beside the bush.

"There you are. I thought for a moment you were trying to lose me, get in first. Wouldn't put it past you."

Bibbi, standing tense and straight, could see the burly form outlined against the pink and orange streaks in the valley, hear the panting breath as he laboured uphill swearing, heavy boots slipping on scattered rocks. Branch held firmly in both hands, Bibbi stood motionless, calmly watching the clumsy

127

progress as Slivitch lumbered up the hill towards him, reeling drunkenly over uneven ground. He stepped back behind the bush as Slivitch approached, bawling, "Goran? Where are you? I saw you a minute ago. Stop mucking about."

He took a few more lumbering paces and tripped over the dark heap, falling heavily with a grunt. Before he could move, Bibbi stepped out and whirled the branch with all his force at Slivitch's head. Stunned, Slivitch moaned and tried to rise but Bibbi brought the branch down for a second blow and then, in a fury of murderous rage he beat both prone figures again and again until, satisfied they were both dead, he kicked them hard before dropping the branch.

He stood shaking uncontrollably as a pale light rimmed the horizon in the east. Suddenly realising dawn was breaking he turned towards the cave. They must move on, find somewhere safe to hide, perhaps once they got over the hill there would be somewhere. Bibbi stiffened his back and forced his shaky legs forward.

Milka appeared in the opening as he approached, pale face apprehensive.

"Everything alright Bibbi? I thought I heard a noise."

"Everything's fine, but we must get further away while it's still dark. It's nearly dawn. Wake the children up." Bibbi stood sentinel as Milka gently woke Radi and Anna, coaxing them into gathering their meagre possessions together. He addressed them as they mustered subdued and silent outside the cave.

"You must do as I say without argument. I'm responsible for your safety since Papa is not here. We're going over the hill while it's dark then hide again in daylight. You must be very quiet at all times. No arguing or shouting. I'll try to find something to eat while you rest, but it might not be easy, so you'll have to put up with it. Come on now." Bibbi led the way as Milka took the children's hands and followed him.

128

He stopped suddenly and turned. Startled, they halted, looking up at his gawky height with frightened dark eyes.

"One more thing. Please call me by my proper name, Misak, from now on." He glared at them sternly, then turned and led the little troop firmly towards the top of the hill.

A Hell of a Place to Lose a Cow

by Sylvie Nickels

The present contains nothing more than the past, and what is found in the effect was already in the cause Henri Bergson, L'Evolution Créatrice (1907), ch.1

From the forest rim a man and a woman gaze down into the canyon. Two thirty-somethings, slim, assured, they seem at ease with each other in the way that evolves with long association. But not in love. An animal attraction perhaps, certainly on his part; but not love.

She glances at her watch. Seven o'clock. The throb of heat is muted now, and the metallic blue of the sky has mellowed to a kinder shade. The sinking sun is bringing texture to the rock pinnacles, as well as deepening colour, so that the weathering of millennia assumes curves and whorls as of man-made sculptures. Temples, almost. Only no human hand has ever wielded a chisel in this unforgiving place.

Hoodoos they call them, these pinnacles of fantastical shapes that characterise Bryce Canyon, created by an unimaginable time span of erosion in America's West.

Hoodoo – to cast a spell.

The man glances at his companion's profile and comments, "We've missed the last shuttle back to the hotel." He notes again that she has cut her hair and that the gamine style makes her younger, more vulnerable, inviting. It belies that intrinsic serenity which has long intrigued him.

"It's not that far to walk," the woman says, still looking down into the canyon. "Especially in the cool of the evening. Well, relative cool." She turns, her still features suddenly illuminated by a smile. "Give us an appetite," she adds, and reaches out to take his hand.

They say there is no deeper love than the first. I wouldn't know as that is all there has ever been. Danny said it was a marriage made in heaven, but then Danny was full of clichés which he pulled out like rabbits from a hat, always with delight and surprise as though he had just invented them. When I explained about clichés, he merely said, well, even if they were so overused by so many people, there had to be more truth in them than all the unique one-liners clever people came out with.

It seemed an unnecessary quibble to point out that we weren't actually married. We'd been together in that squat in Granton since forever. Dad had dragged me away when I was sixteen, but we didn't stop meeting, Danny and I, and as soon as I was eighteen, I was back again.

We'd met in a churchyard. He was into gravestones in a big way and, on a balmy July evening, he found me curled up asleep behind one a couple of days after I left home. Mum and I had been far too close for me ever to live in the same house as her stand-in, though it was a while before I told Danny about any of that. You can learn a lot about a place from its gravestones, he said, and proceeded to show me the several that recorded deaths from a plague: not the Great one but a smaller episode that didn't make the history books. Later he led me to the graves of a whole lot of foreign folk – French prisoners from the Napoleonic wars, Dutch who came to build canals, Italians prisoners-of-war to clear World War Two bomb sites and, of course, hordes of Irish. There was a bit of Irish in him, Danny said.

There was an amazing number of graveyards within walking distance of the squat. If I complained about the distance, Danny said we needed the exercise, so what was my problem. Sometimes, if we were a bit flush, we took the bus. When I got bored watching Danny, I started going into the churches and noticing the stained glass windows and wondering how they were made and why. Well, get some books out of the library, Danny said. That's how he'd learned so much about old gravestones.

You can't actually take books out if you haven't a permanent address, but I got to really like being in the library: that thick silence that's louder than the traffic outside. It was warm, too, in the winter.

With Danny's gravestones and my stained glass windows and the library and the squat, we had a great life. When we needed money, we got casual jobs – there are always jobs if you're not fussy what you do. I wasn't so keen on cleaning loos - well, people can be really *gross*. But the washing up jobs were OK and usually we got some left over grub as well. Then, if the Parks people were short-staffed, they'd take us on: clearing leaves in the autumn, or cleaning up after some public event. During all that time, I let my hair grow until it fell over my shoulders in long dark curtains which Danny would spend ages brushing and shaping. He said I was never to cut it as long as we were together which, as far as he was concerned, would be forever. He had this way of making you feel beautiful even when you knew you weren't.

Others in the squat came and went. A lot ... most ... of them were druggies or alkies, and on the rare occasions they weren't stoned they told us about their lives and why they needed oblivion. We weren't into that stuff, Danny and I. We didn't need oblivion and preferred to know what we were about. So I just knew it wasn't true when they said he was drunk and stepped out on to the street in front of that motorbike. It was late evening and he'd gone out to get a bag of chips. A stupid bloody bag of chips.

132

I was holding his hand when he died a few hours later in the hospital.

The police put out requests for anyone who might have seen the accident; but I knew no one was going to bother much about a dead drop-out who'd brought it on himself. Except I knew he hadn't. One of the druggies told me they saw what happened, knew who the biker was: a toe-rag called Crag Blackmoor who'd been regularly carving up the neighbourhood for weeks. But who was going to believe a druggie? Anyway, by now I was dead too, except I was still breathing and couldn't figure out how to stop. Then Dad came and took me home, and I didn't care enough not to go.

They call this part of Utah State 'red rock' country, but the colours go all the way from rose to cinnamon, lemon to flame, ash to purple.

"If you saw those colours in a painting, you'd say 'yuck'," she observes. She fishes into the sling bag on her shoulder and brings out a camera: one of those tiny digital ones.

"You'll get better sky effects if you leave it a bit longer," he suggests. "And I never say 'yuck'."

She grins at him, and he's charmed by this new, unfamiliar lighter mood. So many sides to this amazing woman. And to think he'd once dismissed her as a saddo. He wonders which of her personae he will be sharing a bed with later for that is firmly on his agenda.

He goes to join her, sitting on a rock looking out over tens … hundreds … thousands … of square miles of rock and desert: a mega construction site as this corner of the earth rearranged itself through ever more awesome upheavals. He finds himself wondering what it must have been like to be the first human to set foot in this extraordinary place?

"Just imagine being the first one to see all this," she says.

So they are telepathic soul mates too. He doesn't usually allow himself to get emotionally hooked by his bed partners. Emotions are dangerous. Better watch it.

It was hard to remember afterwards how long I stayed dead. My stepmother was clearly smarter than I gave her credit for. She just left me lying on my bed for hours, days, maybe weeks. Sometimes she'd come in to my room and switch on the TV, and I'd get up and switch it off again. Then one day I didn't, and there was this programme about gravestones. I think I cried for two days.

Dad was teaching in adult education and said why didn't I do a course. So I cut my hair and took up computing. Danny had always said he'd learn about computers one day, so I did it for both of us. Anyway, if you're going to go on living in a world where everything is www.-this and dotcom-that, you need to find out what they're on about.

Amazingly, I was good at it. Even more amazingly I enjoyed it. No need for face-to-face confrontations with people asking stupid questions. It was magic: just me and the universe linked by a few clicks. I looked in on chat rooms and newsgroups and discovered there were some seriously weird people out there. One day I checked Google and found there were 508,000 entries for stained glass windows, and 423,000 for gravestones. Then I checked Amazon.com for books on the subject; there were respectively 56 and 116 listed, a lot of them out of print.

How about a book linking the two: 'In Memoriam' for all those dead people? And especially Danny. I didn't discuss it with anyone. Anyway, I didn't care what anyone thought. Danny had given it the OK in my head.

134

"Perhaps we should get back to the road," he says, but doesn't move. It's quite addictive sitting on a rock next to this woman looking out over this amazing view. And he has become sharply aware of the silence. It is some time now since they heard distant voices or the hum of a vehicle from the invisible road. Everyone else, it seems, has gone home.

"We can continue along the track and pick the road up from the next access point," she suggests. "Have this view for a bit longer. It's only half … three-quarters of a mile." She leans forward to touch a white flower on a slender stem near his foot. "Did you know that's the state flower of Utah? Sego Lily. You can eat the bulbs, you know."

He didn't know. "You have a storehouse of the most irrelevant facts," he teases. "It's all that time you spend with Google."

"I don't suppose it seemed irrelevant to Ebenezer Bryce and his family when they were hungry."

"You're making him up," he accuses, and it seems all right to slip an arm round her shoulders, draw her a bit closer.

"You obviously haven't read the brochure. Ebenezer Bryce and his family moved here in 1875 and made the road up to this plateau to harvest the timber. So they named the canyon after him." She slides gently away from his arm and stands up to look out over the canyon. "Apparently he said it would be a hell of a place to lose a cow." The colours are truly vibrant now. Give it another half hour ….

"Another half hour and it should be perfect," he says. "Yes it would be. A hell of a place to lose a cow." He takes her hand loosely and she does not pull it away.

Within six months I'd created a huge database, immaculately cross-referenced so that you could check any common denominator between the burial rites, say, of the Aztecs and the Inuit, at the click of a mouse. I couldn't have done it

135

without Danny's help. He was there all the time, encouraging, urging, suggesting; seemed to have an instinctive affinity with computer technology though in his lifetime he never as much as touched a keyboard, let alone a mouse.

By now I'd moved into my own place, a mews flat behind the market place, near the library. This was perfect as I'd taken a part time job in the library. It was at the time they were putting in a new computerised system, so I learned a lot as well. All this I discussed in the evenings with Danny after we'd finished our stint of surfing the 'Net. His presence became so real that for long periods I truly forgot he was dead, and the shock of remembering each time was like a new bereavement. Sometimes I wondered if I might be going just a little bit crazy, but it didn't feel like that.

It was quite a while later and the book was at the almost-ready stage when a headline in the local paper blared out *Local Man Claims World on Full Throttle,* and the name Crag Blackmoor leaped out of the page. There was a picture of him: smiling, cocky, blonde, good looking. They gave his website - www.fullthrottle.uk.net – so I went straight to it. Clearly he had travelled a very long way indeed in every sense since those days of carving up a neighbourhood in Granton. I followed a series of links leading to Crag Blackmoor testing ever larger, sleeker and shinier motorbikes in ever more unlikely parts of the globe looking ever more debonair.

And alive.

It was then, as though a switch had been thrown, that old unresolved grief turned into new all-consuming hatred.

Somewhere on www.fullthrottle.uk.net Crag Blackmoor announced he was planning a series of books on worldwide biking, so if anyone had any experiences they would like to share ..... there followed his email address.

Hi Crag, I tapped out barely stopping to think. Then explained how I knew my way round the 'Net like no one else,

136

and I guessed he could do with a research assistant; and, as I thought he was the coolest thing since MS-DOS, there wouldn't be any charge. And that, while I had no biking experience, I was a fast and willing learner.

As I suspected, the prospect of a research assistant, especially an admiring and free one, appealed to the Crag Blackmoor ego. Within no time we were emailing several times weekly. Two years of sifting through the gold and the garbage of thousands of websites had made me ace at turning up the least likely facts in the fastest time. I soon acquired a working knowledge of the biking world and began to pepper my emails with casual references to the comparative specifications of the latest Yamaha and Suzuki. Then there was the impending Harley-Davidson centenary and all the razzmatazz to be associated with it. It was not hard to impress Crag Blackmoor who clearly knew more about speeding than surfing. After a while, and not very subtly, he began trying to find out more about me – age, partner status, interests. Just about everything except ask for my photograph. Finally he came up with *I guess it's time my own private Brainbox came out of the closet.*

Thank heavens for email anonymity. I had needed to go no further than the local telephone directory to check out that Crag Blackmoor still lived locally: now upgraded to a leafy suburb a couple of miles away. And, yes, my gradually unfolding plan still had a long, long way to go, so perhaps it *was* time to come out of the closet.

Crag suggested the Princes Bar of the King's Head on a Friday lunchtime. This was just across the market place from my mews flat, and couldn't have suited me better. I made it sound as though I was doing him a favour, said I could do the small detour on my way to stay with friends in the next county. He'd find me sitting in the bar reading a computer

137

magazine. But I made quite sure I was late and that he was already at the frowning-at-his-watch stage when I showed up.

I had spent some time deciding on and creating a suitable persona before we met. It wasn't hard. Danny had insisted I grew my hair again, but now I drew it back into a tidy, no-nonsense knot, applied careful make-up to tone down the usual clear-eyed healthy glow; modulated my voice to clipped-efficient. I reckoned the effect was clever, reliable and distinctly un-bedworthy, and it was soon clear that Crag Blackmoor had reached a similar conclusion. He was charming, attentive – and showed no hurry at all to meet me again.

But I'd only just begun with him. Where it was all going to lead I had no idea, but how it was all going to end was beyond any doubt.

I set about making myself indispensable. My research skills had clearly impressed and we were in ever more regular contact. Crag was beginning to get commissions from biking magazines, especially in the U.S. and when he let slip how much he loathed having to meet deadlines, I magnanimously offered to help out. So I started a new career in ghost writing. I also began emailing him during his frequent travels with titbits about the latest 'in' places to eat, drink, sleep, with or without a partner.

Then I suddenly announced I'd been approached to do some new work and regretfully would have to withdraw my services in a couple of months time.

"Risky," Danny said, looking over my shoulder as I composed the email. I'd had to work hard to talk him round into grudging support of the whole enterprise.

"I know my Crag," I said.

He replied with the speed of desperation. "For Chrissake, can't possibly cope without you now, Brainbox," and named a figure by way of a retainer that it would have

138

been insane to turn down, even if I had ever had the intention of doing so.

It was some months before we met again. In the meantime *In Memoriam* was completed and made an unexpected impact. It was never going to make the best seller list, but 'the heavies' wrote flatteringly about the author's impeccable research and it became a 'must have' for reference libraries throughout the English-speaking world.

"Clever Brainbox," Crag said when I showed him some of the reviews at that next meeting. But I could see his mind was elsewhere. For this time I had loosened my hair a bit into a bouncy ponytail, adjusted the make up a little, introduced the hint of a drawl.

"You look different," he said, putting a hand over one of mine.

"Do I?" I said, withdrawing it.

High in the evening sky, a turkey vulture circles and is joined by another. And another. Soon there are five.

She gives a small shudder. "Revolting creatures. But fantastic flight."

He follows her gaze, says to the sky "I think I'm falling for you."

She pats his hand. "I'm not your type," she points out. "And don't forget, after all this time, I'm fairly familiar with what your type is. Or should I say types."

"I've changed."

She looks sceptical.

"Well, what's so odd about that? God, no one could have changed more than you. Right little mouse potato when I first met you."

"Thanks."

139

"I'm serious." She sees that he is. "I can't imagine life without you now."

She looks thoughtful. "OK, we'll talk about it, when we get back."

The next succession of steps was obvious. I gave up the library job, as I was doing more and more ghost writing and it was to everyone's benefit if I became Crag's fellow traveller in the literal sense. By now he was getting showered with freebies, and no one was going to question a minor celeb's need for a companion/p.a. Nor, I guess, would anyone have credited that said p.a.'s duties firmly stopped outside the bedroom door. Crag needed me too much in all other respects to risk jeopardising our working relationship.

In the following years, the world became our oyster as Danny repeatedly put it. As clichés went, it was pretty appropriate. We travelled all over Europe, a swathe of the Far East and did three big trips to the Antipodes.

And then came America. One of their top travel magazines wanted a series to cover all fifty States, a couple each month. Arizona was third on the alphabetic list, and they'd paired it with neighbouring Utah. As always Danny and I did our research very thoroughly, and so we came upon Bryce Canyon National Park. And I knew the time had come.

"They have fabulous national parks over there," I told Crag.

"I leave all the planning to you, Brainbox," he said.

I worked out a dream of a route, starting in Phoenix, where we'd pick up the bike, and make our way gradually north via Grand Canyon and a series of national parks to Salt Lake City. Though it was still early summer, it was hot, hot, hot. Neither Arizona nor Utah legally enforce the use of helmets for bikers over the age of 18, which needless to say Crag thought was really cool; but this wind-in-your-hair stuff

140

is grossly overrated when the wind is straight off the desert and the thermometer is topping a hundred. By the time we crossed into Utah I was wanting out.

Our hotel was just outside the national park. We took the shuttle bus and reached Inspiration Point on Bryce Canyon's Rim Trail towards late afternoon. There was still a fair scattering of visitors draped in cameras and binoculars; well, these were views almost anyone would be reluctant to leave. They silenced even Crag for a while and he settled beside me in the shade of a pinyon pine while we waited for the worst of the heat to drain out of the day. But I could feel his eyes were as much on me as the view. And I could feel my pulse beginning to race a bit, too.

Then he said "We've missed the last shuttle back to the hotel." And I said "It's not that far to walk," and held out my hand.

He says "I guess this is the moment," and she peers into the viewfinder as he arranges himself elegantly on the cliff edge. "How's that?" His smile is confident. He knows he looks good, blonde hair ruffling slightly in an updraft from the canyon, head slightly on one side.

Later she runs the sequence of events through her head like a video set endlessly on 'repeat'. She remembers saying 'OK, just one more. Let's go for a close-up', and taking a step towards him; but is convinced she does not touch him, though it is her next intention.

She sees him shift into a more theatrical pose, his arms flung out as though he would embrace the world. He blows her a kiss. Then he seems to lean back. Almost as though someone is tugging from behind – only, of course, there is no one. Only space. The smile changes to a look of surprise, then alarm, as he feels his balance begin to go, and that is the last thing she remembers of him: his flailing arms and the shout rising to a scream that shuts off into silence.

She puts the camera carefully down on a rock and goes to the edge; kneels there, gripping a tree stump so she can lean over as far as possible. The heat is like a warm hand on her shoulders.

Nothing seems remotely out of place down there among the debris of immeasurable time. It is just as she had hoped: Bryce Canyon is a hell of a place to lose anything.

Alphabet Diet

by Jo Cannon

The nurse says, 'Congratulations, Mick. According to the computer you are no longer morbidly obese.'

Her eyes, quick fish in a fine net, slip towards me and back to the screen.

'So what am I now?'

'Just obese.'

I try not to sound crestfallen. 'I suppose that's a good thing.'

'You've done really well. What is it this week?'

'Kippers, kit-kats and kiwi fruit.'

'Unorthodox. And next week?'

'Lamb chops, legumes and lettuce.'

'I think you should discuss it with the doctor. But I think she'll be pleased. Our surgery has the fattest patients in the city.'

'How do you know that?'

I stand up so she can stretch a tape measure round my waist. For a moment I imagine she is embracing me. I have never smelt a woman's hair without paying to be close to her.

'Pooled data,' she replies, mysteriously. 'We also have the most cases of depression. It's probably the long wait in the waiting room. People get fat and miserable sitting there for hours. And maybe the doctor is a bit lowering.'

I say, 'You should make the doors narrower to keep us all out.'

She is pressing keys again. On the screen, a graph of my body mass index trails gratifyingly downwards.

I say, 'what happens if I keep on losing bits of myself? What happens when my body mass index hits zero?'

'We'll cross that bridge when we come to it.'

I run at night; a fat man jogging is too conspicuous in the daytime. An alarm clock is unnecessary. I wake naturally, with a jerk, at 3 a.m: a time without perspective or reason, when shadows from outside break in and enter me with deep, levering grief. I'd rather be up and out of the house. Downstairs, cold light from the TV flickers across my father's face. His eyes are glassy with fatigue, but at least he is distracted from himself. Far worse are the nights when he wanders from room to room, stray words of love and longing escaping from some recess in his mind that he is ashamed for me to see.

Running at night I am invisible, my existence marked only by security lights that switch on and off as I pass. A yellow mist hugs the streetlights. In the deserted park someone has scattered broken glass at the foot of the slide and twisted the swing seats too high for a child to reach. A stitch makes me walk for a while. Frost crunches beneath my trainers like snail shells. In the day I avoid the park; I know without being told that a lone fat man is not allowed near children.

Letting myself back into the house, I find my father at last asleep in his chair, his face, creased like linen, supported by one hand. I slide my arm under his.

'Come on, Dad. Time for bed.'

He leans against me. 'You're wasting, son.'

'I'm just slimming.'

I handle him gently, like a fragile crawling creature that might shed a leg. Pushing his bedroom door open with my shoulder, I guide him to the bed. Every surface and most of the floor is heaped like a memory game with incongruous items. Magazines in unopened plastic covers; ancient tins and packets of biscuits; batteries; cooking implements; toys. A pile of shirts in different sizes; women's toiletries. I frisk his

144

pockets for the day's shoplifted spoils: six teaspoons and a bottle of kahlua.

The night recedes like a tide; in another hour it will be dawn. My father will sleep now. I fry a kipper and eat slowly, trying to imagine something else, but am defeated by its inalienable fishiness. These days food fantasies move around my head like shapes in a fog. I dream of feasts, and ordinary things: cornflakes, sandwiches, apples. There is a metallic taste in my mouth and my pores emit a sharp, unfamiliar odour that I disguise with deodorant. It is alarmingly easy to lose stone after stone. I am unwrapping like a parcel. As each layer is stripped away I fear what may be exposed, but when the final packing is removed I suspect there will be nothing inside at all.

Although it is only seven when I get to the shop, Gavin is there already. The bucket of sand by the back door is littered with fag ends. 'BLUE LIZARD COMPUTERS': the logo, which I designed, fills me with ambivalence. I never expected that at 42 years old I would own a computer repair shop and live with my father. But then, I had so few expectations. Customers see an immaculate white area with laminated notices and technical photos, but behind the counter Gavin and I spend our days in a nicotine stained backroom among piles of computer towers.

'Rabbit-woman was back yesterday,' he says. 'The motherboard is fused again. Third time this month.'

He shows me a cable, nibbled neatly in two by rodent teeth. There is something wrong with Gavin; I am glad he is not my son. His eyes slide and fix disturbingly at chin level. When I am out he scans customers' files for salacious material as though rummaging through a lingerie drawer. I am astonished that porn is left so trustingly on hard-drives. Perhaps people see us as servants, paid to ignore the goings-on

145

upstairs, or as monks in our austere cell. I won't look at the images he unearths. Pictures of women splayed out and poked about fill me not with desire, but dismay. In the newsagents I avert my eyes even from the tabloids' front-page girls, looking instead at the bored women in the queue. I cannot imagine any of them posed like that.

But then, I know nothing. My sexual encounters can be counted on the fingers of one hand. Honed by imagination, they re-play like well-worn videos behind my eyelids before sleep. Embellished, not with lurid detail, but with tenderness: a woman's fingers in my hair, a hand on my cheek. At other times I do not allow myself to think of them. A hard cyst of shame encloses the reality: lumbering, sweaty acts in dingy rooms. Drugged women with eyes empty as water. I couldn't get my clothes back on fast enough. Once I paid a woman twenty pounds extra to say she loved me. As she mouthed the words, I saw the disgust that until that moment she had carefully concealed.

During lulls in the day's work – when not checking out our customers' tastes in porn – Gavin trawls news sites for articles on large blubbery animals. He pins the printouts on the wall: our only joke. I identify with both stories he has found today. Moscow, Gavin informs me, is so cold this winter that zoo elephants have been fed vodka from buckets to warm them. Pity the poor tuskers: even fat creatures feel the cold. I imagine the huge pets staggering about plastered, innards unfathomably on fire, when all they really need is a warm stable. Then there is the whale that got lost and swam up the river Thames. Expecting something akin to a submarine, I am disappointed that the animal is so small: an insignificant fishy thing winched onto a barge to die. Perhaps, deprived of plankton, it lost not just its way, but itself. Perhaps its body mass index shrank to zero.

146

Body Mass Index 29. The nurse is delighted.

'Well done! You are now merely overweight. What's on the menu this week?'

'Sausages, satsumas, sweet potatoes.'

'How vile.'

As she wraps the blood pressure cuff around my arm I ask, 'what do you think of speed dating?'

'Aren't you a bit shy for that?'

'I could be good at it. You only have to talk for five minutes. I've prepared a short talk on large mammals.'

'You'll slay them.'

I wait until she turns to the screen before I say, 'I wouldn't know what to do with an ordinary woman.'

'It's time you had a girlfriend, Mick.'

An hour after the speed-date session I sit beside Irena in the pub, dazed and dizzy at the pace of it all. She is tiny, late thirties and exhausted; her eyes lie in dark saucers of bone. If I had a type, she wouldn't be it. Her rapid speech and eastern European accent are baffling at first, but like difficult music, become clearer.

She says, 'why aren't you married?'

'No-one would have me. I'm too fat.'

She looks surprised. 'You're not fat.'

The conversation moves so fast I am disorientated. Used to my lugubrious father and Gavin's masturbatory ramblings, I cannot believe how much ground we are covering. She talks of Albania. Something about a husband who drank and went away. A sixteen-year-old daughter left behind to finish school. But the story is hard to follow, with confusing gaps and many years unaccounted for. My life sounds dull, each year the same as the one before. She shares my concern for the hypothermic elephants and the emaciated whale; I watch her teeth and lips, amazed there is so much to

147

say. Her wrist is delicate as the stem of her wine glass, my hand beside hers blunt as a flipper. I think how hard it is to tell the truth, to open drawers and show the broken things inside. A cool sweat slides under my shirt while I tear a beer mat into mushy pieces.

She reaches up and touches my face.

A cavity opens in me. I push back my chair, mutter something and leave the pub. Then I am running. I can run further and faster these days; my thighs don't chafe and I no longer have breasts that wobble. There is a rock in my throat. The streetlights swim in my eyes and suddenly I am twelve: the night Dad and I went out to look for my mother, searching the streets, calling.

My father, crying.

Police cars outside in the night.

I barely remember my childhood after that. The house filled up with silence and unusable shoplifted goods. I was hungry all the time with a drilling, rooted want. My body changed: the padding around me got thicker and thicker. My eyes in the mirror no longer looked like hers. And a zip opened up in me that would never pull closed.

My father didn't expect me home so soon. He looks up from the TV, alarmed by my distress.

'What's up?'

'How did she do it, Dad? No-one ever told me.'

He sighs, as though dropping something.

'She walked in front of a lorry on the bypass. She was wearing her best dress.'

Because we are quiet men, there seems nothing else to say.

Next day, I return late from Blue Lizard. My father is leafing through a recipe book: today's pointless booty, no doubt. He is more animated than I have seen him for years.

148

'Your friend Irena's here.'

'Where?'

Remembering she is very small, I scan our kitchen, bemused.

'In bed. I sent her to bed.'

'What?'

'She's shattered. She could hardly keep awake.'

As I head, perplexed, for the stairs, he calls, 'she's really nice, son.'

Irena lies on my bed asleep. Dusk has entered the room ahead of me, smudging the edges of things. I make out her shape on top of the covers and when I lean over, the blurred details of her face. She looks both older and younger than when awake. I feel myself slide and am suddenly lonely: for her, for myself. Lying down carefully on the bed beside her, I inch closer until she is in my arms. Gently I move her limbs, arranging her arm around my neck and her hand in my hair. And then I sleep.

Even as I wake I know she has gone. The duvet next to me is cool and pulled smooth. It is 3 a.m: the hour when everything hurts. She must have been repelled, frightened, to wake beside my bulk. I remember Gavin's jibes about sows so heavy they must be separated from their piglets in case they crush them. Something inside me undoes like stitches pulling apart; I need to get out of the house and run.

As I stand at the top of the stairs in my baggy tracksuit, I hear my father moving around in the kitchen. And then, the first time in our house for thirty years, a woman's laugh, and his murmuring reply. I open the door to find a party in progress. Irena and my father sit at the table with a pot of tea. Purloined packets of food, probably years beyond their sell-by dates, and unlikely liqueurs surround them. My dad is smiling, biscuit crumbs all over his face. You'd think he was drinking tea with an angel.

Irena has opened the cookery book at the index.

'We're all going on your diet,' she says. 'Can't wait for G. Listen to this:
Greek salad, guacamole, guinea fowl.'

'Gnocchi, guavas,' intones my father. 'What the hell are they?'

I say, 'I've done G already; I've nearly finished W. But if you wait long enough it'll come round again.'

Irena pushes towards me a bottle of dubious-looking liquor. The label is too dusty to read. Without even considering the alphabet, I pour a drink and celebrate.

Underground Springs

by Susan Biver

"Hullo, Mr Gordon. It's me, Brenda."

The old man in the armchair turned his gaze from the window and smiled as promptly as possible, gathering his consciousness in from the frayed fringes where it had strayed. *(Brenda. Bob's wife. Where's Bob?)*

"Where's Robert?"

"In hospital. I told you." Brenda tried to keep the exasperation out of her voice. He had asked her that last time.

(That's right, she told me. And I'd forgotten. About my own son.)

He looked his anxiety at her, mutely pleading for information.

"Getting on very nicely," Brenda said kindly. "You know, appendicitis operations are perfectly routine nowadays. You hardly ever hear of cases of peritonitis any more, do you?"

(Peritonitis. My brother died of peritonitis. He was twelve. I was fifteen. How old am I now?)

"Robert didn't get peritonitis?"

"Oh no, he's fine. He'll be home in a couple of days.

(A couple of days. Evening, bed, morning. Evening, bed, morning. Bob will be home. And I'll still be here.)

"And how are you feeling, yourself, Mr Gordon?"

He grunted, deprecatingly. Brenda took off her coat and laid it across the foot of the neatly made bed. She sat down in the spare chair and drew it a little closer to Mr Gordon - not too close, he did have a rather unpleasant smell. Nothing definable, just oldness. If you could know what caused it, perhaps you could do something about it, with soap or pills or something. But it just seemed to ... emanate from

151

him. Not as much as from some of the other residents, though. Thank heaven Robert had been able to get him a room to himself – and lucky he preferred to stay in it all day, too. She had had to hold her breath as she hurried through the patients' sitting room on her way up, distributing smiles and greetings and constantly glancing at her watch to explain her hurry, excuse her rudeness.

She realised with irritation that he was sinking into that awful abstractedness again. She'd better talk to him.

"How's your arthritis today, Mr Gordon? Not too bad?"

"I've seen the physiotherapist."

He was surprised, pleased, at the way the difficult word tripped off his tongue. Then wondered if it was the right word after all and peered anxiously into Brenda's face for signs of suppressed mirth, pity, contempt. No, it must be the right word, then. Psychiatrist. He must remember it. No, *not* psychiatrist...

Brenda, reaching absent-mindedly for the list of the week's menus lying on the desk, commented, "Oh, the physiotherapist, that's nice. They can do you a lot of good. Did he give you exercises, or massage?"

"Both. He came this morning."

(No, it wasn't this morning. It must have been yesterday. At least yesterday - maybe the day before. But don't correct yourself. She won't know. Physiotherapist.)

Brenda was perusing the menus.

"I see you had veal and creamed broccoli for lunch. Was it nice?"

"I *hate* broccoli!"

She glanced up, surprised at his vehemence.

(Mother, always making both of us eat that hateful broccoli. When he had his appendicitis, Jacky was sure it was the broccoli that had brought it on. The doctor said no, but he

152

still thought so. And then he died.) "Broccoli can't cause appendicitis, though."

Brenda tried to follow his train of thought. "Oh, I never give Robert broccoli, he doesn't like it. Takes after his dad." She smiled affectionately, thinking of Robert and aware of being kind to his father.

(What's she talking about?)

Brenda saw the bewilderment in his eyes and turned to the menu again.

"It's Sunday tomorrow - let's see what you'll be having for lunch. I expect they do something specially nice for you on Sundays, don't they?"

"It's always *cold.* The cooks don't come in on Sundays."

(Damn, she thought with annoyance, I can't get anything right today.) "Well, cold chicken sounds pretty nice, doesn't it? You'll have Russian salad with it. And Danish pastries to follow - you like them, don't you?"

(Sunday. No trays served in rooms on Sundays. Have to sit at that noisy table, watching the disgusting table manners of George and Rita. And then Irene falling asleep with her face in her plate, like as not.)

"Danish pastries - you like them, don't you?" Brenda insisted. She couldn't understand what was the matter, what she had said wrong, why he looked so unhappy. She felt pity for the poor old man, and wished Robert was there to talk to him. He was rather hard on his father, but he did know how to communicate with him.

"Mr Gordon?"

The old man raised his eyes and slowly smiled, gathering in his consciousness once again.

"I'm sorry, my dear. I was thinking of something." *(I probably was, too, but I couldn't for the life of me say what. Funny: one's mind never stops, but nowadays when I want to*

153

look into it, it just empties itself. Like when I used to try to remember a dream. The thoughts just go to pieces and swirl around and disappear. Like lavatory paper when you pull the chain. They don't have chains any more. But even Bob still says 'pull the chain'. I wonder if Brenda does too? But you can't ask a lady.)

"I'm sorry, my dear. I was thinking of something." *(Didn't I just say that?)*

"Penny for your thoughts!" said Brenda, rather wildly.

Mr Gordon laughed cleverly, and Brenda joined in.

*

Robert looked up and there was Brenda, coming towards him. He put his book on the bedside table and cautiously stretched both arms towards her. With a smile, she slipped off her coat and entered his prudent embrace. He winced. She saw it and pulled away.

"Do be careful, Robert. You don't want those stitches to split or something."

She sat down on the plastic chair, maintaining her kind, cheerful smile. Two hospital visits in one afternoon were a bit too much. What she needed was a good brisk walk in the open air. This place smelled. Not as bad as the old people's home, but still, not quite clean and pure under all the disinfectant.

"I didn't think you were going to make it today. Been to see Dad?"

"Yes, I've come straight from there."

"Poor girl, you're getting your chores over in one fell swoop, are you? What a life! Well, how was he today?"

"Oh, so-so. Much the same as usual. Not interested in anything except his food and his aches and pains." She tried to keep the exasperation out of her voice.

154

"What else is there in his life nowadays?" he retorted, rising to her resentment. Then, remorsefully, he told himself she couldn't be expected to understand about hospital life. Even here, just for this short stay, he himself was getting just like his father, waiting for the next meal, the next painkiller. But it wouldn't do to let her see it, evidently – he must be bright and chatty. As if *he* were the visitor.

"I've nearly finished that thriller you brought me yesterday."

"Already?"

"Yes – can't put it down! I've no idea whodunnit, I suspect absolutely everyone. Even the detective."

Brenda laughed. "Shall I tell you the murderer's name and put you out of your misery?"

"Just you dare!"

The three other patients in the ward, visitorless, looked wistfully over to the laughing couple, not so young but obviously still in an enviably loving relationship to each other. The two of them prolonged the laugh a little, searching for something else to say. For want of ideas, Robert reverted to his father.

"I suppose you didn't see anyone on the medical staff when you called at Grant House, did you?"

Brenda hesitated. Not thinking he would ask, she hadn't yet decided whether to tell him now or wait till he was convalescent. But suppose that turned out to be too late? She took the plunge. "I did, actually. I ran into Dr Bowers as I was leaving and had a word with her. Actually, *she* stopped *me* and asked if I could spare her a moment."

Robert noticed the two 'actually's and mentally parsed this: *"Embarrassment. Bad news."*

"What did she say?"

"Well, you know that slight stroke your father had – "

"He hasn't had another one, has he?"

155

"No, no, it's not that. But Dr Bowers says he *may* have another one."

"And - ?"

"Well, actually, what she said was that if he did have one – not that she specially thinks he *will*, mind you, or anyway not necessarily soon – it might be … Well, it could be very serious."

"Fatal?"

Brenda hesitated, alarmed by his sudden pallor. She had no idea what one should say in such cases.

Robert insisted. "It would be fatal – that's what she said, isn't it?"

"She said it was possible."

Robert found he was straining forward. He relaxed carefully against the pillows.

"So we have to be prepared – is that it?"

"Yes, Robbie. That's exactly it."

He thought this over for a moment.

"Did Dad look … ? Did he seem more … ? "

She helped him out. "Look, I told you he was very much as he always is – well, as he has been ever since his stroke. A bit vague, a bit lost – you know what I mean."

Robert sighed. "Yes of course. He's been going downhill pretty rapidly, lately."

"Yes, poor dear. And you know, at times he's aware of it himself, it's quite obvious. Just as I was leaving, you know what he did? He stopped me and apologised for not being any good at conversation any more. He said he knew he got a bit muddled nowadays, he was very sorry, he just couldn't help it."

She suddenly chuckled.

"Then he said something quite funny, though I don't know whether he realised it."

"Something funny?"

156

"Yes. He said: 'I can't help it, I don't know *what* to do about it, I'm at my wits' end'."

She chuckled again. Seeing that Robert didn't join in, she broke off.

"Don't you see? A pun. Even if it was inadvertent. *'At his wits' end'* – you see? Of course, what he meant was 'not knowing what to do', but it's also a pretty good description of what has happened to his mental powers. Isn't it?" She paused. "He's come to the end of his wits, his mind – you see?" She waited. "Well?"

"That was a really *horrible* thing to say, Brenda."

Her eyes widened. "Why? You don't suppose I laughed when he said it, do you? Of course I didn't."

"But you're laughing now. You're laughing at him."

"No I'm not! It's the pun I'm laughing at. I find it objectively funny, and clever if it was intentional, that's all. You know how witty he used to be, often. - Oh, come on, Robert! It's not because there's sadness and pain and so on in the world that suddenly *nothing*'s funny any more. You've said as much yourself before now, you know you have."

"Maybe. But wait till *you* are in the 'sadness and pain' group, that's all."

She felt the unfairness of this, the hurtfulness. Robert must surely know she had no intention of being cruel. But again she was struck by his pallor and his evident anxiety and, resolving not to add to her crop of gaffes today, she said, "I'm so sorry if I was tactless, darling. It was only because your father always used to be so witty, it was as if he'd had a sort of flash of his old cleverness, even if it escaped him the moment he'd said it."

Robert looked at her remorsefully.

"Sorry, love. It's just that I'm a bit worried about Dad, and that makes me touchy."

"Of course it does, Robbie. It was stupid of me to - Well, look, - " she glanced at the ward clock – " I ought to be going now or the cleaner's will be closed." She stood up. "I'll be able to come earlier tomorrow and stay much longer. Anything I can bring you?"

"Yes, something more in the way of light reading – something by the same fellow, if you can. By tomorrow I'll know whodunnit." He tapped the book with a smile.

Miserably going over her ill-timed joke in her head, Brenda took a wrong turn in the hospital corridors and found herself at a back exit instead of the main one. She stepped out into the bright April sunshine and hurried along the path, telling herself she'd better calculate her route, what with the shopping to do and the stuff to pick up at the cleaner's. At the end of the building, she turned left – and stopped short.

A cherry tree. In full bloom. There beside the path. In full bloom. There.

She stood and stared. Her mind had stopped. She saw the tree, the white froth of blossoms, and the vision struck straight into her heart. For a whole instant of eternity she just gazed and felt.

At last she gave a tiny shake of her head and murmured, as if the words were forced out of her, "God, how beautiful." And the words, the framing of the thought, broke the spell. She actually felt the magic scatter and vanish, as time and context restored themselves around her. She stood and stared at the flowering cherry tree, splendid in its softly shining whiteness, and willed it to work its spell again. But it was no good. The moment had pounced on her, dazzlingly, and now it had gone again.

"*Well!*" she said to herself as she walked on, "That was an aesthetic experience and no mistake! Gone as soon as you try to get hold of it, as usual. I wonder *why*? It's just like

158

nice dreams, the way they go to bits as soon as you try to remember them. Why is it? Aren't we *allowed* to experience this kind of – kind of joy?"

She quickened her pace, looking at her watch again, mechanically. "Well, here I am, wasting time when I really can't afford to."

But she knew that time had had nothing to do with the matter.

*

Old Mr Gordon sat in his armchair, muttering to himself. I said something funny to her, to Mavis. No, not Mavis, that's Tom's wife. Brenda. I said it to Brenda. She looked as if she was going to laugh. And then she didn't, because she thought I hadn't meant to be funny. What did I say? It was sad as well as funny, I do remember that. Pity. Lost it. Yet I feel much clearer in my head now. Why? There *are* moments. But then, so often my mind gets tired, it just seems to sit down and say 'You go on without me.' – That's quite funny, too, quite clever. I could bring it out some time, if I can remember it. Not to Brenda, though. To Bob, perhaps. He'd understand – he'd laugh. Brenda would be afraid to, in case I thought she was laughing at *me*. But Bob's in hospital. She had to remind me, Brenda, I'd forgotten again. Now, I can *remember* I'd forgotten. Isn't that strange? It often happens after someone visits me, my head clears a bit, I can think better. He swivelled his chair towards the window and looked down into the garden, still muttering his thoughts aloud to help himself preserve this precious moment of clarity and concentration. Nice garden, lots of flowers. Those two cherry-trees are lovely, just the best time. And a few of their flowers scattered on the grass. Like stars. *Amid the guests star-scattered on the grass...*

He became aware of the perilous fork in the path of his thoughts and paused.

Cherry trees in flower. What was that Zen story? I used to know such a lot of them. But it's years now since I gave them a thought. What *was* it? Something about a priest and a garden. No, a monk - *two* monks. Ah, that's it, got it! I've got it! The old monk, the abbot or something, making the young one sweep and tidy the garden, again and again. Never satisfied. 'That's not right – do it again.' 'That's still not right.' And the young one finally throwing down his broom and –

Mr Gordon leaned forward.

There's that bossy nurse, Karen. Bet she's going to open the big doors. Yes, there she goes. Soon she'll be pushing the wheelchairs outside. Spoil the view, lot of old dodderers sitting around. She's not going to get *me* out there. I *hate* old people! I'd get away from *myself* if I could.

He swivelled his chair round angrily, turning his back on the garden.

What was I thinking about? Lost it again. She's spoilt my concentration.

He clenched his hands in his lap.

Think, you fool, *think*! You were looking at the garden. Flowers, *star-scattered on the grass...Turn down an empty glass.* No, that was the wrong path. The cherry-trees. Flowering cherry-trees. Japan? No. – Yes! Yes, it *was* Japan! The monks, that's right – the Zen story. Got it! The young monk who can't make the old one say the garden looks nice. And in the end he throws down his broom: 'I've tidied up everything five times over!' And the old monk smiles and goes to the cherry tree and shakes a few flowers on to the grass: '*Now* it looks nice.'

Mr Gordon smiled too. Then frowned. No, it wasn't flowers, it was leaves. Must have been autumn. Probably makes a difference. For a philosopher it would make a difference.

- *Psychiatrist* – why couldn't I remember that? No, it was *physiotherapist*. And I did remember it. Don't undermine yourself, you fool.

And don't slip off sideways again, keep straight.

That story. Well, no, I'd got to the end of it, whatever it was. Yes, the philosophical one about the monk in the garden, sweeping up too well. What does it mean? Nature and art. The art of art is to tidy up nature, only not too much. No, that's not quite it. The art…

What was I saying?

The art of nature. No, doesn't make sense. The art of beauty. No, the nature of beauty. The art of the nature of beauty…

Lost it. Keeping at it too long - nothing makes sense after a bit.

I can't stand this modern art. They say art doesn't have to have anything to do with beauty any more. That way, anyone can call himself an artist. I could myself. You don't know which way round to hold a paintbrush ? - it doesn't matter!

I hate modern art, hate modern music, hate modern architecture. The modern world – I don't fit in. The thing for me is to die.

The doctor said I would die soon. Well, she didn't say it. But she made a face at the nurse. She thinks old people can't read faces. She'll see, when she gets to my age. No-one talks to you any more, or if they do you can't hear them properly – you're bound to read faces. Obvious. And the nurse made a face back. She knows I'm going to die, too.

I suppose I'll die here, all alone. If I *can* die.

- What do you mean, you old fool: *if you can*?

No, I did mean something. I don't know *how* to die, that's it. You have to be able to pray or something. Make *something* of it. But I can't. I can't pray, can't imagine God, I never could. Not any God who would take a personal interest in anyone. Not one who'd see you into the next world, if there is one. Well, same thing: there can't be a next world if there's not a God.

Are you there, God?

No, that's stupid. It embarrasses me, I can't ask seriously. Anyway, it's no use asking questions, you have to supply the answers as well. The responses. Like in church. Jacky was a great one for church – he really did believe. Well, he was only a little boy. Lucky for him, I suppose, to be a believer. You could say he died well, if there's a God. Or even if there isn't. It's believing that makes the difference to the person who has to do the dying. But how do you die if you *can't* believe?

- Ah! That was it! That's what I was trying to remember! That other Zen story, that was it. The old man who knows he's dying and sends his daughter to his old friend, the Zen monk. "Ask him how to die, daughter." And she comes back with the message: "Tell him: Just die." And he does just that. He just dies, as simply and peacefully as you like.

That's what I'll do, when the time comes. I'll just die. If I can only remember to.

Old Mr Gordon sank into hazy thoughtfulness. Birdsong and mumbling chatter seeped up from the garden, through the open window. After a time, he lifted his hand as if for silence and made a statement, aloud.

It's not dying I'm afraid of. The only thing I dread is senile dimension.

He chuckled briefly.

No, not *dimension*, though that's quite funny too. Another dimension of the mind that you slip into. What's the word ? *Dim*-something.

He chuckled again...

And that's funny too, I certainly am getting dim. Pity I won't be able to remember all these funny things to tell Bob, though.

Try another way of putting it. Yes. Mental collapse – that's what I'm afraid of. Why, though? If you really do collapse, I don't suppose it bothers you. Not if I judge by these spells of absent-mindedness I keep getting. Longer and longer, I think, though I can't be sure. You can't tell how long it's been, when you get back from them. It's not like what I *used* to call absent-mindedness, that was just daydreaming. Now, it's *really* absent – my mind's just not there. *I'm* not there. 'He's not all there' – that's what they'll say.

Again he chuckled.

And that's funny too. Everything's funny today, and I haven't got anyone I can tell it to. Who ever would have thought senility was so funny? – *Senility*, that's the word I was looking for! No, it wasn't. It had something to do with being dim.

Anyway, absent-mindedness doesn't worry me, not while it lasts. It's only when I come back again mentally – then I feel embarrassed, I wonder what people will have been thinking of me. It's humiliating.

No: what I'm really afraid of is the loony-floor. That's what they call it here, even some of the nurses do, I've heard them. When you get to be really a nuisance, that's where they send you, up to the top floor, the loony-floor.

– Senile *dementia,* that's it! I've remembered it! Well, I suppose as long as I can still find the word, I haven't got the condition. I couldn't stand being sent up to the loony-floor. Maybe James is still up there, and Elsie and Heather, after all

163

this time, still drooling and mumbling away. But supposing you were still all right in your head *sometimes*, and suddenly found yourself up there? Supposing you realised where they'd put you?

It makes you think of those awful stories where they dig up an old coffin and find the lid scratched all over on the inside......

*

"You're late," yawned Robert, heaving himself into a sitting position. He gave Brenda a perfunctory kiss and poked into her canvas shopping bag.

"Got another book for me? I've finished that other one."

"Yes, I have. Not the same author, though, they didn't have any more."

"Just as well. I didn't think much of it's being the maid who did it in the end, did you? A bit feeble, both the motive and the method. Far-fetched. A maid with a broom – I ask you!"

He fished out the book, then groped in the bag again.

"What's this – a camera? You surely weren't thinking of immortalising *this* scene?"

He made a small gesture of disgust around the ward.

"No, it was just for a tree I saw."

"A tree? What tree's that?"

"There's a cherry tree by the path behind the hospital, it's in flower. It looked really beautiful yesterday afternoon. I thought I'd take a photo of it."

"For me?"

"For you? Oh. Well, yes, of course for you. And maybe a print for your dad too."

"Have you taken your photo?"

164

"No, not yet. There was such heavy rain in the night, the tree looks a bit sorry for itself today. And without the sun on it, it's… It has … It looks quite different…"

For a split second, the ghost of yesterday's aesthetic experience gleamed in a recess of her brain and she shivered.

"Robbie, tell me: have you ever … ? - There was something yesterday evening … I don't know, but it was …"

"Spit it out, love, you're not being very clear."

She laughed and took a deep breath, relaxing. "What happened was this: I went out of the hospital by the wrong door – I'd got lost – and I came across this cherry tree. It was in full bloom."

For a moment, she felt her voice strangled in her throat. She gave a high-pitched gasping cough and continued: "And I don't think I've ever seen anything so *beautiful* in my life. It gave me a sort of shock – do you know what I mean? I just stood there, and I…. - Robbie, has it ever happened to you?"

"Well, there were a couple of cherry-trees in our garden at home - Dad planted them - and I do remember thinking how pretty the flowers were in the spring."

"Yes, well, the cherry tree was just an example. What I meant was: have you ever had that sort of *feeling*?" She thumped her breast-bone with her fist. "A sort of shock? A sort of - almost like fainting, except that you don't feel your body at all? And you sort of just stand there and want to *thank* someone?"

He had put his head on one side and was watching her shyly excited face.

"I think I know what you mean," he said. "In those early days, in Rochester – you remember? Every time I looked at you, I went all dizzy. Crazy, it was!"

Brenda was touched, pleased, frustrated. She wasn't getting it across to him. "That's how I felt when I looked at

165

you, too. But that was just sexual attraction. What I mean is something … aesthetic. An aesthetic experience – you know?" Robert's mouth was trembling: there was evidently another tremendous yawn coming and he was doing his best to stifle it, out of consideration for her excitement. She felt forlorn and slightly foolish, and muttered awkwardly, "Oh well, it's not important."

He swallowed his yawn. "No, of course I know what you mean – I was just thinking back. But no, I can't say I've ever had *that* kind of aesthetic experience."

"What other kind is there?" It was almost a snap, and she regretted it at once. He looked so humbly appeasing.

"I was thinking perhaps music… But of course I'm not musical enough really. Probably means I've never had an aesthetic experience at all. How would I know?"

She shrugged one shoulder, smiling.

"No, tell me," he insisted.

She looked sharply into his eyes, eliminating the possibility of mockery, then gazed over his shoulder at the wall. Words were hard to find.

"Your mind goes completely empty, and you're filled with beauty… And then you sort of come to again and want to *thank* someone."

"To thank God?"

"Well, yes."

"But I'm the one who believes in God. You don't."

"No, that's what I always say. But when *that* happens to me, God suddenly has to exist. Just so that there's someone to thank. Otherwise I'd – I don't know – I think I'd explode or something."

He was laughing, but awkwardly, confessing at once a blind spot and his faith. "Perhaps God sends you those experiences to manifest himself to you. With me he doesn't bother – I already know he's there."

166

Brenda said humbly, "I envy you. I'd *like* there to be a God, I wish I *could* believe."

For a moment, they looked at each other in silence, reliving instantaneously a debate of many years.

Robert suddenly became aware of at least one pair of half-open eyes fixed inquisitively upon them. He picked up the book Brenda had brought and looked at the spine.

"Craig Mellis," he read, speaking more loudly. "Never heard of him. Well, perhaps it'll be less of a let-down than the other one." He reached over wearily to push the book inside his locker. "That's the trouble with detective stories. Even if they're quite enjoyable, you can't tell till the very last page whether they were worth reading or a waste of your time."

He yawned again, mightily.

Brenda eyed him sceptically. A *waste of time*, what did he mean? Lying here in hospital, what else could he do with most of his time? You can't *think* profitably all day long. And the other patients didn't look as if they made very stimulating company. They seemed to do nothing but sleep.

There was a tap at the door and a nurse came bustling in. Robert looked round, and the three drowsers opened their eyes expectantly. But it was Brenda the nurse wanted.

"Could I have a word with you when it's convenient, Mrs Gordon?" she said. "There are some administrative papers that ought to be signed." The explanation was given to the ward at large, and loudly, but only Brenda caught the note of warning.

"Certainly. I'll come straight away."

She followed the nurse out, wondering, apprehensive.

*

"Hallo. You've been a long time. I've had a nice nap."

She sat down slowly beside him. "Robert…"

167

He was at once alert. "Anything up?"

"Yes, I'm afraid there is."

"Go on, tell me."

Hesitating, she tucked in a stray corner of the sheet.

"It wasn't the administration that wanted me. The nurse took me to the intensive care unit."

"Dad?"

"Yes, Robbie, I'm afraid so. They brought him in this morning. He's had another stroke or something."

"He's not - ? You don't mean he's - ?"

"No, no. I saw him, and he's conscious. But I think…I think perhaps…"

She broke off, gesturing helplessly.

"*What* do you think, for God's sake?"

"Don't sit forward like that, Rob, you'll hurt yourself."

He took hold of her wrist and gave it a little shake.

"Tell me," he said. "I'm OK. Just tell me how you found him."

"Well, he seems to be wandering in his mind."

"But surely he's always like that nowadays?"

"Yes, I know, but he seems completely *lost*, this time. *Completely* confused."

He considered this. "What did the doctor say?"

"I couldn't find a doctor. But when I asked the nurse she made one of those gloomy faces ."

"A 'he's going to die' face?"

"Not exactly, no, I don't think so. Though he's very weak, of course."

"*What* kind of face?"

"She sort of screwed up her mouth and rubbed her temple, sort of apologetically. I got the impression she thought this time his brain was badly damaged."

"*Very* badly, do you think?"

168

"Well, as I say, he seemed terribly confused."

"He did talk to you, then?"

"Yes, quite a bit. Except that it wasn't really to *me*. He was looking at me, but he kept saying 'Jacky'."

"That was his brother. He died when he was quite small."

"Yes, you told me."

"You think he thought you were Jacky?"

"I'm not sure. He was certainly looking at me, and he did say 'Jacky', several times. But then he called me 'daughter'."

"Called you *'daughter'*? He's never done that before, has he?"

"No. There again, I didn't have the feeling he was really talking to *me*."

" 'Daughter …'. I wonder what he had in mind. Can you remember his exact words?"

"Oh yes, perfectly. He just said - twice - 'Daughter, go to him.'"

"Go to *me*?"

"Well, that's what I thought. I'm not sure, though."

"Did he want you to bring me a message?"

She said, uncertainly, "Well, he didn't actually talk about a *message*…"

He had noted her hesitation. "But he did add something?"

"Well, yes, but it didn't make sense."

"What did he say?"

Suddenly she lifted both hands and in an oddly vehement gesture dropped them in her lap again. "I can't remember. It didn't make sense. And then the nurse said I'd have to go because I was tiring him."

After a thoughtful silence, Robert asked, "And he hadn't said anything else at all?"

169

"Well, there were some other things too, but nothing I could make head or tail of."

"What, for example?"

"Oh, all sorts of things, but just broken fragments. He kept going on about a cherry tree, for instance. – I thought that was quite peculiar, actually, because of that tree I saw yesterday. I wish you could have seen it. The flowers were so … they were so…"

She broke off, moving her hand in a helpless little gesture. He took no notice.

"What else?"

"Oh, he said something about a garden, and about some stars. And about a priest or a monk or something."

"He wanted to see a *priest*?"

"Oh no, I don't think it was that. That wouldn't be like him at all, would it? No, I got the impression he was sort of *seeing* this priest, this monk, in the garden."

"With the cherry tree?"

"Well, yes, perhaps. That's what it sounded like."

"At night?"

"No, I don't think so. Why?"

"You said he talked about stars."

"That's right, he did. But as I said, nothing made any sense."

They sat in silence for a moment. Then Robert said, "If he gets over this, you know what will happen to him, don't you?"

She sucked in her lower lip, hesitating. "You tell me."

"They'll send him back to Grant House, and the matron will have him banished to the loony-floor – you know what *that* is. And if he's not completely gaga when he arrives, he certainly will be after two days. You've never been up there, have you?"

"No."

170

"I have, just once. I never told you about it. Dad made me go and see if I could do anything for that friend of his, James, when he first got sent up there. They wouldn't let Dad go himself – bad for the morale of the troops."

"I've always thought it must be pretty horrible up there."

"It is! You go through two doors to get there, one after the other. They're both soundproofed, and when you get out the other side you know why."

"Please. Don't tell me. I honestly don't want to know about it."

There was a pause.

"You're a bit squeamish, aren't you." It wasn't a question. She flared up.

"Look, I go and visit your father, I try to be nice to him, I listen to those aches and pains that he tells me about every single time. Do I *also* have to hear about the loonies on the top floor?"

"Sorry, sorry!"

Robert glanced uneasily at the other beds. No-one seemed to have noticed Brenda's outburst.

Her anger died instantly. She lowered her voice. "No, I'm the one who has to be sorry. He couldn't help it, poor old man."

"Couldn't help what, exactly?"

She made a vague gesture. "Oh, everything."

"No, come on, you had something particular in mind. You've been tiptoeing round it ever since you got back just now.

She sucked in her lower lip again.

Robert laughed. "When you start nibbling your lip like that you always give yourself away. Come on, tell me. What's on your mind?"

"Honestly, Robert, I'd rather not. I don't think it's something I *ought* to tell you."

"Why on earth not?"

"Oh, for heaven's sake, do you have to keep on at me?"

"Shhh, do try to keep your voice down, love. Look, I really want you to tell me. I think it's probably the last message I'll ever get from my father, and I have to know what it was."

"I never said there was a message."

"No, and you didn't say there wasn't one, either. Come on, Brenda, out with it."

Brenda considered.

"If he was just a little further gone," she said, looking stern, almost belligerent, "I'd say he was sniping at you from behind his tombstone."

"Brenda!"

Robert sat up sharply and winced with pain. Brenda glared at him.

"All right, he did give me a message for you. You really want to know what it was? It was horrible. He was just like Alcestis's husband, I can never remember his name."

"Just a sec., who was he?"

"You know, that Greek who didn't want to die and got the gods to let him substitute his wife for him when it was his turn."

"Did he? The pig! But what's that got to do with Dad?"

"He's *jealous* of you, Robert! He's jealous because you're young – well, a lot younger than him, anyway – and you're going to live, while he's old and he knows he's at death's door. He'd like you to take his place! Or if he can't, then he'd like to take you with him. He's the dog in the manger!"

172

"What on earth did he say to give you that impression? - I'm sure you got hold of the wrong end of the stick, it doesn't sound like him one little bit."

"Oh no, he said it twice, very clearly. It's the only thing he did say twice, and it was practically the only proper sentence he managed to put together."

"And it was - ?"

"Well, if you really want to ruin your picture of your father at the last moment, I'll tell you."

"Go on."

"He said – and he said it *twice*, mind you – 'Go to him, daughter. Tell him: *Just die.*' There!"

To her astonishment, Robert sank back into the pillows with a smile of relief. His face was quite transfigured with tenderness as he shook his head and said, "You've got it all wrong, love. If I've heard that phrase once, I've heard it a dozen times – it's the punch-line of one of those Zen stories he used to collect when he was younger."

Brenda, ruffled, felt foolish.

"He never told me any of them."

"No, and I hadn't heard any of them for years either. I thought he'd completely lost interest. – I'm quite glad to know those stories are coming back to him now, actually. He told me once they gave him great spiritual comfort – those were his actual words, I remember them quite clearly. *Great spiritual comfort*, he said."

Resentfully, Brenda muttered: "You might at least tell me what his message meant."

"Oh, it was just an allusion to a story about a couple of old men."

"Well, go on. Aren't you going to tell me the story?"

"You'd really like to hear it? OK, just a sec., let me think a moment."

Robert gazed at the ceiling, collecting his thoughts.

173

Brenda looked out of the window. It was beginning to rain again, and she thought sadly how bedraggled her tree would be looking.

*

The intensive care unit seethed with a quiet urgency of beeps and burblings. A nurse, passing Mr Gordon's bed, glanced at the monitor screens, frowned and paused. She listened a moment to his irregular breathing, then went on to the next bed.

Mr Gordon, smiling wordlessly up into the cherry blossom above his head, drew his monk's robe more closely around him.

FINIS

And when Thyself with shining Foot shall pass
Amid the Guests Star-scattered on the Grass
And in Thy joyous Errand reach the Spot
Where I made one – turn down an empty Glass!

From Edward Fitzgerald's version of *The Rubaiyyat of Omar Khayyam.*

A Day's Outing to the Reservoir

by Caroline Davies

It was so faint I thought I was imagining it. When I closed my eyes there was the sound of bells far down, submerged by the water. The surface of the lake was unruffled but I saw things moving in the depths. I didn't tell anyone else on the coach trip. They would have thought I was mad. The water all goes to England you know, to Birmingham, who would have thought it? Perhaps they don't have rain there, not like here.

I come back every year on the longest day. I have my own car now. I don't know what gave me the idea of reading poetry – it sounds so silly – but they liked it. I went for the obvious choices – the Thomases, RS and Dylan. I could sense them listening; hanging on every word. I've been branching out lately with more modern stuff, Gwyneth Lewis and Menna Elfyn. It's like an epiphany; with me reading while they gather round fluttering like angels' wings. When I've finished they sing, mostly hymns. Then I get out the thermos and some Welsh cakes while they chat. I can't tell what they're saying, a general hubbub, all of them talking together, Mam, Taid, Nain and all my cousins. The water is so deep it drowned all the houses in the village and all the graves. Dad was glad when we were moved out: we got a brand new Council flat in Swansea.

This year they were waiting for me. That was a bit different. It normally takes a little time before they start to emerge. I can't really see them of course, just a blur at the corners of my vision. "No poems this year," I said, "Not got the energy."

The doctor said it was inoperable but they'd make sure I wouldn't be in any pain. What does he know?

I'd brought the family bible with me, so very heavy it was like my heart as I walked past the sign saying Danger deep water. But I thought why not take the bible back to where it belongs. It was easy once I was in the water, like a baptism with the minister's hands pulling me deeper in. The roaring in my ears as they sung me back home. Then I could hear the bells louder and clearer than ever before.

"Must be ringing for someone's funeral."

A Chamber of Commerce

by William Wood

Arthur Slade woke feeling pretty pleased with himself. He'd done it. Not bad, really. Not bad for a man of his age. He'd broken out of his routine all right. Surprised himself, too. Learned a bit about himself, and all.

An urgent need to pee forced him out of bed. He went to the bathroom smiling. It was good to empty his bladder. Almost a pleasurable sensation, a kind of tingling in his penis.

"Not surprising, eh, Arthur," he told himself. "You dirty old man!"

He pinched his scrubby moustache between forefinger and thumb and went back to bed. He switched on the BBC World Service. The programme was "Jazz for the Asking."

"What a time to play jazz," he thought. "Early Sunday morning!" He stayed in bed a while. There was not much to do in a strange city on a Sunday. It would already be too hot to go out. Only one more weekend to endure as the sole occupant of the mining company's town house. He would go down to Labadi Beach later, have a bite of lunch and catch up on some of the paperwork in the afternoon. It was too hot out of his air-conditioned room to do much else. Then after dark, well, he could always repeat last night's performance.

"Practice makes perfect," he thought sheepishly. Involuntarily he moved his hand under the bed clothes to scratch his scrotum, but the itch seemed further up, deeper in. He squeezed his flaccid penis, setting off a stab at once pleasurable and painful of pins and needles in its core.

"Too much excitement, Old Lad," he thought, but a faint anxiety fluttered at the back of his mind and made him throw off his covers and get up. He made some breakfast. A good strong pot of coffee, a papaw, a slice of sweet, puffy Ghanaian bread with pineapple jam.

Next time he peed it felt as though it were burning him. He put it down to the coffee, ignoring the suspicion waving frantically to him from the back of his mind to catch his attention. He looked the other way. Nevertheless, he wondered if he *had* caught something last night, and if he had how long it would take for the symptoms to show. He opened a pamphlet they had all been given as part of their briefing material, entitled "Health Where It's Hot". There was something about sexually transmitted diseases in it, if he remembered right. He turned to the sentence, "If you do not intend to expose yourself to sexual contact there is no need to read the following chapter."

Too late Arthur read the chapter avidly. The advice was down-to-earth. "Do not diagnose yourself. See a doctor immediately if you suspect anything."

In a moment of panic Arthur thought he had the lot: everything from syphilis to scabies, from hepatitis to herpes, not to mention the ugly gonococcal family. Then he came across a table of incubation. The soonest anything could show, he read, was two days after infection.

"So, there's nowt the matter with me, then," he concluded dogmatically. "I've checked, haven't I?" he wheedled to himself, pinching at his little moustache. "Just got over-excited. A bit sore, what do you expect?" He slapped himself on the thigh with a chuckle meant to reassure and made preparations for the beach.

Labadi Beach was a popular resort at weekends. Arthur brushed off the boys hiring out mats, chairs and surf boards. He declined a drink. "Later, later," he said, rubbing oil into his belly. Very soon he went into the sea, enjoyed splashing about in the surf. Not exactly cool, at least the immersion cleared his head and his worries. It was good, this embrace of water around him. And people. He wondered what Daphne was doing back home.

178

What the weather was like. He'd surprise her with his unseasonal tan.

"And you said you'd been working hard," he could hear her saying.

When two girls approached him in the beach bar he felt sick with fear. A real wave of nausea as though his subconscious were trying to float a warning to the surface.

"White man. You want to buy us a drink," simpered the younger girl, slim, high-bottomed and highly scented. She was dressed more for a party than for the beach.

"I've got to get back."

"Take us with you, then," challenged the girl. She looked directly at him. There was a hard edge, a business edge to her voice. "We'll give you a good time."

"I don't think my wife would like that," he tried to joke.

The other girl, who hung back a little, was eyeing the plump, middle-aged man critically. She blew a bubble with the gum she was chewing, popped it and caught her friend's attention. Without another word they turned and joined a group of young Lebanese men who were drinking around a makeshift table. Bubble-gum slid onto the bench beside the best looking and put a hand on his thigh. He went on talking to his friends, neither acknowledging her presence nor rejecting it.

"It's broad daylight," thought Arthur, brushing the salt from his moustache with his forefinger. "Daphne won't believe this."

Arthur's own act, his own premeditated act of lust had taken place surreptitiously in the night. He had planned his undoing under cover of darkness. He envied these Lebanese lads their insouciance, their utter arrogance.

Arthur had set out deliberately to get a whore. At the age of forty-something he had decided to find out what he'd been missing. Even for first-time Arthur it was easy in this city to find

179

a companion. His guest house was ideally placed for it. It was surrounded by a network of tree-lined avenues frequented after dark by "ladies of the night", as Arthur had quickly observed. Many of them stood in groups, for safety, he supposed. But there were bolder, single girls in the shadows. The whole stretch of the road, he realised, was a kind of shopping street for whores, a drive-through brothel. Not many cars came this way, but of those that did, one in three stopped to deposit or pick up a scantily dressed package of flesh with handbag. He wondered where they went to do it and what they did. And he wondered what it cost. He resolved to find out.

Arthur went through the rest of the morning like a man in a daze. He allowed a boy to rent him a mat, he rubbed oil into his flabby white body, drank a bottle of beer or two, waded into the sea from time to time to wash off the sand and the sweat and the anxiety, and also because there was no public urinal on the beach. Only when passing water amidst the splashing throng did real time impinge painfully on the indelible reality he was revisiting, the action or perhaps the inaction replay of yesterday's sexploits and what led up to them. He was still laboriously finding his way towards the agonising question, "Why did I do it?" He had got no further than the preliminary, "What did I do?"

Arthur had planned his pick up as meticulously as if it were the Great Train Robbery. Or the perfect murder. Nothing was to be left to chance. He had no idea what it would cost him. He guessed £40 or £50. Since the largest denomination Ghanaian note was worth only 50p he filled a big brown envelope with money and put it in his bedside cabinet. If he carried the money with him in the vehicle he stood a fair chance of being mugged. It was his intention to pick the girl up and take her back with him to his room where she would earn the money "honestly" and receive payment. He certainly did not want to linger longer than

180

necessary under those trees where the girls gathered. Neither did he intend being lured off to a hotel room somewhere.

Before he left the room in the guest house he made sure the curtains were closely drawn, left only a table lamp on to give a subdued light and set out a whisky bottle and two tumblers on the sideboard. He had planned for everything, even for hand towels in the bath room. Everything but a condom, assuming they were part of the stock-in-trade, together with whips and creams and small gadgets. Why else did all the whores carry hefty handbags?

He got into his Land Rover to drive round the circuit. A thrill electrified him from the pit of his stomach to the top of his skull. The thrill of the chase charged with primitive lust. He was on his own with a double bed, a bagful of money and streets of fancy women to choose from.

He pinched at his moustache, smoothed his thinning hair and drove round the circuit on an initial recce pretending he was going somewhere, looking for an address, a house number. Even though it was dark and no one was with him, he tried to look nonchalant.

He couldn't help noticing them, though. A very tall, thin woman in a tight mini-skirt stood in a lay-by where in the daytime the tro-tros stopped for their passengers. A gaggle of girls, as young and nervous as school children, smoked and chatted together beneath a street lamp. Novices, probably wanting to be taken first to a disco or night club. Further on older women stood on their own, still, grim and patient, some of them women his own age. Disgusting!

The second time round Arthur was beginning to sweat. He'd have to stop this voyeurism, face reality and actually pick one up. His stomach turned over. He wanted to go to the lavatory.

By now they could not fail to recognise the vehicle and realise this white man was scouting. He tried to force himself to cruise up to a group. He could always ask for a street name, pretend he was lost, see how it all panned out. There was no need to be too direct at first, after all...

The palms of his hands were slippery on the steering wheel. A car overtook, stopped suddenly only a hundred metres or so in front of him and reversed quickly back to a huddle of whores. There were several young men in the car. Arthur had no choice but to drive on past. A lively conversation was going on around the stopped car, some of the girls bargaining eagerly, some hanging back. They might have been haggling over loaves or bread or iced water. Sex was just a commodity. It was all so natural, so effortless. Effortless for some.

He noticed too late a simply dressed woman under a tree. She didn't look too threatening. He'd try her next time round. He picked up speed, and as he did a young woman in a short skirt and high heels ran out excitedly from a drive-way, tried to flag him down. She might have been any girl late for a party stopping a taxi. Only a Land Rover, even in the dark, could not easily be mistaken for a taxi and on this street there could be little doubt that what she wanted was business. Arthur's throat went dry, a stab of fear and excitement pierced his gut and he applied his brakes. At this moment, the young men in the car sped past, just missing his vehicle and all but knocking the girl into a storm drain. The near accident unnerved Arthur. He drove on sick with relief. Relief that the car had missed him, relief that he had an excuse to go back to the guest house. There was no sense in this kerb crawling. Not at his age. He felt sick, sick...

The rest of Arthur's Sunday was marred by further anxiety. His physical discomfort fed his mounting panic which in turn increased his physiological disorders. He escaped for a few hours by sleeping off the morning's sun and his lunchtime beers.

182

He awoke with a groan and scurried to the medical book again, flinging it away in despair moments later. He could have caught almost anything.

"Get a grip on yourself, Lad," he told himself. "It's probably no more than a urinary infection or summat." He got out some papers, brought his report up to date and worked up a spreadsheet on his laptop. He also had to prepare for tomorrow's interview at the Ministry of Trade. All this gained him a few more hours. Then his mind returned to Saturday night and that feeling of failure.

Two night-watchmen guarding the entrances to neighbouring houses had now noticed him. One was pointing while the other stared. Arthur accelerated, no longer consciously in control of his actions. His plan had failed. He switched to automatic pilot.

Around the next bend two figures stood in the shadows. There was a bare patch of earth, a kind of lay-by under the trees that he had not noticed last time round. He stopped. His stomach churned. He really did not want to do this. It was as bad as being stopped by armed police late at night. His head span. Two girls were suddenly at his side window.

"Hello," smiled one of them.

"Hello," he croaked. His throat was dry. "Would you like to come back to my place with me?" The girls exchanged glances and the one in the rear gave a nod to her companion. "How much would you want?" he asked, as she opened the door to climb in.

"Four thousand cedis," replied the girl hopefully, expecting the price to be beaten down. Four pounds! Arthur was so astonished that he said nothing and the girl hesitated, holding the door ajar.

"All right, it's a deal," Arthur heard himself saying. "How long can you stay?"

183

"Let's talk about it in the car." She pulled the door open and got in. There was no step so she had to hitch her skirt high to wriggle in beside Arthur.

By Sunday evening Arthur realised with dismay that he could not do it again. He wanted to, the idea still attracted, the excitement, the lure. But the reality was that he had no appetite for sex. The very thought of wielding his member was if not salt in the wound at least like banging a bad bruise. Instead he drove to the garden restaurant of the Sunrise Hotel where he ran less risk of being propositioned than at the more public Afrikiko or one of the beach restaurants. Pity he was on his own. Pity Daphne was not here, someone to talk to. All he needed was someone to talk to. Perhaps, he thought, with another bowel-quake that left his legs shaky, not Daphne. Not just yet. He'd have to get this sorted out before he went home. This infection or whatever it was. Oh God! What had he done?

This was it, thought Arthur. He'd done it. No doubt about those legs, long and smooth. He'd bought them! They were the most visible part of a slim girl with a good figure as far as he could make out. It was too dark to see her black face properly in the cab of the Land Rover, but he distinguished a smile, a flash of white teeth, and grinned nervously back. He could think of nothing to say and she did not help. She put her hand on his knee and moved it up his thigh. Arthur took his left hand from the wheel and covered hers.

"Not here Luv. Let's wait until we get back." She withdrew her hand immediately, like a scolded child. It occurred to him that she might be nervous, too. She had no idea where they were going or what he would demand of her.

"It's not far," he said, clearing his throat. "Around four or five minutes drive, actually."

"That's all right," she cooed, and leant back, stretching her legs forward as if she were in an armchair. Her skirt was very short. Arthur put his hand on her knee. It was cool, smooth. Arthur himself felt clammy. He felt sure his palm was sweating. He returned it to the steering wheel.

"How long can you stay, then?"

"As long as you want me to."

"I see."

They didn't speak anymore until he turned into the drive of the guest house, which she recognised.

"I went to a party here once," she told him.

"I'm on my own tonight," he replied, grimly.

Arthur awoke on the Monday morning with a strong sense of relief. He felt all right. The knot in his stomach had loosened. Perhaps yesterday had been a horrible dream. There was no actual pain in his penis. He didn't think there was. He swung his legs gingerly out of bed and grasping the sleepy, one-eyed pig by the scruff. He drew back the foreskin and looked it in the face. Exposed, it stared back blearily. Shouldn't it be dry? A phrase from the medical book head-butted him. Penile discharge. The knot tightened again. He went to the lavatory and sure enough, the tingling as he eased himself was intense, almost pleasurable.

Arthur stopped in mid-piss, fumbled for the plastic mug on the shelf above the wash basin beside him, knocking the tooth brush on to the floor. He filled the mug with warm urine and held it up to the light. It was cloudy with bits of stuff floating about in it. Shouldn't it be clear? But perhaps the muck was toothpaste and dust. He emptied the contents into the pan but didn't have much piss left to re-fill it more than a few centimetres. He put the mug down and shook the drips of his penis. Drips or discharge? He looked again at the scowling, unblinking organ.

"It's all in my imagination," he told himself. But no, it did feel very tender. And there was definitely a burning sensation still. One thing the medical book made clear was that anyone suspecting a sexually transmitted disease should see a doctor as soon as possible. There was nothing to loose. Everyone in the delegation had been given a list of recommended doctors. He would visit one straight away after breakfast.

The girl stood beside him as he unlocked the guest house door. He took a look at her and congratulated himself. She was about his height, did indeed have a very good figure with no superfluous flesh. Rather a plain face and, he guessed, about twenty years old. She was quite reserved, he thought, as if she were here on business. As indeed she was!

She followed him in and he told her to sit on the sofa. He asked her what she would like to drink.

"Brandy."

"I've got whisky or beer."

"Whisky."

"With soda?"

` *"Yes."*

She did not believe in wasting time. When Arthur gave her the whisky she drank it straight down. A drink was a formality, a preliminary. Arthur knocked his back in one gulp, too, and sat down beside her. He knew she would not reject him but he did not know where to start. He put an arm round her shoulders and squeezed her, but this seemed inappropriate, a gesture rather of affection than lust. He ran his thumb across her lips, full and unblemished, he noticed. She bit it playfully. There was nothing about her lips, her young face, to indicate she was a whore. He did not know what he had expected, but there were no contusions, no bruises. Yet he could not help thinking what those lips had tasted, what her eyes had seen. He had read somewhere

186

that you didn't kiss prostitutes. That kissing was the only thing that was taboo. In any case he felt no desire for the girl.

He ran his hand over her breasts. They were firm, plump and although she gave a little sound of pleasure it meant nothing and Arthur felt none. Her body was as shapely and as well formed as he might have conjured up in any fantasy: it was living, breathing flesh and blood and it was his to do with as he fancied, and yet for all the effect it had on him he might have been handling a statue or an inflatable doll.

He tried her knees, her thighs. Immediately she opened her legs and leaned back on the sofa, raising her pubis to his touch. Her underwear displayed rather than covered her. A mere string of fabric which he could move to either side of her cunt with one finger. He wondered why she wore it at all. He cupped his hand over the whole sexual package, feeling her springy, wiry hair in his lower palm while his middle finger lay in the crevice of her bum.

"You've got a nice body," he said, like a connoisseur.

"Shall we go to the bedroom?" she suggested.

She followed him into the air-conditioned room, took her clothes off mechanically and lay on top of the bed. There was none of the provocation of strip-tease; nothing erotic except for her attitude on the bed. She looked at him with a let's-get-on-with-it expression.

Arthur felt a fool removing his trousers and pants under her bored gaze. Cheated. This was supposed to be exciting, sexy. Butterflies were careering round in his stomach. He had le trac, stage fright, first night nerves. He only wished his penis would rise to the occasion, instead of hanging limply as though he were waiting for a bus. He climbed on to the bed beside her and pulled her up against him.

The clinic was in a bungalow set in its own compound. Off an airy waiting area corridors led to consulting rooms, an office, a

187

dispensary and bathrooms. A dozen patients of all ages were already waiting while Arthur explained to the receptionist that he had booked an appointment by telephone earlier.

"Yes, please," said the efficient looking woman dressed in nurse's uniform. "You are temporary resident, isn't it?"

"That's correct," Arthur fervently hoped. He couldn't stay here forever but he dare not return to Daph's embraces until this mess was cleared up.

"Please sit," said the receptionist, indicating a small alcove evidently reserved for private patients. Arthur thumbed through some trade magazines whose pages stirred listlessly under the breeze from the ceiling fan. Quite soon a nurse in a slightly different uniform asked him to follow her and led him to a tiny room at the end of one corridor. Another nurse, also in a crisp, white uniform sat behind a desk.

"Please remove your shoes and stand on the scales."

"But..."

"Please!"

He did as he was told.

"Thank you. Sit down. Unbutton your shirt. Roll up your sleeve." She took his temperature under his armpit and his blood pressure. "Have you had a bowel movement today?"

"As a matter of fact, yes."

"How many?"

Arthur was confused. All this seemed unnecessary. For all she knew he might have an in growing toe-nail or boils. How many what, anyway?

"How many times?" she explained.

"Twice."

"How was it? Loose, hard, average?"

"Average, I suppose."

"Normal, then."

"Okay. Normal. But I don't normally go twice," he volunteered.

188

The woman wrote down all her findings on a form, clipped it to a green folder and pressed a bell. Her colleague returned, picked up the folder and led Arthur to a different waiting area outside a consulting room. She disappeared inside with his papers. When she re-emerged she informed him that he might go in when the buzzer sounded, and left him sitting on the hard chair by the door.

Arthur felt he was part of an elaborate, efficient system. It made him feel safe, restored his confidence. Until he saw the doctor, that was.

The girl took over, told him to relax, and massaged him. It was nice, but that kind of thing never turned him on. With Daphne he was always the active one. It did not feel right to be on the receiving end. He tried again with the girl, rolling her first on her back, then on her front, exploring her whole body carefully and curiously, but with a growing anxiety that the natural reaction was not taking place. After all his planning and preparation, after his luck in getting this clean and compliant young woman and not some poxy old cow, he felt no physical desire for her at all.

He got on top of her, felt her springy pubic hair tangle with his, let his flaccid penis flop on to the soft folds beneath. She made little stirring motions with her pelvis and encouraging moans bubbled up from deep in her throat. He wanted to tell her not to pretend, but kept up his own pretence. Rolling off he said, "There's no hurry, is there? Let's just lie together for a bit."

She turned the sound effects off and started to run a finger round his nipple. He took her hand and looked at her.

"What's your name?"

"Sadie."

"Sadie, eh. And what do you do during the day?" She looked at him blankly. "I mean are you a full time...Do you earn your living like this, with men, or do you have a job as well?"

189

"You don't think I am any good, is that it?"

"Don't be silly, Lass. I think you're smashin." He ran a
hand over the curve of her hip. She smiled, believing him.

"I'm a seamstress," she said. "I sew cloth."

"Do you work the streets every night?"

"Mostly weekends. With my friend."

"Your friend?"

"It's safer. I nearly asked you if I could bring her with
me."

"Why didn't you ask me? Did you think I looked safe?"

"No, I thought you would be angry. I thought you would
drive off. And then I would have lost a customer."

He wondered how many customers she had had that
evening. She was sweet smelling and dry. There were no juices,
hers or anyone else's that he could detect. She might have been
any clean young girl on his bed. And although she struck all the
poses and made all the noises and nuzzled at all the erogenous
places, the experience was absolutely unerotic. Arthur, naked
himself on the bed, the purple tip of his useless willy matching
the purple of his nose, his beer belly falling like a deflated
balloon on the sheets, nevertheless was beginning to relax.

"Would you like another drink, Sadie?" he asked.

"In a minute," she said, workmanlike. "Let's get the job
done first."

Arthur felt inadequate. "Look. I'm a little tired today. I'm
not sure I want..."

"Shall I suck it?"

"Go on then, have a go."

There was a croaking sound which, reacting slowly, Arthur
realised must be the buzzer. He opened the door and walked in.
An African in a white coat and thick glasses sat expressionless
behind a desk. He made no attempt to greet his patient, gave no
indication as to whether Arthur had got his cue right or where he

should sit. But there was only one chair, this beside the desk facing the doctor. Arthur sat on it. Like a tortoise emerging from hibernation the doctor moved his head to look at him.

"Good morning, Doctor," he said in his cheery, one-of-the-lads voice.

"Good morning."

"I've come to see you."

The doctor clearly did not think it worth acknowledging the obvious. He let Arthur explain his problem and appeared to lose interest after a few sentences.

"...and it tickles when I p.., urinate," concluded Arthur.

"Tickles! Where?"

"Inside. Like it's burning hot, doctor."

"Ah, it burns," repeated the doctor, taking a bit more interest. "When were you last with a woman?"

"Last night."

"What time?"

"All evening."

"Was she the kind of woman that might have infected you?"

He lay back. Well, it was better than the dentist, he supposed. Quite pleasant, in fact. Sadie nibbled at his balls first, with her lips. Then she licked at the tip of his penis, tongued the opening. At last he felt a slight stirring. The whore was working very hard now. She had his whole penis in her mouth, she was sucking hard, rocking to and fro on her haunches, squeezing his testicles in one hand. It was a double relief to Arthur when he exploded convulsively into her mouth, his body rigid, aware that he was groaning horribly. It was done at last.

"Was she the kind of woman who might have infected you?"

"Quite possibly," admitted Arthur, though Sadie had seemed, if not exactly innocent, at least hygienic.

191

"It is a little soon, but we should test your urine. Can you produce a sample?"

"I think so."

"Good." The doctor scribbled on a pink card which he gave to Arthur before lapsing back into immobility like a puppet hung up after a performance.

"Aren't you going to examine me?"

"No need. There's a laboratory outside. Get a bottle, fill it and bring the results back to me."

"How long will it take?"

"About an hour."

Sadie stood on the floor, looked around and Arthur realised she needed to empty her mouth out. He pointed to a door off the bedroom. When she came back still naked she calmly opened her handbag took out an aerosol can and sprayed the inside of her mouth.

"I will have a drink now."

"You have earned it," said Arthur with sincerity. "Just a tick." He, too, went to the bathroom. He soaked a flannel under the cold tap and rang it out over his detumescent penis before giving the whole area a perfunctory wipe. Then he held his wrists under the cold running water. He felt tremendously relieved.

Sadie was putting on her blouse. He went up to her, put a friendly arm round her waist and patted her still naked, black bottom.

"You're a nice girl," he said. She smiled at him in surprise.

"Next time I'll bring my friend, if you like."

Arthur poured the drinks while she put on her thong and skirt. She downed hers before he had got dressed himself. She was ready to go. Arthur took out his envelope of money.

"Here, I think you said 4000."

192

"Yes." Her eyes narrowed. What was he playing at?
"Take five. Now, what's the drill? Shall I drive you back?"
"It's okay. It's not far. I'll walk."
"Maybe you'll get picked up," he thought. "Goodbye then, and thanks!" Feeling foolish he pecked her on the cheek, rather sorry she was leaving.

When he returned with his pink card on which the lab technician had scribbled his results, the doctor showed no recognition of the white man. However he took the card and for the first time in their acquaintance permitted himself a brief smile.

"I can assure you, Mr..." he glanced at the card, "Slade, that there is nothing wrong with you."

Arthur felt dizzy, almost sick with relief. But a cloud of doubt scudded across his restored horizon.

"But why then do I get this burning sensation when I pee?"

"I do not know what this woman did to you. What kind of sex you indulged in. But any kind of vigorous activity might inflame the ureter. That would make it feel tender."

He'd done it! In a fashion. "Not bad for a start, Old Lad," he told himself in his pub voice, and he did a little dance, stopping abruptly when he realised that he had not used a condom after all. But you couldn't catch anything from a blow job, could you?

A cold sweat broke out. Irrational almost. He tore off all his clothes again and got into the shower. He soaped himself all over. He scrubbed the soap into his genitals. Imagined himself scraping off the saliva, the germs. What if the virus was even now creeping into him. He forced himself to pee where he stood in the cold shower. It was good to feel the cleansing, caressing shower water. He watched it swill away the yellow stain. He

193

relaxed and reviewed the last hour or so of his life. He pictured the girl on his sheets on her back, one leg stretched up, foot resting high up the wall beside the bed, the other leg flat beneath his own knee. And now at last his recalcitrant organ stiffened. He grasped it, masturbating brutally, sucking the shower water between clenched teeth. Another ejaculation would swill out all the germs, all the uncleanness. Come on, come on. He had to sustain this arousal. He thought about the next time. He would have her again tomorrow, take her properly. Tomorrow he wouldn't get undressed so soon. He would insist on undressing her first. He would strip her himself. He would be more forceful. He was hurting himself now, driving himself towards orgasm. Buttocks clenched, he felt his thigh muscles, his calves tighten like a plucked string and loosen with the release of sperm. The sudden limpness of his legs nearly felled him. After a few seconds he soaped himself over again, rinsed the soap away and turned off the shower.

"It's smoking like a gun," he laughed but he was not finished yet. He remembered that he had some TCP in a bottle that he had bought for a small graze. He filled the wash basin half full of water and poured the contents of the bottle in to it. This cleansing soup he stirred with his rapidly shrinking penis.

Arthur laughed aloud. "You've taken a great load off my mind, Doctor."

"Apparently"

"I am sorry I have bothered you."

Again silence. The doctor was beginning to ignore him. But another question was welling up, an unconsidered, unspoken question that had to be asked. Silly, because Arthur deep down knew the answer as well as the question that he had tried to hide from himself.

"Doctor, could I by any chance have caught Aids?" There, he'd said it, named the enemy, expressed the real reason for his panic. He had named the disease.

"If you had sex with an infected person you could have picked up the virus. But I cannot tell you." Arthur wondered if the doctor was prompting him to recount the details of last night. He hesitated, but in a kinder voice the doctor told the confused, podgy white man. "You see, it takes three months to manifest itself."

"You mean that if I contracted the virus today, it wouldn't show for three months?" Arthur tugged at his moustache.

"Correct. If you are worried, you could have your partner tested."

Arthur's driver was waiting patiently in the car-park when he emerged from the clinic. Arthur got into the car without a word. The driver waited for his instructions. Arthur looked at his watch. It was time for his appointment.

"Moses, how long does it take to get to the Ministry of Commerce from here."

"Depends on the traffic, sir."

"I am supposed to be seeing the Deputy Minister now."

"Don't worry, sir. In Ghana time is little bit flexible."

"Well, let's go."

It was business as usual.

The Cleaner

by William English

The tapping at the door is only barely audible. If Mark hadn't reached the bottom of the stairs on his way past the front door to the kitchen he'd not have heard it. Why not the doorbell? Suspicious, he opens the door slowly, just a crack. At first he thinks there's no one there, has time to think that someone's knocked and run away. But, glancing down, he sees a figure, so slight, so short as to be hardly there. More than that, he can see no reason why such a small woman with a shawl over her head and shoulders should be knocking at his door. And carrying what, a bundle of some sort? His right hand finds the back of his head – his reaction to unknown territory. Beggar, he decides. But, looking down further, he finds no hand outstretched, no scribbled note, no empty tin. Instead, he looks (down) into a pair of wide brown eyes gazing steadily up at him.

'The cleaning,' the woman says. The two words give him some information: foreign, but not a specific foreign.

'Oh, yes, the cleaning,' Mark says. The hand remains on his head, rubbing and fidgeting notions, questions, speculation. Of these one insists on some appropriate reaction.

'Er, come in, then.' He doesn't have to draw the door back much, and hardly needs to move aside. The woman slips in and stands looking down at the small reception space made where the bottom of the stairs meets the corridor to the living/dining room and kitchen.

Mark has the usual moment of uncertainty where he's too self-conscious to react immediately. Maybe he's able to hide this from most other people, but here it is: he sees himself as a tall thin man, weak blue eyes, what's left of his hair close-cropped as if for security, dressed (as at work) in a black

196

jersey and black jeans. He worries about how others see him, find him: this tall man now looking down at a very short woman in a shawl, carrying a bundle.

So he has to shift his mind from this undermining, nothing in particular state; has to shift out of relaxation mode because it's Sunday and the day is his own, not someone else's. Not a day when he will be hassled at work from beginning to end, where he feels that he's only just keeping his head above water. He has to get his mind round the notion of cleaning. Yes of course, the advert.

In stepping over the threshold, the woman's shawl has slipped back to show him dark, neatly combed, centrally parted hair tied severely back. Below this her black eyebrows are like finely drawn, almost straight black lines. The bundle she's carrying moves and snuffles. Oh, my god, he thinks, it's a baby.

'It's mostly the kitchen and bathroom,' he's saying, leading the way down the corridor to the kitchen. He's still in Sunday recovery mode. He's thinking, *Shit, why didn't I say thanks but I've already got a cleaner, sorry, bye?* But the truth is that he hasn't. He cancelled the cleaning contract with *H'maids to the Rescue*; house or handmaids, he never discovered. It was just that he didn't feel comfortable with them: things got moved or disappeared; odd smells (not cleaning or disinfecting ones) permeated the place when he got home from work; his clothing looked disturbed; his drink, he suspected, was drunk. Not enough of anything to be certain of – but. They came, they cleaned and they cleared off – anonymous, faceless. What he wanted was a face, someone to visualise, someone to, however briefly, communicate with. That way he could begin to trust.

'They're the ones that need most - ,' he finds himself having to suppress a smile. 'But it's really the whole place.' He thinks he'll have to go through the motions of showing her

197

the extent of the job and then say how he's seeing several other applicants and will have to let her know. 'And, I'd prefer the place to be cleaned Friday afternoon and/or Saturday.' In each room he watches for her reaction. There's little; she merely nods and looks round with her alert wide eyes. He wonders why she doesn't ask about the pay. The bundle, thank god, does not shift or snuffle any more. He wants to ask where the baby goes when she cleans. But his hand continues to hover near the back of his head, moves up over the bald patch at the top he's in denial about, then circles round his mouth and chin, touches his ear, but will not allow such a question about a baby.

The tour has been quickly completed: the kitchen, living/dining room and downstairs toilet, and the bedroom, spare room and bathroom upstairs. They've got back to the front door. The woman's gently, imperceptibly, rocking the baby. An automatic action, he notices, as if it's nothing to do with her. He thinks, I've never touched, never held a baby. The thought makes him shiver.

'Things for the cleaning?' she asks, freeing and circling a helping hand, startling him because they're at the front door and Sunday is beginning to reassert itself. Her voice is surprisingly strong for someone so slight, but slightly hoarse.

'Oh, sorry.' He's already apologised for the state of the kitchen. He leads the way back to the kitchen thinking, H'maids? They must have brought all their own stuff. Bending down, he opens the door beneath the sink and points. 'Haven't looked, sorry, but it should all be there.' Sorry, sod it, he's not sorry. Does he apologise all the time at work? Although he can remember no specific occasion when he used the word, he knows in this very being that he does because he knows he skates on thin ice every day, all week, all the time. He's tall and awkward; he's worried that he's not up to the job; he

198

expects to fail; he expects the boss to call him in and sit him down. The woman genuflects, peering at the clutter of plastic bottles, packets, brushes and cloths.

'Okay,' she says, straightens and turns, leading the way back to the front door. She says, 'Is nice house.' Still he cannot place the accent, even if what she says sounds genuine. He thinks she didn't have to say anything about the house. At the same time realises that he's been looking at it in a more detached way than usual because he's been showing someone else round, looking at it as if through other eyes. He knows that a house – interior décor, colours and tones, furniture, books, nick-knacks – reflects a person's character and personality; precisely how and what it signifies is difficult for its creator to fathom. The last of a succession of women over the handful of years he's been here who lived with him a while then walked out, what, two three months ago? What did the interior of his creation tell them? There's himself and there's this place. Two sides of the same person? He wants to think about this, concentrate on it, hold onto it after the woman has gone, because he's never thought about his before. But there's still the social niceties bit to get through.

'Er, I'm seeing - ,' he pauses, sure that he sounds unconvincing, 'a few other cleaners. Do you have a contact number? Sorry, a telephone?' His hand tries to help by holding an imaginary phone to his ear. The other hand he imprisons in his trouser pocket lest it signal what he sees as his unease, his awkwardness, his assumed ineptitude in such a situation.

The bundle twitches. The woman makes a comforting noise somewhere near the quiet articulation of a foreign word and a universal sound of soothing, then rocks the baby a little harder. She shakes her head.

'I come. Ask in few days.' Leaving the words behind her, she turns head and body away from him towards the door. Mark leans awkwardly past and a little over the woman to

199

reach the front door catch. She slips out through the same small gap. Peering over the bundle, she treads carefully down the three steps to the pavement, turns left and hurries away. She doesn't look back. To Mark she looks as self-contained as the bundle she carries; a parcel of experience and life totally hidden from him.

He's closed the front door on this unexpected visit, intending to get on with Sunday: the papers, a few holiday brochures, telephone his mother, think about contacting friends to fix something up for next weekend, wander down to the Sunday flea market (but resist buying anything) and then a bike ride along the tow path; later, his evening jog in the park. Shit, he thinks, distractions, desperate activity to stuff into a hidden compartment the horrors of the looming Monday morning start of the working week. Instead, there's this other thing: he must walk through his place again in the same order that he took the woman. He wants to look at it as if from afar, as if for the first time, undisturbed by the presence, however mute, of another person.

Okay, same order: kitchen, living/dining room, tiny toilet crammed in under the stairs taking a small bite out of the kitchen, upstairs, bedroom, bathroom and crammed spare room; the decked patio reached from the kitchen is scarcely relevant.

Mark has completed the second tour. He's run a hand along surfaces and will have to wash his hands. He's tried to see his house through the impressionable but fleeting eyes of an outsider. Whether or not it's actually filthy is a value judgement he's not going to get into. But the main thing is that it was hard because of the personal baggage he's dragged with him into each room. For instance, the spare room where Angela camped the last few nights after things had broken

200

down, while she found somewhere/one else. The bedroom cupboard which Lisa had taken over, the bed he'd shared with these women was too small for two, slightly too big for one. The kitchen they'd all sighed about, even though he had done most of the cooking, the dining/living room into which these women had imported their clutter: the flowers, books, magazines and the whim-laden glittering trinkets from practically everywhere they went. And, oh god, the bathroom overwhelmed by their lotions and potions and motions; the toilet blocked by sanitary towels which sometimes floated back, confronting him in his queasy early working day mornings which had always been bloody enough without this.

Conclusion? That he likes simplicity, he likes clean lines – shelves, the mantelpieces, window sills only burdened with a few token embellishments: a Victorian wind-up clock, a strategically placed antique pot here, a treasured pebble there, but clean, everything must be clean. The opposite is germs, disorder, disarray, - confusion which he can only just about tolerate in the kitchen and the spare room. Pacing up and down the downstairs corridor, he things about this, but can't decide whether or not he likes this conclusion. But is that it? What else? Ah, the future; he has to admit that he has doubts. He has to admit that a future with clean lines, order and tidiness, but alone, is something he had not confronted.

While he continues to pace the corridor from the front room past the stairway to the kitchen, irritation kicks in; he wants his Sunday back, he doesn't want to be disturbed from his Sunday routine; he doesn't want to ask who he is and what he is, how he should change himself; he doesn't want to let a small, foreign woman (illegal immigrant?) who he'll probably never again see affect him like this. What right has she - ? The hand is clawing at his head, the other gripping the stair rail, pulling at it, forcing it to creak. Sod it! Get a life, he thinks. Get out and get some fresh air.

201

Monday is the expected hell. One long conflict to get a product on course, on time, on price – and it's all up to the packaging. The thin ice he's skating on can crack at any moment. He'll simply disappear. Yet all round him his workmates seem to exist in an anxious-free state, apparently in control of themselves and their work. Well, all except Jean whose face shows in turn frustration, bewilderment and irritation, interrupted by sighs which paradoxically relax her face for a few seconds. Mark can't remember what she actually used to look like. He had a section meeting at which Jean says nothing, spending most of the time looking down at a ring-bound notebook, occasionally scribbling something. Mark notices that other colleagues glance at her. After a surge, a deluge of objections, negative comments and destructive questions from those at the meeting – everyone seems in a rush to cast themselves in the role of devil's advocate – Mark thinks he manages to convince a majority that it's a good idea to redesign the Bettabreak choc bar packaging.

As they file out of the small office, Mark is assailed by the reek of his own sweat, rising like a malignant genie from his armpits. He discovers that sweat has run down both sides of his chest; he'll have to go to the wash room. As he stands, he sees that Will, who seemed most vociferous in his objections to the proposal is still there, delaying his departure for what Mark immediately sees as a chance to have another go at him, man to man, alone. He feels his heart lurch and begin to race. 'Good idea,' he hears Will say, 'something we've needed to do for ages. See you later.' Mark says as Will's nearly out the door, 'Jean, is she all right?' Will turns and looks back. 'PMT,' he says with a grin, 'but it could be a collapsed relationship. Y'know, pushing forty, the shelf and all that.' Then he's gone, mobile pressed to one ear, living his private, outside life in moments snatched from the very

202

harness of work, leaving in the air a description which Mark thinks could fit himself in all but one regard.

Cleaning up under his armpits in the toilet, Mark tries to think through the meeting. He'll write up his notes, email them to the boss, request a meeting with him. After years of this he still cannot fathom the awkwardness, the bloody mindedness of people. Is it because of him – is he not forceful enough, hard enough? Assertive?

The land phone rings. Mark still has it in its traditional place near the front door. At first he doesn't recognise the woman's voice because it launches itself without the niceties of identity: ' – owe it to you to tell you first. As you know, I was away yesterday. Very low. But – it's Wednesday isn't it? Yes, managed to see the doctor. The long and short of it is that I've been signed off for a month. (Ah, he thinks, it's Jean). He's very understanding (the doctor) and went through everything. Says it's stress. I'm so sorry (the armfuls of tabs he'll have to pick up), I know it'll mean more work for you – the boss doesn't like taking on temps, does he? (He doesn't). But I wanted to explain the situation to you first, personally, because you've always been so good to me.' *Have I?* he thinks. Jean's now getting into her stride. She takes a huge breath and Mark can visualise her cheeks reddening with the excitement of it all, the adrenaline, the high. This is different; this is like a break. 'Monday I thought you were brilliant – those things you said (What?). I wrote some of them down.' There's a rustling of paper. 'Yes, here it is,' she says. 'Clear blue skies thinking, re-engineering the image, pulling up the manhole cover.' (Did I say all this?).

Mark hears Jean taking another big breath. He wonders what she's on, what the doctor has given her; he's about to attempt to assess the impact of what she's said when there's a knock at the front door – modest, tentative, as if there

203

might be no one to answer. With his free hand Mark opens the door just enough to see who it is. There's a repeat of looking down at the small woman with the bundle. He'd thought he'd only opened the door enough to look through but she's already in, standing staring up at him: that carefully parted hair, those large brown eyes, the strong eyebrows now raised to give the high forehead a stave of wrinkles. He feels himself loom over her.

'Jean,' he interrupts, 'sorry, I've got someone here. Phone you back in a few minutes.' He puts the phone back on its stand and thinks, Shit, I haven't got her number.

'I come for de cleaning,' the woman says, and waits for a reaction from Mark. The bundle is still, quiet.

Mark takes a mental breath. Oh, god, the cleaning. No one else has phoned, called or whatever. The place is getting grubby, not just the kitchen and bathroom; this is making him feel grubby as well. 'Yes,' he says, 'the cleaning.' She's nodding, but begins to rock the bundle. She's nervous, he thinks, so am I.

'Okay,' he says, standing in the hallway. He feels bounced into agreeing; he feels irritated; he wants to think about what Jean said. He doesn't like things in the air, uncertain, unknown. He thinks he's getting all these in one go. 'Friday afternoon,' he says, 'and Saturday morning, but not before ten a.m. okay?' Slowly and with emphasis.

The woman nods vigorously; exaggerating the movement as if ordinary nodding is not enough. 'Ah,' he says, 'now let's think about the key - .' One hand has grasped the back of his neck, ready to crawl up onto his head. His eyes roam over the woman's head, scanning the door and the wall either side.

The woman takes a breath. She leans slightly to one side in order to support the weight of the bundle so that she

204

can free one hand. She bends her wrist at what looks like an impossible angle in order to point at herself. She says in her low, hoarse voice, 'Honest, I am honest person,' pointing straight at her heart, nodding, looking him in the eye as if challenging him to deny it.

Mark opens the front door. He speaks slowly and carefully. 'You – see – this - pot (the flowers fading for lack of water)? I – will – leave – the – key – under - it. Okay?' she nods. He says, 'Friday – afternoon – and – Saturday – morning?' She nods and steps carefully down to the pavement. 'Thanks,' Mark says, 'see you later.' The woman hurries away without a word, without turning back. He's left on his own doorstep beset by anxieties and questions unasked. He's plunged into the unknown in a way he's always so careful to avoid; he's trusting (or trying to) someone he doesn't know anything about, cannot contact, and oh god how's she going to do all this cleaning glued to a baby? He'd never get away with something like this at work, no one would. The habitual feelings of failure begin to reassert themselves. He feels himself going down the chute. Then, oh god, I promised to phone Jean back. With resignation he keys one four seven one.

There's no one there on Friday when he gets home. All day he's felt uneasy. *I've hired this nameless immigrant,* he can't tell anyone. *I don't know where she lives, have no contact number, and I've left the key out for anyone to find; I don't know when I get home if I'll find the place cleared out, or fifty illegals squatting there.* In something approaching panic he leaves work promptly. But when he gets home he has to admit it feels different; aromas of cleaning from the bathroom and the kitchen fill the whole place. The ten pounds he left by the phone has gone, replaced by the key. Mark has a shower and feels properly clean for the first time in weeks. Even though it's the end of the working week and he's really tired, his

205

spirits rise. Tomorrow the woman will clean the rest of the house and then Sunday will be pristine and completely his own.

Downstairs, he thinks he'll phone Jean, just to clear tabs at work for the weekend, but really because there's a possibility of more praise. Which he gets because of all her bits and pieces he's picked up or covered, and because he reports on a couple of meetings which she says he handled brilliantly, even if he didn't think so at the time.

Saturday, the bell rings ping pong and he can't think who it is. But it's the woman with the bundle. He expected a knock. Not wanting to hang around awkwardly, he says, 'I'll leave you to it, then – kitchen and bathroom very good.' She nods. He bumbles off into the kitchen where he's washing up the breakfast things. He wonders about the baby, but shrugs. None of my business – if she does the job all right.

Soon he hears the busy but comfortably familiar sound of the hoover. He lets his mind relax, drift where it will. It reaches a folder where he keeps local information: pubs, clubs, restaurants, exhibitions. He'll get out and see a few things this weekend. The folder's in the spare room. As soon as he finishes the washing up he goes upstairs to find the folder. The woman is hoovering in the living/dining room. He runs up the stairs and bursts into the spare room. He's shocked to see the bundle on the small bed – a blotch of pink cheek, a fist jammed into the face just below a tiny nose. He's fascinated and repelled in equal measure because he feels as if he's strayed into forbidden territory; that even though it's his room in his house he shouldn't be there and should get out quickly. The folder's abandoned and this irks him. But after the woman's been paid – she's taken the ten pounds in a strange way, no thanks, just a small nod – and he's out doing a bit of food shopping, he feels he's really looking forward to going back, being enveloped once more in a clean, pleasant smelling

206

house. As he walks back in bright sunshine he tries to think of an excuse to phone Jean, but can't and decides to leave it until next Friday.

Weeks go by. At work the ice holds so that he hasn't yet fallen into the freezing water beneath. Which doesn't mean that he's (mixing metaphors) out of the woods; he thinks in terms of a temporary release. The newly designed product is selling – but it's too early to say well, too soon in the day to relax. On the other hand, the house feels clean, as does he, all the time.

As things happen, there comes a Saturday morning when Mark finds another urgent need to go into the spare room when the woman's cleaning – some map this time, an idea for a walk with Jean – not a date, he's telling himself, just a bit of a social thing with a colleague, like anyone else might do. But this time he asks the woman if it's all right to go into the room while the baby's there.

'Yes,' she says, as if it's obvious. 'But baby not there - ,'

'Oh,' he says, 'so you don't bring it now?'

'Baby gone,' she says, with finality, turning back to dust the mantelpiece in the living/dining room.

Climbing the stairs in his customary way two by two, Mark's stunned by this news. Baby gone. What the hell does that mean? He rummages about in the spare room, in turns forgetting and then forcing himself to remember what he came up for. The impenetrability (if there's such a word) of the woman: my god, I don't even know her name. And still don't know where she comes from, where she lives, if she's married (foreigners don't always wear rings). Nothing. She cleans and gets paid. Simple exchange of labour for financial reward. Nothing else. The woman is a blank, or at best a shadow in his mind.

During the week Mark finds himself repeatedly returning to the mystery of the woman. He brings casual conversation at work round to the subject of cleaners and foreigners and immigrants. No one's interested; he thinks he'll talk to Jean about it when he sees her on Sunday.

On Friday when he comes home, exhausted, deflated but relieved, he can immediately sense something different when he steps into the hallway. No smell of cleaning greets him. Furthermore, the money's still there on the little table. He goes out and lifts up the pot: the key's still there.

At first he manages to prevent himself from getting worried; he tells himself that something must have happened, that she'll be round in the morning. But this is not good enough for him; he has doubts about such optimism. His body, conversely, refuses to accept this absence as a minor glitch in the order of things. He hates this mind/body split; he wants everything to be ordered and predictable. He doesn't sleep well that night. In the morning he's up early as if the long, possessive talons of work will not let him lie in. He leaves the money and the key where they've awaited the woman's arrival (it seems a long time, has become a part of his life), and gets himself organised to go out shopping.

It only takes him about an hour. When he gets back he knows something's different again and looks for the money. It's been replaced by the key. For a moment his heart lifts, he feels better, energised: it's all right, the world has not after all veered off course; she's here, cleaning, she'll say 'Sorry, some trouble,' or something like that. The phone's right here, he could call Jean and tell her. He has to wait a few seconds for the knee-jerk reactions to simmer down because he knows it's not so: there's no smell of cleaning, no calm murmur of the hoover in a room somewhere. The house is empty. Empty, yet he still has to check, still has to look in every room, but there's

208

nothing missing, nothing disturbed, no clue, a blank. She came and took the money; the replaced key says goodbye.

Mark's standing in the bathroom, washing his hands, aware he's peering back at himself from the wash basin mirror. The tears streaming down his cheeks take him by surprise, as if he needs this reflected image to tell him that he's weeping. He stands and watches vertical glazed lines develop into lazy drops which fall from his chin into the wash basin. He doesn't want to reach for the towel to one side; instead, he wants to hold on to this moment so that he can distil understanding from the unrefined emotions which prompted it.

What's squeezed out comes in notions of grief, inadequacy and personal failure. He watches his hands rise to his face, pressing from both sides so that his mouth is distorted in an effort not to say, sorry, sorry, sorry. He will not articulate the word, as if his whole life depends on killing it. But watching the man in the glass makes him want to tell him something: look, we're all like this. We all hate uncertainty, we want everything to be predictable, organised, certain. We want someone to tell us we're great, someone to show us we're not about to fail, disappear at any moment because there's at least some solid ground beneath our feet. That others in the street, at work, next door are as nameless and faceless as we are, and we can't always expect to be understood, or to understand. People will always come and go in our lives, vanish without trace, with or without a baby. With no explanation. A mystery.

The front door bell rings, ping pong. Mark's heart gives its customary lurch in the face of the unexpected. He hasn't yet told the face in the mirror everything. Ping pong. The face is still waiting, but he knows he cannot bear to ignore the bell. Ping pong, a third time and he cracks. Reaching to his left for the towel he quickly dries his face and runs down the

209

stairs two by two. He opens the door to a woman of about his mother's age: grey face and hair, grey coat (in such mild weather), and wreathed in the smell of fags.

'Allo, love,' the woman says, smiling as if she already knows him. She even sounds like his mother. 'I come about the cleaning. Saw the advert weeks ago, but what with one thing and another -,'

The phone next to Mark rings. With a sense of premonition he reaches for the receiver and tells it the last six digits of his number. There's an earthy giggle the other end. 'Sorry,' Jean laughs, 'misdialled. I was trying to get my mum.'

'Hold on a moment,' he says to the phone, 'don't go.'

Purdown Abbey

by Michael Heery

One

Brother Anselm wrapped his cloak tightly around himself. It was always this cold in the big church on winter nights. Vigils had been rung and the monks were all present, intoning the appropriate chants. Brother Gilbert led the monks, using his strong voice to conjure images of praise and hope for the saved, and the vision of hell for the damned. Anselm usually liked the singing. It was a time when he could forget all the troubles of daily life. It was also the time when the monks seemed to act together, as one organ beating in support of the Lord. Their own petty differences became submerged under waves of chants and prayers. It was as if God felt the weak ripples of their pleas and sent back to them His flood of forgiveness. His grace washed and purged their souls, reminding them why they were here. Anselm had noticed before that it was often after vigils that the monks seemed to be most at ease with each other.

However tonight his thoughts were distracted. He simply could not concentrate. He was just too worried and needed to seek reassurance, which was something he couldn't do here in the church.

Usually, life in a close religious community seemed as natural to Anselm as God's own order. After all, he'd been here for years. However, it could also become an obstacle, especially for those with a burning conscience. There was little privacy in the life of a monk. For several minutes he muttered the responses, troubled by his thoughts. Everything was wrong. Tonight, in his agitation, the choir carvings seemed more rustic than ever, insulting to a learned soul. Why were the teachings of Church fathers so often reduced to these platitudes? Why were so many of the monks nowadays ignorant of church history? Most of them had probably never even heard of papal teleology. It was all so irritating. He looked up into the gloom of the choir. The church candles fluttered, shadows flickered and the low rhythmic voices of the monks unsettled him.

Suddenly, he decided. He made the sign of the cross, told the monk next to him that he was feeling unwell and got up to leave. 'But where are you going?' asked his neighbour. 'I need air,' he replied. As he left the bench he was aware of the eyes of the other monks upon him. What could they possibly know of his concerns or of the problems of the outside world? Mostly they had fled here to escape the reality of the secular world. Whether young or old nearly all of them were ignorant of life. They were wary of the Abbot and were easily intimidated. What advice could they possibly give to him? Unlike them, Anselm understood the relationship between the Church and the power of the state. Why else had the Abbot nominated him as his successor?

Anselm gasped as he walked out into the freezing night air. His cloak, as usual, was useless in the face of a strong wind. He crossed the small square and entered the slype, a dark passageway leading from the devotional to the household quarters. Ahead of him the dim rectangle of light at the end of the slype was misty grey. As Anselm reached the end of the passageway he looked up in surprise. Simultaneously, a crossbow bolt smashed into his chest, splitting his diaphragm. He died almost immediately. For a life dedicated to nurturing a rich dialogue with God it was a cruel death. In his long life as a monk he had spent many hours meditating upon the final transition that would take him from this poor simple life into the majesty of the next. Suddenly, those spiritual preparations were past, with none of

212

the prayer he'd envisaged. We can never know what brief thought flew across his mind as the bolt was released. Did he cry out? Did he try to dodge? Did he even understand what was happening? Or did he just silently accept the inevitable conclusion? What is known, however, is that thirty minutes later the other monks came out from the abbey church to find Anselm lying on the frosty floor with a crossbow bolt embedded in his body.

Two

It was far too early for his liking. DC Parker turned into the grounds of Purdown Abbey at 5.00am. He turned off the Oasis CD, realising as he did so that it was probably playing much too loud. So, only his second week on the Bristol force and he lands a murder investigation in a Catholic abbey. Not what he ever expected, even in his wildest dreams. Hardly why he spent all that time in training. Those role play sessions about arresting inner city drug barons. And yet this could be a real opportunity. He desperately wanted a good start to his new job and here he was facing a real killing. Or so it seemed. His professionalism told him not to jump to conclusions. This would have to be handled one step at a time. And still, he couldn't help smirking. If only those bastards who'd doubted his talent could see him now! That awful Super in the Gloucestershire force, not to mention his mum, dad, older sister and every teacher he had ever had to run rings around.

As he reached the end of the driveway, he began to realise that he didn't know anything at all about Catholics. How many of them were there? Were they all Irish? Or were they really posh? And what did they do at those masses? Didn't they worship statues or something? And a *monastery!* Hadn't Henry the Eighth done away with all that nonsense? Who knows?

213

As he pulled up Parker saw a couple of uniforms talking to some people in dark robes. Monks, presumably. At the same time he heard from HQ that DC Butler was on her way to assist. Parker had met her only once, mainly because she'd been off with flu. It seemed that she was to work alongside him. Sooner she got here the better. The point now is that he's here on his own, facing a lot of monks and expected to appear business-like. Bit like Morse or one of those other TV guys. He got out of the car, nodded to the officers and asked everyone to keep calm and to take him to the scene of the crime.

The Abbot introduced himself to DC Parker and offered to take him to the slype. "The what?" asked the detective. "Oh, it's a special type of passage. It leads between the spiritual and the secular realms of the monastery." Parker felt a pang of anxiety but put it down to nerves. He decided to take charge. He inspected the body, noting that the wound had bled a large amount of blood. The dead monk was old and grey but didn't seem to have been moved.

"Crossbow bolts are an unusual murder weapon these days. Pretty powerful from what I hear. In the Middle Ages I guess they must have been commonplace. But they certainly aren't in Bristol in 2006. Do you think someone is making some kind of special point in using this weapon? Like a ritual or symbolic killing?" So began DC Parker's questioning of the Abbot.

For his part the Abbot tried to keep calm. "What on earth do you mean by saying "ritual or symbolic killing?" We are a very respectable foundation, established in 1882. We have lived here peacefully for years, doing God's work without any trouble whatsoever. This is not, you know, one of your drug inspired mafia killings! We are simply monks doing God's bidding and we don't have enemies. For goodness sake this is a real tragedy that we need your help with. I can't cope

214

with accusations. It's so upsetting. Can you possibly imagine how we are all feeling? A maniac is on the loose out there! Who's he going to kill next?"

Even though he'd only recently been appointed, Parker sensed that the interview wasn't going well. But, just as he was about to reply to the Abbot, a door opened and DC Butler swept over towards them. She completely ignored Parker and went straight to the Abbot, saying, "I am *so* sorry about this terrible news. You must be distraught.Is there anything we can do to help?" The Abbot audibly sighed with relief, even though he knew that his problems were only just beginning. DC Parker, on the other hand, felt his heart beat quicken and his muscles tense. Unknown to him, he was experiencing the very first physical signs of what would prove to be a stressful and enduring hatred.

Three

"For God's sake, Michael, what is this? A tribute to Umberto Rankin or something? I know I said you should try out a new genre, but I meant one genre at a time. What's going on? Are you *trying* to mess me around?"

These words show my tutor reacting to my homework. I was halfway through the second term of the Certificate in Creative Writing. In many ways Geoff Piggott was a good teacher. He had read a hell of a lot and understood about plots and characters and so on. To most of his students he seemed to be really committed to helping everyone write well. He knew what he wanted to achieve. He knew what he wanted *us* to achieve. But he was impatient to get results and this made him excitable. He didn't cope well with surprises. He liked us to absorb his message, go away quietly to work on our assignments and then come back the following week full of enthusiasm and bristling with written evidence of what we'd

215

learnt. He liked a hearty class discussion but only if it was positive. In that sense he was like every teacher you've ever met. I guess that for him it was all about the lesson plan. And getting his pay cheque.

The serious trouble started with Margaret, an older member of the class. She was hard as nails, sharp as a spike. She seemed to know enough about literature to have an opinion on absolutely everything. She also had - how shall I put it – an exaggerated sense of irony. Or to rephrase it, she took the piss all the time. "Geoff, are you saying I should replace the word *wanker* with *troublemaker* throughout my story?" "Geoff, are you inadequate or something?" "Geoff, how do you *know* that's not how a raped woman feels?" "Geoff, are you trying to tell me to shut up?" "Geoff, do you ever go out into the real world from this classroom?" And so on, class after class, throughout the late winter months. I felt sorry for Geoff. We all did. But we laughed a lot too.

Despite our sympathy for Geoff, Margaret's words worked upon us, like the subliminal message in an advert. After a class some of us would go to the pub together, where we'd agree how much we pitied Geoff having to put up with such a bolshie student. But when I got home, alone in the company of my computer, I began to use *her* as my tutor, not him. I became subversive, secretly looking for ways to undermine Geoff's ideas. I increasingly wrote in pastiche, I made jokes, I assumed all manner of voices. Or to put it another way, I began to take the piss.

By the time spring came around I'd had enough. I knew I wasn't achieving anything. Certainly not the literary skills I'd dreamt of a year ago when I signed up for the course. I felt that I wasn't getting anywhere. I was dissatisfied with the whole class. I'd had enough of Geoff, enough of Margaret and more than enough of creative writing. When I looked at my kids I felt the pull of other responsibilities and I knew I could

216

do without all that effort, that cynicism. I needed a break. The mild, wet weather seemed to be pointing westwards. At Easter we all took a short break in Cornwall. We had a great time and the only creative writing I managed was a postcard to my mum. Afterwards I signed up for an intensive French refresher class and in July I took my family to Brittany for a summer holiday. Sandcastles, food markets and lots of good French wine. We all enjoyed it and for me it was totally liberating. The only book I read was Harry Potter. In fact we all read it, my wife, the kids, Grandma, everyone. One time we even read it aloud in the garden sunshine, laughing at our attempts at amateur dramatics, admittedly after one too many glasses of wine.

Now, looking back after several years, I sometimes wonder if I should have stayed in the class. These days I write a bit of poetry, I belong to a local poetry group and I've even had a short poem published, in *SERVICE! o*ur company's staff magazine. Occasionally I enter a poetry competition. It's all very part-time and small-scale but it gives me some satisfaction. However, one day I'm determined to write more prose. I'm gradually working up to it. I've even bought a notebook where I jot down ideas. I know I have a good prose style - everyone tells me so – even if I'm writing departmental reports. I need to knuckle down to it. Maybe I'll start with some memories of my childhood. I came from a poor family and I think people would be surprised to learn of the difficulties I faced as a child. My upbringing certainly never prepared me for my present position as a successful personnel manager.

Or perhaps I'm just kidding myself. Still, it's a plain fact that nowadays I keep thinking about Geoff's class and wondering what would have happened if I'd stuck with it. I simply can't help myself. It stays in my mind. And it's not just when I begin to worry about what to do when I retire in a year or two. Or what I should do when my joints insist that I give up cycling. It's also whenever I read yet another sparkling review of one of Geoff's novels in the Sunday paper.

Four

Dear Michael
Thanks for your email and kind words about my new novel
Utopia. Your writing class was a long time ago (one of three I
was teaching at the same time if my memory is correct!) and
I'm sorry to say that I don't recall you. I do remember a
lively student called Maggie (or was it Margaret?) Got some
good ideas from her.
All the best
Geoff Piggott

Dear Mr Smith
Many thanks for your long prose poem The Purdown Murders.
On this occasion we are unable to accept it for publication.
We receive about 800 requests for publication in the magazine
each quarter and can only take the very best. We use a points
system whereby each submission is awarded points out of 10.
Your work achieved a score of 2, whereas at least 8 is
required for publication. Please try to remember to include a
stamped addressed envelope next time.
Best wishes
Annie Montgomery
Editor, POETRY WEST

Hi Michael
Lovely to hear from you. It was a joy to read your poem
Purdown Abbey Blues, which I found both amusing and
innovative. The rhythm fits well with a twelve bar blues style,
hence, presumably, your title. However, I'm so sorry to have

218

to say that your poem doesn't fit the terms of our entry
requirements (see the bureaucracy is catching up on us yet
again!!) as our competition is strictly for under-14s only. I am
therefore returning your £1.20p
With Love
Harry Quint

Hi Mike
I am sorry to report that your haiku Pared Down Purdown
was unsuccessful in our 2005 competition. We had over 600
entries, all of a very high standard. We'll keep you on our
mailing list. Better luck next year.
Anthony Lefevre
West of Ireland Haiku Competition

Dear Mr Smith
We don't usually accept email submissions or indeed reply by
email. However to save time I'm happy to break our rules just
this once. Your draft novella Purdown Abbey Mystery isn't
suitable for publication. Although you can create good
descriptive passages, the work as a whole is too derivative.
And if I'm being honest (well – I am a publisher!) you fail to
develop your characters and so the plot ultimately fails. My
advice is that you try a creative writing course.
Yours etc
Emma Porthouse
Assistant Literary Editor

Dear Mr Smith
Another bumper crop of sonnets! The results of the twenty-
third annual Prestatyn sonnet competition are as follows:
  1. *The Tiptoe Man by Hal Evans*
  2. *Giant Strides in a Welsh Landscape by Lizzie Patel*
  3. *Creative Writing for Beginners by Margaret Burton*

219

I am very sorry if you are unsuccessful this year. Better luck next time.
Owen Jones

Dear Mike Smith
You ask for feedback on your poem Purdown Breakdown. We usually charge for such a service, but just this once I am willing to make a couple of comments. Firstly, 170 lines in rhyming couplets is extremely ambitious. Even a professional writer would find it daunting. A lot of your rhymes seem rather forced. 'Diaphragm' and 'dying man' and 'crossbow bolt' and 'juddering jolt' are just two examples. Secondly, in my opinion the murder mystery is not best served by a traditional verse form. Have you tried writing a short story? I wonder if you would benefit from one of our intensive residential courses here at Wells-next-the-Sea. They are only £750 for one week, or two for just £1400. I'm confident that we can really help your literary style! I look forward to hearing from you.
Ingrid Pritchard
Creative Writing Solutions
Wells-next-the-Sea.

Dear Michael
Thanks for entering our Short Story Competition and for your £8.00 fee. Unfortunately your story Purdown Nightmare was not short-listed by our panel of judges. However, for a further £6.00 we will be happy to re-read your entry and to provide a full critique of it.
Dan Berkeley
Banff Literary Society

Mr Smith
I'm sorry but it is strictly against our rules to explain why
your entry was not a winner in our sonnet competition. And
No, I'm not prejudiced against the English. However I will
readily own up to an intense dislike of execrable poetry.
Owen Jones

Hi Smithy
Yes I do remember you from school. However I can't possibly
accept your piece Monastic Crime-wave for the magazine,
notwithstanding our old school ties. (By the way, I don't think
you ever repaid me that £1.00 I lent you at the school prom)
Bill Longley
Editor
Modern Policing Monthly

Dear Mr Smith
No, you cannot have your £6.00 returned to you. What we
have provided are the honest, objective, professional
judgements on your work of myself and my colleague Mary
Watchet (whose short stories, by the way, are widely
published) What do you expect for £6.00? Flattery?
Dan Berkeley
Banff Literary Society

Hi Mike
I am sorry to report that your haiku Purdown Fever was
unsuccessful in our 2006 competition. We had over 600
entries, all of a very high standard. We'll keep you on our
mailing list. Better luck next year.
Anthony Lefevre
West of Ireland Haiku Competition

Michael
I am very happy to accept your application for a place on our
creative writing course. Didn't you take Geoff Piggott's
course some years ago? Fine man, good writer too. You may
remember me from the class. Well, as you've probably heard I
am now teaching the course myself. Looking forward to
seeing you again in September.
Margaret

Dear Mr Smith
I am delighted to confirm that you have a place on our new
intensive course Return to French. See you in Septembre!
Au revoir
Catherine Villebois

Dusk

by Wes Lee

She idles, she lolls, she lies on Liam's chaise-longue outside on the veranda. She listens to the birds, she spies on the hens in the garden, she knows all of the hens by the names Liam has given them. She knows they have a complex life, most people never take the time to notice their habitual circuits throughout the day, but Liam does, he sees the minute but important changes in their routines; their infractions and collusions. Something as simple as someone walking through the garden at an unfamiliar time sends out ripples, causing them to roost in a different place at dusk.

"I'm lost," she told Liam.

They were sitting on the veranda surrounded by the heavy perfume of Liam's favourite rose, *Amber Light*.

"Those two words have come back to haunt me," she said. "Sam Frost told me the same thing ten years ago, I can't believe it's been ten years, I can't believe that so much water…"

"Who's Sam Frost?" Liam interrupted.

"I worked with him, I used to give him a ride home."

They'd been sitting in her car as it was turning dusk, she'd pulled up outside Sam's house and neither of them had moved. It had felt romantic and sad and the darkness was coming. She'd felt like it was a decisive moment, that if someone didn't make a move they were probably never going to go any deeper. That's when he'd told her he was lost.

"Did you go out with him?"

"No," she said. They had teetered on the edge of jumping each others bones for weeks. "It was just a moment, one of the ones that you remember. One of the ones with words that come back to bite you."

"What happened to him?"

"He had four kids, a wife, a dead end job, his life was sewn up. He should have said I'm trapped, *I'm lost* was a cover . . . his eyes looked stricken in that rear vision mirror."

"Were you sitting in the back seat?"

Talk of other men always frightened Liam. She knew he was calculating the proximity of their bodies, imagining Sam jamming her up against the steering wheel. Torturing himself with visions of infidelity.

"I was in the front watching his eyes in the mirror . . . that's all I remember."

But she remembered something smug, something unforgivably stupid, flying out of her mouth. She'd told Sam she would never allow herself to get that pathetic. That she'd never feel lost. It's funny, in a choking kind of way, how it all comes around.

"You're not lost, you're just grieving," Liam said.

"I'm fucking lost!" she shouted. "And days like this depress me."

Perfect days, impossibly beautiful days, delphinium blue sky days, blinding-white-sun-filled - too intense days.

"Why?"

"Whatever I do it's never enough, I can never make the most of a day like this."

"I feel the same."

She knew he didn't. She knew he'd never felt the same. He was a different kind of animal. She could never have been with an animal with the same stripes.

"How *do* you feel?" she pushed him.

"The old existential chestnut . . ."

"Don't hide away in a stock phrase, what's in your heart? Open your mouth and words might just flow out."

She knew he was terrified of opening his mouth, he had to think through everything he said. He was afraid of

224

spontaneity, afraid of what might travel out of his mouth. Some people were like that; when they uttered things they believed them, they spoke from some kind of plan where things fitted together. She'd never been like that, she would say one thing then contradict it, she'd offer two opposing opinions in the blink of an eye, it never bothered her - everything flowed out. And Liam was always there to hear it. He said he liked to listen to her, he said she was exciting; that he never knew what would come out of her mouth. But she wasn't sure he liked it, how could he like someone so different? She mostly knew what would come out of his mouth, there was safety in his responses, it was something she needed. She was the water he was the rock, that's what her mother had said. *You are the water that flows around him, he needs you.*

She remembered the feeling of total safety lying in bed as a child; headlights flooding through her bedroom window, illuminating the edges of furniture. Shadows moving forward in a surreal elongation, pushed by the transit of the car as it slowed down to a stop. Voices hitting the chill air. A door slamming, then the slow slide of shadows back across her wall as the car moved off, until darkness again.

Her mother walking through the front door, through the house. Her voice calling out, *I'm home!*

What a word that was. *Home.*

She has one here with Liam, but it could never be like the other home. The first home. The home where the fridge was always miraculously full. The home that felt like it was part of your skin.

The weather outside is fragile, the weather inside is fragile, changing from moment to moment. She feels the weather deeply on her skin. Deeply in her heart. She feels the light on her skin; she is sensitive to the changes in light, she sits all day and deep into the dusk feeling the change of light. She has become like one of Liam's hens, habitual in her continuous circling of the veranda, she seldom moves off it. She is paralyzed yet still breathing, covered in a savage cloying scent. People call it grieving but it doesn't near cover it, one word can never encapsulate it. It should be a blank wail. When people say the word they might as well be grunting, making animal sounds, a low incoherence. There is no word for it, this strange bombardment of images and feelings; travelling into a maze that never unravels; only goes deeper, a journey into some strange story that she called her life.

The Day Simeon Cantilie Stopped Smoking

by Paul Hansbury

*Some days there would be a ring at the doorbell and a man in
a suit would ask if he could count on my mum's vote at the
election. My mum would close the door in their faces if their
rosette was blue or yellow. She had no time for blues or
yellows. She said the men couldn't read because we had a
poster stuck up in the window by the front door which read
'Vote Labour.'*

This is a story about a murder. It all happened back when I
was a child, and I didn't understand people and things. The
whole affair fascinated me because my consciousness wasn't
evolved enough to understand it. I can *see* that now, like I can
see a lot of other things too.

Simeon Cantilie fascinated me above all else. I
haven't seen him for going on ten years now, yet still his
image is as clear to my mind as a reflection in a mirror. The
tall frame walking slowly with a scholar's stoop, the shoulders
bent inwards like a moulded coat hanger, and the arms
dangling uncomfortably by his sides. He was tall but must
have had short legs because he wore the bottoms of his
trousers turned up, like he didn't know how to sew.

I'd come home from school and Simeon Cantilie
would be seated on the wooden bench on the square of green
outside the flats. There were three trees in a line on the green.
There had been four up until the storm in eighty-seven. This
was round the time the tree branches looked as if they were
dabbed with cotton and the scent of the blossom sweetened the
air. The sky was eternally bright and cloudless; the colour of
cornflower. When I came close and Simeon Cantilie saw me
he'd make to punch my stomach with the outside of his balled

227

fist. 'How's it hanging, kid?' He always called me kid; too many American movies, I suspect. We'd chew the fat for a bit but only after he had lit his pipe. Even now I can see his right hand patting his breast pocket, then reaching in and drawing out the tobacco pouch. There would be a look of intense concentration on his pale, heavy face as he tamped the tobacco into the pipe. Nothing diverted him. Sometimes I'd tug on his sleeve but at most he'd straighten his little finger towards me, gesturing that I must wait. Then, only when he had inhaled his first draught of Golden Virginia, was I allowed to speak.

'Who was the lady you were with the other day?' I asked. My mum had mentioned it over dinner the previous night.

'A girl? You shouldn't be up as late as that,' he said knowingly.

'Mum says…' I can even remember what she'd said: 'Ol' Simeon's messing with a girl again. He can't keep his hands off them. He should just let them alone.'

'That's my girl, Julie,' Simeon Cantilie said.

'Are you and she married?'

'Oh no.' He might have laughed lightly at the suggestion. He closed his eyes and raised his pipe to his mouth. There was a raggedy strand of tobacco dangling over the edge. 'Julie's already got a husband. But they don't get on so well.'

'Why don't they get on so well?'

'That's not my business. I suspect they argued a lot, and then he left her, clean walked out in the middle of the night.'

'Will *you* marry Julie?'

'I can't. Not when she's already married. He got her before me.'

'I think that's sad. Julie already being with someone. Does it bother you?'

'Sometimes. But I'd be more worried if she hadn't been with someone. I'd think there was something wrong with a girl who could turn forty and not have been in love. It's difficult when you're older, all the girls are spoken for.'

The corner of his mouth turned up. He was staring into the distance.

'It took me a long time to win her over,' he said sadly. 'She said she'd go back with her husband and she had no time for me. I knew though.'

'What did you know?'

'That he was bad for her and she'd come to me.'

'Where is he now?'

'I don't know. But he lost her. It hurts when you lose...' He held his pipe by the bowl-end and stabbed quickly at the air. A memory of bitterness flared in his eyes, frenzied. 'Still, you'll learn about these things later, kiddo.'

'What were you thinking about when I came up to you?'

'Same as everyone at the moment. Who to vote for; you know about the election on Friday?'

'Yes, I know. Mum says "People *have* to vote Labour." I ask why and she sighs, says "I've always voted Labour." It doesn't seem a very good argument. Why should people vote Labour?'

'Shall I let you in on a secret?'

I nodded. With hindsight I wished he hadn't told me, for a long time in my heart I thought him telling me started it all off. If he hadn't told me my mum might have seen things more calmly.

'Okay but you mustn't tell anyone. Not your mum: not your friends: and certainly not the narks.'

'What are the narks?'

'If you don't know, then it's safe to say you won't tell them.' He drew on his pipe, drew out the moment of

229

revelation. 'What I'm going to let you know is this: Old Simeon Cantilie is going to vote Tory.'

In my memory I gasped, though probably it wasn't really like that. I'd never heard anyone say they would vote Conservative before. And I was shocked to hear him describe himself with those exact same words: "Old Simeon Cantilie": just like my mum had called him. 'But why?' I asked.

He patted his breast pocket, where his heart was...and his tobacco. 'It's about taxes. The Government gets our money when we buy tobacco and Labour take more of it than the Tories. It's a selfish reason to cast a vote, but it's also a very good one.' His eyes widened, and I knew he was a man who knew his place in the world. His mind was expansive and alert.

'Come on now, Jamie!' My mother was leaning from the window of our flat. She had a tea towel clutched in her hand and her knuckles were white. My heart plummeted because she had caught me talking to Simeon Cantilie. She said, 'Your tea's ready.' I concentrated on the thought of food and sprinted up the stairs to our flat. I was breathless when I reached the slice of pizza and bowl of salad on the table.

'Wash your hands first, Jamie.'

I went to the sink and turned on the tap.

'You've been talking to him again. I've said to you before you mustn't, mustn't, *mustn't*.' Her voice shook as she uttered the sentence. 'I want you to have nothing to do with him. He's a layabout and a weirdo.'

I rubbed the soap to a lather between my hands.

'You hearing me, Jamie?'

'But *why* can't I speak to him?'

'You're too young to understand even if I told you.'

As I was eating my mum sat in the corner reading *the Sun*. 'All it's about is the election,' she moaned. 'No one

230

wants to read this stuff, not when it's pushed out all the interesting news. It's not fair.'

'If I was old enough I'd vote Conservative,' I said, probably because it sounded like an adult thing to say.

'Not if you live in this flat you won't! I'm having no Tory voter under my roof.'

I lowered my head and concentrated on the food.

'What ever made you say that, was it *him*?' she asked.

'I've been thinking.'

'Not properly you haven't. Do you know what they do to us, the Tories?'

'It's about taxes,' I said proudly. I think the exchange must have continued for a little, because I have an idea I repeated the statement: 'It's about taxes.'

'What nonsense has that man been filling your head with? Did *he* tell you to say that? I bet he did, I *know* he's a Tory man. Let me tell you one thing: he doesn't know what the hell he's on about! Spends too much time sitting outside pretending to think. He should be spending more time with that tart he's supposed to be going with. God knows what she sees in him! And I tell you another thing: her husband's still clawing her back, still getting a piece of her if you ask me. She's trouble that one - a good for nothing -' She stopped to catch her breath. 'Look Jamie, what I'm saying is, I don't want you talking to him anymore and filling your head with things you don't understand. You hearing me?'

My face was hot. I'd told mum Simeon Cantilie's secret. I pushed the plate across the table away from me, half my pizza uneaten, and got up to go to my room.

Two mornings later I awoke to my mum whistling. She started to sing a song out-of-tune and I found her dancing round the kitchen, like a child, I thought. The TV and radio were both turned on.

'You seen this, Jamie? We did it! Labour won by a landslide.'

I didn't say anything. At school it passed unmentioned; I guess our teacher thought we were too young to care about politics. It was only in Assembly that Mrs Marsh said all us pupils had 'only lived under a Conservative government. It has been a long time in coming,' so she said. Nothing seemed to have changed and I wanted to know what all the fuss was about. When I turned into my street my gaze instinctively picked out the bench where I expected to see Simeon Cantilie. It had come to me that I might ask him about the election result. But there was a problem. Simeon Cantilie wasn't there.

I blinked and looked again.

The bench was empty. I walked across the square of grass and the air wasn't steeped in its usual whiff of Golden Virginia. I couldn't have imagined beforehand how strange it would seem not to see him, like he was supposed to be there. I lowered my head and kicked a crushed beer can along the blossom-strewn grass ahead of me.

There was only one day over the following weeks when I saw Simeon Cantilie. I went into our flat and mum was fiddling with a Walkman in the corner by the TV.

'Where did that come from mum?'

'I found it on the bus this morning. I think it needs new batteries.'

'Are you going to take it to the police?'

She looked at me sharply. 'No. Someone's left it behind, they're not going to come back for it.'

A new voice came in through the door, which I had left ajar behind me, 'Don't you feel bad about taking it?'

I turned to see Simeon Cantilie standing in the doorway.

'Keep away from my son,' she warned.

232

'The kid's right, you should hand it in to lost property.'

'I'm warning you, don't lay a finger on Jamie.'

It seemed unfair. Simeon Cantilie was simply standing in the doorway, doing no wrong as far as I could see.

'I'll take it to the lost property, if you want, mum.'

My mum shook her head from side to side. 'It's not fair. I've had things stolen and I've never got them back.'

'That's a very selfish attitude. And I thought you claimed to be a Socialist? This dog eat dog approach isn't....' He broke off, contemplated. His hand scratched his rough unshaven chin. 'Did you feel upset when you were the victim of theft?'

My mum frowned. 'What's this got to do with you? Get away from my flat!'

'Won't the person who's lost their stereo be upset,' I said. She was getting herself worked up, I could tell that from her face.

'People are dishonest in this world. Why should I be honest?' She continued, putting the Walkman down and clenching her fists until the knuckles whitened, 'Even if I hand it in, it's not going to change anything. Things don't change.' Then she must have remembered the election. '*People* don't change.'

'That's so negative. Why are you so *pessimistic*?' said Simeon Cantilie, coming fully into the room now.

'I'm realistic, that's all.'

'But don't you think things could be better?'

'No and let go of me. What's wrong with you? Let me go... Let me go!'

She shook herself free of his clutch. Simeon Cantilie stood still, controlling himself from trembling. Mum scowled and he dropped his head, turned, and shuffled along the

233

corridor. He had spoken with a passion and resentment I'd not witnessed before. He was revealing himself to me.

About a week later I spoke to Simeon Cantilie for the last time.

'Come along, Jamie.' My mum took hold of my hand.

'Where are we going?'

'I have to go out. I can't leave you here and I can't take you with me. I'll have to leave you with the weirdo.'

'Wait here a second.' She went back into the flat and came out again with a new hat artfully angled on her head. She quickly looked at herself in the mirror beside the front door and picked away a speck of dirt with her fingernail. Then she dragged me along the corridor and we stopped outside Simeon Cantilie's door.

'You've got to look after him,' she said as the door opened. 'You say anything to him and…'

'And you'll what? Kill me?'

'Look after him. Ok?

'All right, kiddo?' His words came weakly, lethargically. I can't remember if he made to punch me but I don't think he did.

Mum marched away from us. She was wearing heels and they echoed down the corridor. Simeon Cantilie led me into his lounge and slouched in his chair. I was fascinated by the unfamiliar space. The layout was identical to our flat but it felt so different, like all the same pieces had been shaken up and rearranged, like in a kaleidoscope tube. There were piles of magazines and newspapers by the telly and the carpet was worn and stained. There was an old ink-stained desk in the corner with a block of wood under one of the legs where a castor was missing.

'Where is she off to?' he asked.

I shrugged my shoulders. He just sat there, staring into space.

234

'Are you ill?' I asked, puzzled.

He shook his head. He didn't have any games to entertain me with. He showed me a book of art and then found a cardboard box of paper straws in a cupboard. They were artists' straws. They kept me occupied but there was something more, something seemed to be on his mind.

'Do you know where your mother's gone to?' he asked again.

'No.'

'She was dressed up some. Do you think it's for a man?'

'I don't know.'

His question had a strange resonance to it. 'She shouldn't leave you like this. It's not fair on you. She should be here.'

I said, 'Why does she go off like this?'

'She's done it before, kiddo?'

'Last week she took me to my nan's.'

'All dressed up the same?'

My silence was as good as a nod.

'She's no better than a child. She doesn't *see* things.'

I don't think I saw Simeon Cantilie again for the whole summer. Occasionally I heard his TV through the thin wall between our flats; late at night when all else was quiet. And one time I heard him arguing with a lady, who I guessed was Julie, 'his tart' as mum called her.

When did I realise? Not for a couple of weeks. I just thought he'd changed his routine. Then the school holidays came and other things occupied my attention. It was the lack of an odour on passing his front door that finally struck me. Simeon Cantilie had stopped smoking.

I sat on the bench one day toward the end of summer. My legs didn't reach the ground and I kicked them back and forth

235

aimlessly. It was a little cold, the sun was dipping behind the buildings, a few birds twittered in the trees. A billboard across the street had a torn red poster, not taken down or covered over since the election those months before. I caught sight of Simeon Cantilie walking along the pavement opposite. His hair had grown longer and fell over his turned up jacket collar. His hands were thrust into the pockets and he wore a baseball cap pulled down low on his forehead - which was dipped to the ground, he scarcely lifted his feet from the pavement as he shuffled along. He just walked on by as if he didn't live here any longer. He looked sadder than any man I ever saw.

Some months later I awoke to a noise. It was pitch dark in my bedroom and I felt my way across to the window and tugged apart the curtains. It was a moonless night and the room remained thickly dim. As I walked into the hallway I noticed the front door was open, and the bright lights of the corridor pushed boldly into the flat. I wandered out, my eyes adjusting to the light, my bare feet quickly stepping across the cold terrazzo floor of the communal corridor. The door to Simeon Cantilie's flat was ajar. I knew something was amiss but my actions were clinical and calm. I stopped outside the open door. I looked in through the gap. The woman was lying on the floor, not moving. Cold and still and silent. I was afraid of stepping across the threshold.

It was the last time I saw into Simeon Cantilie's apartment. There was the TV and there were the piles of magazines and newspapers all round. The lamp on the inky desk was turned on. A few white cotton shirts hung on hangers along the picture rail. He had taken up the carpet so there were bare floorboards.

A chill ran through me as I saw the cricket bat covered with blood on the floor beside the woman. I keep telling myself my memory tricks me, that really it was lacquer from

236

the hard ball. Why couldn't it have been lacquer rubbed off on the smooth willow surface of the bat? But I know it was blood. The morning was cold and still and silent.

My mum was angered to find me there.

'Go back inside! You'll catch cold,' she exclaimed, hurrying up behind me, herself in night gown and slippers.

'But I want to see. Where's Simeon Cantilie?'

'You get away from here now. You must get away from here.' Her voice was panicked. Her hands pinched my shoulders and I'd been dragged clear away from the doorway. It was the time I saw how much my mum found it intolerable to have to protect me from the world. Intolerable because she herself didn't much understand it. I didn't *feel* anything.

'What's going to happen mum?'

She looked at me. It was all she could do.

Everything just happened and my senses were numb.

Then I saw Simeon Cantilie's tall frame slumped against the wall further down the corridor. A bottle of whisky held loosely in his near hand. A shadow seemed to come over him. He saw me, looked at me, and a gleam came in his eyes, and went, like the fleeting shimmer of a dropped silk handkerchief. He might have been laughing or he might have been crying. I think he was laughing but sadly.

'Hurry, get back inside!' snapped my mum, pushing me towards our door. I tried to look back at Simeon Cantilie but my mum stood between me and him, desperate to keep my eyes off of him.

'You're all mine Jamie. Don't go near him, ok.'

The sirens closing in on the block brought it home to me. Later I heard all the details, saw the diagram in the *Camden News Journal.* My mum kept telling people about it on the phone. I think she liked the attention. You'll have realised from the outset who the victim was, I never have made an effort to disguise the fact. A motive was there too,

237

from the outset: Simeon Cantilie had murdered Julie because she had been seeing her husband again, behind his back, and he didn't know how to deal with it. This was the one version, the one given by the newspapers at least.

'He always was a weirdo,' mum told reporters.

But there was more. My mum was very cagey when the reporters asked about her friendship with Simeon Cantilie. It wasn't until some time later, on the day of the Court case, that I answered the door to a journalist, and learned the rest. The journalist wore a beige overcoat and he had thick-lensed glasses. He crouched down in the patronising way grown ups will when they want to use you, like they're demonstrating how they're on your level. He spoke in an undertone:

'Is your mother in?'

I nodded. I turned to get her but I felt my arm tug back.

'I'll speak to you first, if that's okay, young man.'

I nodded again.

'Some people say your mum was bitter because Mr Cantilie was with another woman. She and he were — I'm led to believe — shall we say — *intimate*, at one time...'

I swallowed.

'Jealousy does things to people, sometimes it makes people become competitive. Has your mum been seeing anyone lately?'

I swallowed again. Mum *was* always going out, dressed up smart, though she never left me with Simeon Cantilie after the first time. He wasn't there any longer. The journalist pressed me harder,

'Come on, young man, you can tell me.'

My mum must have heard something. She came hurrying to the door and pulled me away.

238

'What are you questioning Jamie for? He's eleven years old. You have no right! No right to talk to him without my permission.'

'I was merely asking if...'

'Piss off now. I don't want to talk to you or anyone from your poxy Gazette.'

As she closed the door he said, 'You'll grow to be a tall lad, Jamie. I'll bet your father is a tall one.'

That was about ten years ago now. Whenever I catch the familiar smell of Golden Virginia, I remember Simeon Cantilie. In my head he says 'How's it hanging, kid?' and bends over, lightly punching my stomach with the outside of his fist. I imagine him in his prison cell. I tell myself one day I shall go and visit him, but I know I shan't.

Mum has become addicted to scratch cards, if you ask me. Sometimes she wins five or ten pounds, but mostly she loses. I asked her about it the other day:

'Sometimes you get lucky,' she said.

'Don't you worry about always losing?'

'You have to be in the race, Jamie. Otherwise what's the point: being idle gets you nothing in this world.'

I think she's had her share of luck already, but she can't see that. It isn't in her to see it, which is a perverse sort of blessing.

'I feel sorry for him,' I said. For a moment I didn't think she knew who I meant.

WILD THING

by Michael Limmer

1

Norman Briscott pushed away his empty plate, leaned back in his chair and contentedly patted his stomach. He had enjoyed a superb breakfast, easily comparable with those served up by his dear late mother.

Norman checked his watch. It said 8:24 a.m., time to head for Raitt & Fitton, the large factory where he worked as a wages clerk. He had been there since leaving school; a matter of twenty-two years, ten months and two weeks.

As he tucked his chair beneath the table, the door to the kitchen opened to reveal Elspeth, his adored wife of three blissful months. Auburn-haired, apple-cheeked, with a delightful freckled nose, she looked demure in her 'World's Best Housewife' apron.

"Your sandwiches are ready, Norman dear."

"Wonderful. What are they today ? Smoked ham and Dijon mustard ?"

"Oh, you'll be so disappointed. All I've done is tuna and dill."

"But they're my absolute favourites. As well you know, darling girl."

They beamed at one another, and Elspeth disappeared into the kitchen to fetch the sandwiches.

As he walked through to the hallway to don his jacket, Norman glowed with pride. He had been terribly alone after his mother had died. Poor mother. She had never approved of any girl he had brought home, particularly after his father had run off with one and was never seen again. Otherwise she had idolised her only child, and he had dutifully nursed her through her last illness, the whole six years and seven months of it.

He had met Elspeth at the library. Their eyes had locked as she had stamped his books. They had got talking and learned they were both enrolled in the same rug-making class at the local community college. They both progressed to transcendental meditation the following term, by which time romance had well and truly overtaken them. Elspeth confided that she had been married before, to a violent and demanding man, a builder who had died in a fall from scaffolding. She had moved south, resumed her maiden name and taken a job as a library assistant, looking for a fresh start. As things turned out, she and Norman could not have met at a more propitious time.

Elspeth joined Norman in the hallway, handed him his briefcase containing sandwiches and an apple and reached up to straighten his tie. They exchanged pecks, wished each other a pleasant day, and Norman made his way out to the car with an undeniable spring in his step.

He walked round to the driver's door brandishing his key and immediately leapt back in alarm. A man was crouching beside the car, out of sight of the house. Seeing Norman, his face split in a stupid grin and he got to his feet. He was tall and swarthy, with dark, unruly hair and dressed in scruffy parka, jeans and trainers which had once been white. He reached out and snatched Norman's briefcase. Instinctively Norman snatched it back.

"Go away," he snapped peevishly. "Go away, I tell you. This is private property."

For a moment the man looked bemused. Then his smile vanished, he dug a hand in his pocket and brought out a knife.

He jabbed it in Norman's direction, and Norman hopped back with a little screech. Out of the corner of his eye, he saw Elspeth watching with horror from the doorway.

The man pointed at the briefcase and Norman quickly handed it over at arm's length. It was whisked away, the knife pocketed, and before Norman could blink the man was escaping up the road at a laboured run, the briefcase tucked under his arm.

Norman's legs wobbled as he collapsed against the car. Elspeth was by his side in seconds. "Oh Norman, darling, are you all right ? What happened ?"

He looked up at her blearily and fought for words. Old Mr. Jameson came hobbling across the road from the house opposite.

"I saw it all. You've been mugged, young Briscott. Come along, my dear, let's get him indoors and then I'll call the police."

By the time the police arrived, Norman was sufficiently recovered to give them a good description of the Wild Man, as he and Elspeth had tagged his unkempt assailant. Elspeth wondered if he might be a disgruntled ex-employee of Raitt & Fitton, and they promised to look into it, although it appeared that Norman had simply been the victim of a random mugging.

In any case, Elspeth would not allow him to go to work and phoned the chief cashier, Mr. Murgatroyd, to explain what had happened. Fortunately she didn't work on Mondays and concentrated on looking after her husband. She fussed over him for most of the day, because he looked so pale and didn't want any lunch, which was unheard of for him.

But at tea-time he devoured six crumpets with raspberry jam and contented himself with listening to the radio. Even so, Elspeth was shocked when she came into the room halfway through the shipping forecast to find him doubled up in his chair with laughter.

"Norman ? What*ever's* the matter ?"

"Matter, old thing ?" Norman replied between huge gulps for air. "It's the Wild Man. I hope - tee hee! - hope he's pleased with his haul."

"But weren't there important documents in your case ? After all, you *do* work for the Wages Department."

"That's just it. Ha, ha ! No, there weren't. All he got were - oh my goodness ! - *my tuna sandwiches*. Oh - and an apple - "

The laughter seemed to do Norman so much good that Elspeth joined in reservedly. But secretly she was troubled that they might not have seen the last of the Wild Man.

2

As the week progressed, life resumed its even tenor. Norman returned to work, although he noted with grim amusement that Raitt & Fitton doubled the security presence on the days he visited the bank: two OAPs in ill-fitting uniforms, rather than the customary one.

Elspeth worked her ten-till-two shifts at the library, and in the evenings Norman settled down to his stamp and coin collections, while Elspeth began reading *War And Peace* in between knitting them matching jumpers with N and E monograms.

They chatted about their day at work over their bedtime Horlicks, and then Elspeth took Norman's breath away by presenting him with a brand new leather briefcase engraved with his initials *N.A.B.*. Gradually the Wild Man and the mugging became things of the past.

In a bid to erase the incident from their minds altogether, Norman suggested they spend the weekend away.

243

However, Elspeth had promised to work Saturday morning at the library for a colleague and, as Sunday looked like being a glorious day, she suggested they take a picnic to the local park. She busied herself preparing for this, and Norman found himself salivating at the thought of strawberries and cream, cucumber sandwiches, treacle tart and Victoria sponge.

Sunday did not let them down. They found a parking space close to their chosen picnic spot, and the contented couple eagerly carried folding table and chairs to the shade of a clump of poplars. Elspeth started to set the furniture in place while Norman, resplendent in Hawaiian shirt, white chinos and moccasins, strolled back to the car for the picnic hamper, joking with his beloved that he should have taken a body-building course to enable him to lift it.

As he opened the boot, he heard a rustling noise beside the car. He told himself it was probably a squirrel and immediately felt apprehensive.

He knew he was being foolish: but his own uncertainty had ignited a spark of fear in him. Oh, it was ridiculous, because there was no way on this earth that… Surely to goodness… But he had to set his mind at rest. Tentatively Norman peeped round the car.

He froze. The Wild Man's moon-like face illuminated with a lunatic grin, and he staggered to his feet. He looked even more dishevelled than before, and there was a pungent smell about him as if he had been sleeping rough.

Norman heard his own heart pounding massively. He felt distinctly unwell, his legs like jelly as he backed away, fighting for breath. He glimpsed Elspeth, fifty yards distant on their grassy knoll, hand clasped to mouth in alarm as she saw the Wild Man advancing upon him.

"No," Norman heard himself bleating. "Not you. Please - please, no."

244

The Wild Man was still grinning as, unchallenged, he lifted the hamper from the boot. Paralysed, Norman watched as he turned and made off across the park.

He became aware of Elspeth beside him, clutching his arm, her voice dull with shock. "Oh Norman, it can't be him again. Please say this is a bad dream."

At that moment Norman came to his senses and found that something terrible was happening to him. He was growing angry, felt himself burning and shaking with rage, aching to exact a terrible vengeance. He had not felt like this since his schooldays, when Albert Tunnicliffe had pinched his marbles in the playground.

Elspeth stood aghast at the sight of him. But he took her gently by the shoulders and steered her towards the car, pulled open the passenger door. "Lock yourself in, dear." His voice was steady, but Elspeth noted the underlying steely command.

"Oh my darling, do be careful."

"He stole our picnic," Norman explained reasonably. "He cannot do that. I will NOT have him messing up our lives. He has gone too far with me, Elspeth."

"Oh, *Norman!*"

She gazed after him in admiration as he set off in pursuit.

He had narrowed the distance between them to about thirty yards before the Wild Man chanced to look round.

Seeing Norman puffing towards him, he became alarmed and, hoisting the heavy hamper on to his shoulder, broke into a loping run. Not far ahead a hump-backed bridge spanned a river and Norman, suddenly guessing the Wild Man's intention, upped his pace.

The Wild Man stopped on the hump of the bridge and placed the hamper on the parapet. He looked back at Norman and gesticulated madly at the hamper, then shoved it off the bridge. It entered the water with a gigantic splash, and the Wild Man treated Norman to a demented grin before making off across the park.

Further pursuit was useless. Norman, lungs bursting and heart thumping, leaned against the parapet and watched the hamper flounder and sink, its demise heralded by a welter of bubbles. He was exhausted, close to collapsing, glad of Elspeth's support as she rushed to meet him.

"Thank goodness you're all right," she panted.

They trailed back to the car, where Norman slumped exhausted into a seat.

He was utterly bewildered. "Is he mad? What *is* he trying to prove?" he kept mumbling.

His wife was more practical. "We must go to the police at once. Norman..." Her voice faltered. "Oh, my dear, I'm afraid he might be trying to kill you."

Norman, in mid-wheeze, immediately perceived a symbolism in the drowned hamper. He felt faint and signalled his agreement. "Then the police it is," he replied anxiously. "Er, will you drive, old girl?"

3

The police shared Elspeth's view: it appeared that the Wild Man might have some grudge against Norman.

Round-the-clock surveillance was out of the question, so Detective Sergeant Braine suggested that the couple might take a holiday, firstly to put some distance between themselves and their personal *bete noire* and secondly to give the police more time to locate and apprehend him.

Mr. Murgatroyd at Raitt & Fitton was most sympathetic, and so it was, within twenty-four hours of the ill-fated picnic, Norman and Elspeth were embarking upon a ten-day break in Madrid.

They spent the first day of their holiday casting nervous glances behind them wherever they went. But as they enjoyed their evening meal sitting on the sun-dappled terrace of their hotel, sipping a delightful *oloroso*, the Wild Man seemed hundreds of miles away and they made a pact to forget about him until their return, a whole nine days distant.

The holiday proved to be everything they could have wished and on arriving back at Heathrow, Norman telephoned Sergeant Braine. He reported that the Wild Man had not once been sighted and felt sure that he had left the area. Norman and Elspeth, both wonderfully relaxed, took that as a positive sign.

The taxi dropped them at their door on a pleasant sunlit evening. Mr. Jameson waved to them from his garden, neighbours were walking their dogs, children were playing in the road and there was not a wild man in sight.

The following morning, Norman got ready for work. Elspeth cooked him his usual gargantuan breakfast and prepared his sandwiches: tuna and dill, his favourites, a back-to-the-daily-grind treat.

There was now, however, one break in their routine. At 8:22 a.m., two minutes earlier than usual, Norman put on his jacket and went to fetch the car from the garage. He had not wanted to tempt fate by leaving it on the drive.

He reconnoitred carefully up and down the road to ensure the all clear, then backed the car out, locked it and went back inside to collect his briefcase and say goodbye to Elspeth.

He was walking up the path to the front door when he heard the scream.

The sound took his breath away. Then he realised with horror that it had been Elspeth who had screamed, and that she was in danger.

Norman dashed through the hallway and into the kitchen. The back door stood ajar - his wife had obviously

247

been on her way to the dustbin - and the next sight which met his eyes was that of his sandwiches strewn across the kitchen floor and being trampled into the linoleum as Elspeth grappled with the Wild Man.

He was wilder and dirtier than ever, angrier too, his face beetroot red, and Elspeth was trying desperately to fend him off as he attempted to fasten his hands round her throat.

Norman shot across the room and grabbed the Wild Man by the shoulders. The ferocity of the assault succeeded in separating him from Elspeth and, staggering back, the Wild Man shoved Norman away and gesticulated frantically at the sandwiches. Then he turned back to Elspeth, who was cowering by the sink.

Norman launched himself again at the intruder, leaping on his back and clinging to his neck. Enraged, the Wild Man swatted at him with his huge fists, loosening Norman's grip. Then he swung round and enveloped him in a bear hug.

Norman gasped as the breath was squeezed out of him. His lungs were at bursting point and he wavered on the point of passing out, when suddenly Elspeth, pale and frightened, appeared behind the Wild Man wielding a carving knife, which she plunged between his shoulder blades.

The Wild Man's lips stretched back to reveal his gums as his mouth tore open in a silent scream. He flung Norman off him on to one of the kitchen chairs, which promptly snapped under his weight. He turned upon Elspeth, thrashing his arms about like a drowning man and then, as she squealed and fell back against the sink, he spun round, crashed face downwards across the kitchen table, breaking it in half, and subsided to the floor. He lay still.

They all three remained as if frozen in a tableau for minutes which dragged by like hours, Norman and Elspeth staring sightlessly across the kitchen at one another. Her face

248

was pale and pinched with fear, and his breath came in loud, racking sobs. He fought for words, finally grinding out, "Police - ambulance - call them !" And she, nodding feebly, mewling like a stricken animal, hauled herself upright and bolted from the room.

Norman, uncertain as to what motivated him, crawled across to where the Wild Man lay face down across the shattered table. One eye twitched, and as Norman came into focus, the Wild Man tried to sit up, tried uselessly to form words. But Norman, horrified at the sight of the knife protruding from the man's back and the red stain spreading over his rumpled clothing, could not understand what he was trying to communicate. And as one vast tear formed in the man's eye and rolled languidly down his cheek, so did Norman sit upon the kitchen floor among his ruined sandwiches and cover his face with his hands.

*

The police and ambulance both arrived quickly and, under Sergeant Braine's supervision, the casualty was borne away.

The sergeant returned the next morning to inform Norman and Elspeth that the Wild Man had died in the night.

"Oh, thank goodness."

Norman understood his wife's reaction. The fact that they would no longer be plagued by their tormentor was a great relief. But strangely he didn't feel that way himself. He'd hated and feared the man, but all he experienced now was an indefinable sadness.

Sergeant Braine went on to explain that they had identified the Wild Man from documents found on the body.

His name had been Desmond Galloway and he had been a deaf mute. He had been looked after by his elder brother, and when the brother had died two years previously,

249

Desmond had been taken into care. He had escaped recently and had been living rough, leaving behind him a trail of thefts, mainly clothing and food.

"I'd say he resented the fact that you stood up to him on both occasions he stole from you, Mr. Briscott," Braine went on. "He'd never been known to have a violent nature, but I should think the pressures of life on the road and the death of the brother on whom he'd depended forced him to act out of character."

Norman was further saddened by this. If he'd known that all the Wild Man had wanted had been food and clothing, he'd have given it freely.

But he was not allowed to dwell on it. Braine added that there was a possibility that Elspeth could be charged with manslaughter.

"Not while I have breath," Norman announced staunchly, and he enveloped his wife in a protective embrace, noting that she looked very pale. "It was not only self-defence, sergeant. She also saved my life. She's a brave little woman, and I can promise her this: today is the first day of the rest of our life together."

4

"And you're sure you'll be all right, dear ?"

Elspeth nodded and smiled bravely as she closed the door. She walked back through the hallway and into the living room. From its place among the cards along the mantelpiece, her certificate stood out proudly. How Norman had beamed on the day it had been presented to her. Far from charging her with manslaughter, he had joked, they had presented her with an award for her bravery.

She had saved his life.

250

Elspeth's smile was tinged with sadness, as she plucked his photograph from its place beside the certificate and sat down holding it in her lap.

But not for long.

The trauma Norman had experienced during the Wild Man episode had brought on his first heart attack. The second, only weeks later, had proved fatal.

But then, he had suffered a great deal of stress, and he had been seriously overweight.

And - she grinned wickedly - she supposed the naughty lingerie she'd bought in Madrid hadn't helped.

But everything had been Desmond's fault, not hers. He had escaped and somehow traced her. He knew she hadn't pushed his brother off that scaffolding. How could she, she'd been working in the library at the time, in front of two dozen witnesses ?

But he'd suspected her of poisoning Clyde's sandwiches, so that he had felt increasingly unwell, and had contributed to his death in that way.

She shrugged. *Well, he'd been right there.*

Tuna and dill. Nice and tangy, masking the taste of the arsenic, particularly when administered in small doses, which added up to one very large dose in time.

Desmond had obviously suspected she was doing the same to Norman, and that might have put the wind up her if she had. But she hadn't.

Yet.

All in all, Elspeth supposed, she'd come out of it pretty well. Clyde and Desmond couldn't harm her now, she'd even received a certificate for murdering Desmond, and dear Norman had left all his worldly goods to her. His stamp and coin collections alone were worth several thousand pounds.

She gazed down affectionately at Norman's photograph. He'd been a good man in many ways, she

251

supposed. She'd felt safe with him, and he'd only started to bore her ever so slightly. She'd wait a few weeks, as a mark of respect, before she embarked upon that world cruise.

It was something they'd often talked about. What a pity he wasn't coming with her.

She stood up and carefully replaced his photograph on the mantelpiece among all the messages of condolence.

She sighed.

Poor Norman.

It's A Different World

by Pam Eaves

Brilliant gold leaves floated down on a soft breeze, twinkling in the sunlight. Charlie clapped his hands together, chuckling as leaves fell onto the rug tucked round his legs. Wait 'til Mummy sees all the gold I've got. I told her I'd be rich one day.

He frowned suddenly. Where is Mummy? She's always here to cook my tea when I bring my wages home and I'm so tired. Such a long day and no one to cook my tea and there's all this gold to show her.

His face crumpled, eyes filling with tears.

"Mummy," he bawled. "Come here. Look at all this…"

What? What was he going to show her? Harsh tears oozed from faded blue eyes, running down his creased cheeks; then he smiled as he saw the gold leaves lying in his lap. Oh yes, show her… Show her what?

He couldn't remember.

"Mummy," he called again.

Frantically turning his head from side to side dizzily trying to focus, he saw Mummy fast asleep in the chair next to him and leaned towards her, managing to touch the recumbent figure. The wheelchair lurched forward and he grabbed at her for support as he nearly fell, clutching her knee.

"Mummy, it's me, it's..."

What's my name? Charlie's eyes filled with helpless tears again, then he smiled as he looked up at the wrinkled face and silver hair.

Oh look. A piece of gold has settled on her head. Lovely silver gilt hair shining bright. I love the sun on

Mummy's hair. She lets me stroke it when I sit on her lap and it feels all soft like her silky dresses.

His hand touched rough fabric. Bewildered he stared at the strange old hand lying in the lap.

What's that hand doing stroking Mummy's dress? Why isn't she wearing her silky dress? I like the sound it makes when she moves, all whispery. Bemused by the rough feel under his fingers, Charlie rubbed his hand up and down over the rug.

"Now, Charlie," said a brisk voice behind him. "I keep telling you not to touch the ladies. You'll wake Grace up and frighten her."

Charlie stared uncomprehendingly up at the round, red face bending over him as the nurse, her stiff blue uniform crackling, manoeuvred his wheelchair away from the sleeping Grace. Nasty person. I want Mummy. Why's she asleep?

"Mummy!" he bawled, flapping his hands weakly in protest.

Vaguely hearing the commotion, Grace stirred, peering around with blank eyes and gazed at Charlie shrieking and throwing himself about in his wheelchair. The buzz of tinnitus blurred his shouts and she calmly watched the whirling arms until her lids drooped again.

"You'll be alright now, Grace," the brisk voice announced, returning to tuck the blanket round her legs. "He'll settle in a minute. He soon forgets."

Grace smiled vaguely. Thank goodness that screaming child's gone. Slipping into a reverie, she scanned the smooth sweep of lawn across to the dark blue line of trees in the distance.

Perhaps Lily will bring tea out here today so we can have it together. It's lovely when Madam and those dratted kids go out; we get some peace and quiet. That little toad exhausts me; insolent perisher, and the girl's not much better.

254

School will knock some discipline into them. I can't for sure. Still, I shall miss this garden when I have to get another position – and Lily. Dozing off, Grace was unaware of the semi-circle of wheelchairs under the tree.

Florence, her hands busy, looked in disgust at Grace sitting slumped with a happy smirk on her face. That one's a lazy so and so. You can tell by just looking at her sitting there all day doing nothing. Pampered bitch.

Bending over, she stitched industriously, removing invisible pins as her hands moved along the blanket edge, carefully sticking them into an imaginary pincushion. Mustn't drop one, they cost a fortune these days. Her fingers stiffly plodded on, even though her back was aching and shoulders stiff.

I must finish these curtains for Mrs... Blast! Can't remember the woman's name, demanding cow, but there would be more work from her if she was satisfied.

A flash of pale blue caught the corner of her vision and Florence looked up, surprised.

"Tea Florence?"

Florence glared at the blue and white check overall. What a nerve, calling me by my Christian name. Rude woman. I don't know her. What's she doing in my house anyway? Never seen her before.

"Florence," the woman said gently. "Would you like some tea?"

Bending over and offering a cup, the tea lady watched the busy fingers kneading and stretching the blanket that covered Florence's legs.

"What are you making today?" she asked.

Florence glared up angrily without replying.

She's stupid too. Anyone can see it's curtains. How else do you keep body and soul together if you don't earn a bit. I've got to save for my old age. Nobody to look after me. She

255

folded her lips grimly, refusing to answer. Still, the tea was welcome. Not that she liked anybody poking about in her kitchen. How'd she get in, and why did she bring that horrible cake? I like proper cake, fruit cake.

Flexing stiff fingers she peered at the tea and cake on the table by her side then looked around. How come I'm outdoors? I don't work outdoors. Could get marks on the material. Outdoors is dirty.

I'm going inside. She tried to get up but firm hands pushed her back in her chair.

"Now, now Florence, you just sit here in the nice shade and enjoy your tea in the fresh air, otherwise we'll have to put you to bed."

Bewildered, Florence looked up at the stiff, blue figure and meekly responded to the voice of authority. Taking the proffered cup, she tried to remember what she was doing before this woman came. I must have been doing something. I'm always busy.

A leaf fluttered down into her tea, a dark brown boat floating on the milky beige liquid. There. Outdoors is dirty. I've always said so. Can't drink that now. Shakily pouring the tea onto the ground Florence looked around.

Where am I? Am I ill? Is that a nurse? I want to go home. Miserably her head drooped over the tea dregs spilling into her lap, the sewing forgotten.

A slight, military figure marched smartly past the comatose group towards the sweep of open lawn, stick swinging. Got a few miles to cover today but I'll manage. No pack to carry this time. Should be an easy one, not like that trek over the mountains last year or hacking through the jungle. Cor, those blooming mosquitoes didn't half bite, and the snakes… These lads don't know they're born with an easy patrol like this. Good camp terrain for tonight if the weather stays fine. Not like some places.

256

Suddenly John stopped and looked round. Where's my pack? Someone must be carrying it for me. He started marching again. They're good lads, looking after old Jacko. They know I'm slowing down a bit; must up the pace and catch up. As he increased his speed, John scrutinised the trees ahead. They can't have got that far ahead. Got under cover of the trees and waiting for me to catch up probably. They're a grand bunch - know I get a bit tired so they help out, but then, I've done my share in the past.

He broke into a shaky trot as he heard shouts behind him. Must make those trees - give me cover boys. Where are they?

As he stumbled behind a bush on the edge of the wood, John caught his breath and peered across the field.

Must be the enemy. None of ours over there. But what's that woman in blue doing out there? They've pushed her ahead to try and fool me. Why else would she call out? She looks evil. Wants to cut me off but I'm not falling for that. Come on Jacko; must get out of here old chap.

Panting after his retreating figure, the stocky nurse stopped to catch her breath, then shouted, "John, John, come and have some tea. Don't go off again. You're wearing me out."

Watching his erect figure trot out of sight through the trees, she pressed her hand to the stitch in her side and turned back.

"I'll have to get a couple of the boys after him, they've got younger legs than me," she muttered as she strode towards the house. "He's too tired to get far this time. He's been on the move all day."

Fancy sending a woman. Amateurs! John snorted contemptuously as he reached the far edge of the wood. Didn't take much to lose her. He inspected the wire fence. Is it electrified? Wish I had my pack. Where are the chaps? Fatigue

257

overcoming him, he staggered suddenly and leaned weakly against a tree, sliding down as his legs gave way.

Please don't let the others see me like this, he prayed silently. They think I can still hack it. Just have a blow for a minute, and then I'll be all right. He slipped gently to a sitting position. Just rest a minute.

He awoke as strong hands lifted him into a wheelchair. Struggling vainly, he complained, "I'm not wounded. I only need a bit of a blow."

"Now then, John, old chap. You can't sit down out here, you'll never get up again."

Manhandling him gently into the chair, the beefy orderlies trundled him back to the semi-circle.

Nurse Mason waved them towards the house.

"Take him to his room and put him on his bed with the side up. He's absolutely exhausted himself today with all that walking and he'll only be off again if we have him out here."

The men turned towards the house. John, bewildered, bumping along in the chair.

Where are my chaps? Someone ought to tell them I'm wounded. Where'd these medics come from? I don't remember getting hit. Oh God, I'm so tired. This war seems endless. I'm so sick of it, always on the move.

He sank into slumber as he was lifted onto his bed.

"We'll have to wake John up for supper, otherwise he'll sleep right round again." Nurse Mason, breathing heavily, lowered her bulk into a vacant chair, and accepted the cup of tea Olive passed her.

"I'm getting too old for this type of nursing. You need to be young and strong. Thank goodness most of them are sedentary, not like John, always on the wander."

Olive sat down into the chair next to her, nursing her own full cup.

"I shall be glad when winter comes and they're all indoors. It's getting to be a real problem for me too trundling this tea trolley round on the grass when they're all outside, what with my arthritis and all. I suppose the fresh air is good for them but none of them seem to know whether they are indoors or out. They're all away with the fairies if you ask me. I don't know how you have the patience. Still, I suppose they're happy enough in their own way, poor souls, though goodness knows what they think about all day."

The two women sat sipping their tea in companionable silence enjoying the peace of the warm, autumn sunshine flickering through thinning leaves onto the semi-circle of empty faces staring into space.

Willow and the End of Times

by Stephen Firth

Unlike many other fat people, Willow Linehan was quite aware of the disfavour with which she was regarded by others. A certain reluctance for physical contact, a tendency to keep her at arm's length, and, above all, the fact that she had never been able to form close relationships with others, all testified to the distaste with which she was viewed by the majority of people. But Willow was indifferent: she was a member of the human race, but refused to join the club. She was not a joiner, but went her own way. For she had a gift which others prized and sought her out to benefit from. She was one of those who can twitch aside the veil of Maya and see into the heart of shadow. Whether reading a palm, scrying in a crystal, or simply reading the cards, Willow was wiser than her unpromising appearance would have suggested. Part Celtic, part Saxon, like many others in these islands, it was her Irish blood inherited from generations of wise women, which gave her the powers which had drawn some to her for many years. Even these whom she knew well never became close: she preserved a strict client relationship with them, while permitting a slight loosening of formalities with her favourites.

The little house in Railway Road, bought with a legacy twenty years before, had become more than just bricks and mortar; its essence had become something other, transforming it into a shifting gateway between worlds, so often had Willow parted the mists that divide the dimensions to peer into the past, future, and universal consciousness.

She had never had any interest in men, and her only experience of coupling with one did not encourage further exploration. It had taken place on the stairs of the deserted lower level of the car park at the run down shopping centre in town, and could have been called rape but for the fact that Willow hadn't protested or resisted, She thought afterwards, restoring her nerves with a soothing cup of tea, that she had gone through with it out of curiosity, a trait which was, after all, essential to her line of work. It was odd, she thought, that the swarthy, quite good looking young man who had forced her into the act was choosing to have sex with her rather with a pretty girl nearer his own age. Perhaps it was her long hair, the dark tresses hanging voluptuously down her back, which caught his eye. As her mother and grandmother had done all their lives, she brushed it out one hundred times every night until it shone with the lustre of burnished ebony.

After that, she decided against any further exploration of the carnal, and as if to reinforce the decision, her hymen grew back, so that she was, in her own eyes at least, still a virgin. She was a tall woman with good cheekbones which would have made her handsome, had it not been for the superfluous flesh which hid them. She dressed in the loose flowing patterned dresses favoured by the mystically inclined, with good jewellery, rather than the garish type normally seen amongst the spiritualist, New Age, charlatan tribe of which she was reluctantly, by default, a member. Willow, however, treated her calling as a profession with her own self-enforced codes and standards, and she had never been tempted to deliver a false prophecy or reading. On the rare occasions when the spirits were obstinate and nothing came through, she would tell the client so, and not charge them anything.

This more than anything else was what told her faithful adherents that she was the real thing. She had no fear of the shades she conjured or the visions she saw, even when malevolent spirits threatened to get out of hand. Secure in the defences she had learned over the years, she banished, controlled and subdued them with the confidence of a Magus,

261

although the only spells she practised were the charms she was sometimes asked for by clients.

"Meg!" she called "Come on, Meggie, good girl!" The more wayward of her two Labrador bitches was harassing a squirrel, which chattered at her from a safe distance high up in a tree. Meg, a beautiful golden creature, had a very wilful nature and took her time over responding to instructions, unlike Merry, the black one, who was as obedient as Meg was self-willed. She walked them every morning before breakfast in the wilderness at the back of the houses which had once been the railway cutting, and which had been allowed to revert to scrub and woodland. The part they were walking on at the moment had once been the course of a Roman road, which is why, Willow thought, one of her most recent spirit guides was a Roman woman called Agrippina. Rupert, the Burmese cat, sometimes accompanied them, as he did today, walking sedately at Willow's side, his tail erect, apparently choosing to be unaware of the dogs' foolish behaviour. During her sessions with clients, he sat drowsing on her lap, or under the table, sometimes coming to life when particularly frisky spirits were encountered. Then he would rise, apparently perturbed and prowl around the room, almost as if he was on guard. If he hissed or growled, Willow would know to be on her mettle: Rupert's instincts were infallible and she could expect a nasty visitor, one which would need to be banished back to its realm, pronto.

Today was one of those soft, wet mornings which she hated; drizzle, mist and a nasty gusty breeze which caught at her rainhood, pulling it off every so often. All of a sudden the dogs ran back to her, hiding behind her knees as if alarmed, and at the same moment Rupert came to a halt with his ears flattened, as he sometimes did during one of her sessions. Ahead of her the mist seemed to waver and then congeal into vague shapes, which came closer with what sounded like the faint braying of trumpets. The dogs ran off into the trees while Rupert's ears became even flatter on his head, and he showed his teeth in a faint snarl. However, he didn't growl or hiss, so Willow knew that the manifestation wasn't a particularly threatening one. The shapes began to take on form, and she stood to the side of the track as what appeared to be a ghostly army materialised marching towards her down the old Roman road. So close that she could have touched them, had they been real, the spectral legion swept past, the clank of metal faint but clear, and the brazen trumpets and horns raising the hairs on both her own neck and that of the cat as they passed. She made no attempt to count them, but wondered to herself how many men were in a legion; a thousand? Ten thousand? The host of marching soldiers took several minutes to recede into the distance so there must have been a large number. Willow supposed that they must have passed this way on their way to an ancient battle. Could this have been the lost legion which vanished without trace in the third century AD? Or was that up north somewhere? Rupert rubbed his wet muzzle around her legs as if to say that it was all over, and she called the dogs to her, waiting patiently while they decided the coast was clear before slinking nervously back to her side.

Later that day, during a reading for a regular client, Agrippina appeared in the room, not just in Willow's mind's eye as she usually did, but as a full manifestation. Even the client, an unimaginative woman with no apparent psychic powers sensed something.

Willow reassured her. "It's only Agrippina, love. Nothing to alarm you."

All her clients were familiar with the mention of her most recent spirit guide, but few had the sight to see her. The second sight is a gift so rare that those, like Willow, who possess it, consider themselves to be the elect. Many make claims about their abilities, but the majority are charlatans for whom Willow had only deep contempt.

The reading went brilliantly that day and the client was delighted.

"Such a gift, Willow dear. So lucky to have found you after the impostors I've been to in the past!"

But when the client had gone, Agrippina was still there, smiling at her.

"I have come with a special purpose today, Willow, to give you great news. The Age of Osiris is imminent, when mankind will be judged, and only the elect will be saved. Already the four horsemen are abroad and it will not be long until the Pale Rider has claimed his own; he comes with the legions of Hell at his heels, snapping up souls as they run. You have been chosen as one of those to be saved and to inherit the New Age of Paradise!"

Willow gaped at her guide, not sure what to say. She wasn't very clued up about the End of Times theories currently so fashionable with Christian sects, but she was pretty sure that Osiris didn't figure in their calculations.

"So the Apocalypse isn't just a story then? And I thought that Christ would return to save us, not Osiris."

"The saviour has many names; Christ, Osiris, Quetazcoatl, Enkidu are some of the names men have called him, but all know him as a Saviour who will come at the End Times to save the righteous. I have come to tell you that you are chosen to live in Paradise with them. Dead souls are rising, as you saw this morning, and more will come to be reaped by the Pale Horseman as the four ride abroad."

"But why me, Agrippina? I don't think of myself as particularly good."

"You give much to others, and want no more than a just reward; you do no harm, and you respect life, and the spiritual realm. Take your animals, and supplies for a month to

264

a high place and wait with the others you will meet there. Do not leave that place, whatever you may see happening and you will be safe until the coming of the saviour. A great battle will rage far away at Armageddon, so great that you will see the signs and hear its roar even here, but stay quiet on your high place and the floods and fires will not affect you."

Agrippina was gone, while a thousand questions crowded in on Willow's mind. She was vaguely aware of the turmoil in scientific as well as religious circles over catastrophic events such as earthquakes, volcanoes, tsunamis, hurricanes and superbug epidemics, and what they might portend, but hadn't paid much heed, occupied as she was with her own spiritual quest. And she, Willow Linehan, had been chosen while millions of others would be dragged down to the sulphurous pit! She who had got so used to being despised, or merely tolerated, had been *noticed* by the Great Ones. She made a cup of tea, to avoid doing anything else for the moment.

Agrippina hadn't said how long she had got. And where was the best high place around here? She supposed it was the parish church, built on a knoll which rose high above the surrounding levels in an ancient time when winter floods were the norm.

She did *not* want to leave her comfortable little cottage to shelter in a draughty church, even for the promise of the pleasures of Paradise.

She fed the animals and had another cup of tea. Then she squared her shoulders and set about packing essentials for a month-long siege. Cat food, dog biscuits, tinned food (and a tin opener), biscuits, of which she had a gargantuan supply, tea, powdered soup, a kettle; she would have to be ruthless, or she would never be able to transport it all. The car would take her to the outer wall of the church, but all the stuff would have to be carried from there to the porch without any help.

265

Rupert and the dogs were baffled by this unscheduled trip, and the cat loathed cars, as most felines do, regarding it as a mortal insult to be shut up in one. He howled all the way to the church, only ceasing when Willow had switched off the engine at the lych gate. She was only halfway out of the car when she heard a voice.

"Want a hand with that, love? It's Willow isn't it? From number six?"

She looked round for the source of the voice to see Mr Farrar from the other end of Railway Road, who she had known to say 'good morning' to for twenty years. That's as far as their relationship had gone until now, and the same for her other neighbours, apart from Dick and Zoe, the hippy couple next door who she was rather fond of.

Now, he was apparently another of the saved, and behaving as if it was the most normal situation on earth. The spirit of the blitz she supposed. She wondered if others were taking it the same way, and was not surprised when she saw that out of the dozen or so others gathered at the church several were clearly distressed by the situation. Apart from Mr Farrar, Dick and Zoe and their little boy, she recognised only two others; a young man from the baker's shop and Petunia Wirrall, an occasional client of hers, who had a penchant for the scrying crystal.

"Some of us have had to leave nearest and dearest behind, dear, which accounts for some of the tears," confided Mr Farrar in a low voice.

"What about your wife?" asked Willow looking round.

"'Fraid not; she's not been chosen. I hate to judge, but I often warned her."

Willow enquired no further, and allowed him to help her up to the church porch with her suitcases. People had already claimed spaces inside the church; a whole old-

266

fashioned pew made quite a good space to live and sleep on a temporary basis. Side chapels offered more spacious accommodation while the vestry had been claimed by two couples who presumably got on well together. There was no sign of the vicar, an obnoxious power-mad woman, universally disliked, which surprised no one. She had refused to allow Willow into the church since becoming the incumbent two years previously, accusing her of being a witch.

Willow tried hard not to crow to herself at her fate, but found herself giggling out loud at the thought of the coming retribution.

Everyone had brought their pets, which caused some trouble for the first few days, until the animals came to an accommodation with each other. After that, the dogs stopped hungrily eyeing the rabbits, the cats left off intimidating the goldfish, and a large iguana found itself a ceiling beam where it could bask under a light fitting, free of harassment. The church had a lavatory and running water, so life could have been worse, and, for relative strangers, all the chosen got on quite well. A long future of rapture stretched before them all, and it would be unfortunate if things were to be otherwise.

The next few days passed surprisingly quickly, considering that none of them could leave the sacred tumulus, and there were fewer quarrels than might have been expected. Willow supposed that that was because they were all outstanding people in some way who had been chosen for leading lives of a blameless nature! That's why they had been chosen, after all, or, if not that, people who had led orderly lives and been kind to others.

She herself spent most of her time on the tower looking out for signs of the Final Judgment, her animals sitting quietly by, but for the first few days there was little to see. There were spectacular and frequent lightning flashes and some dramatic Turneresque sunsets, but Willow didn't really

267

know what to expect any more than her companions. On the fifth day, a great noise roused them from sleep at dawn. Rushing outside with the others, Willow saw below them on the plain a numberless host of people rushing pell-mell in great turmoil across the landscape, pursued from above by huge birds like crows, and on the ground by the four spectral horsemen. She could see quite clearly which was which; on horses the size of skyscrapers rode the figures of Plague, Famine, War and Death. Willow shivered with a dread not dispelled by her knowledge that she was one of the saved. Above them thunder rolled and lightning cracked, and behind them flood waters rose furiously in great surges. In the distance flames and smoke rose into the air from great volcanic eruptions, and beneath them the earth shook like an angry giant. The hill where they had found refuge seemed hardly affected by the apocalypse below, but terror forced many of her companions back into the safety of the church. Willow was used to confronting her fears, and stayed outside to watch, even when the surging waters had begun to lap at the church wall.

By this time there was no further sign of damned souls, just the flood and eruptions of fire in the distance. Other hills rose above the waters like distant islands, refuges for others who had been saved.

For some days after that, there was no further activity, just the now barren plain below and wisps of smoke drifting across the horizon. Then, about three weeks after they had arrived on the hill, Willow saw the sky change one dawn. She called the others to come outside. By now, they had all acclimatised to their new situation, and stood watching with her. The sky had become a vivid scarlet, darkening to an ugly purple in the East, and from that direction came the sound of battle and the flashing of giant tongues of flame.

268

"The final battle has begun," said Willow, who the others now regarded as their guru, "the great Beast will make his stand at Armageddon and confront the Saviour. If he wins, he will rule the Earth and take us for his slaves, marking us with his sign of 666; if the Saviour is the victor, then we will soon be in Paradise."

"Surely there's no doubt about the outcome?" asked Mr Farrar anxiously.

Willow knew no more about the prophecies, and couldn't answer.

There was little conversation for the next two days as the final battle raged in the East. All the speculation and the pooling of what knowledge they possessed between them of apocalyptic matters was stilled while they anxiously awaited the outcome.

On the fifth day after the battle had begun Willow noticed a lessening of the noise and flames, and for the next few hours the world seemed to become a calmer place, with the winds dropping, the waters receding, the sky lightening and gradually turning blue. From the warm glow she gradually became aware of inside, Willow knew the outcome. The Revelation had been fulfilled and the Saviour of the world, whether Christ, Osiris, or Buddha, had returned, bringing lasting peace and love. She felt younger, and as she looked down at her body, it was that of a girl, the girl that she had been, before she became fat and reviled. Looking round at the others, she saw the same changes in them; the careworn faces acquired over lifetimes of worry and sadness now smooth and youthful.

The blue of the sky was suffused with a golden light, and from the heavens streamed a host of the Great Ones, the angels, the cherubim, the ancient gods, Christ, Osiris and the prophets. A soft yet powerful music thrilled through their new bodies and filled them with unimaginable joy. Willow laughed

269

out loud, a warm and melodious laugh which expressed the rapture they were all feeling now. She danced in the churchyard, circling lightly like a corybant, free of the rolls of fat which had been her curse, the others following her rapturous dance. She, Willow, was now a Lord of the Earth, a free spirit, free from the disfavour of others, free for her soul to expand in everlasting light and joy.

A Kind of Freedom

by Wes Lee

Naomi tried to look like a concerned friend listening to the woes of another friend, across lunch, across small side plates, across thinly buttered bread, across condiments and stained cutlery, across the narrow space between them that was supposed to mean something.

"It's not healthy to keep raking over your relationship," she told Sara.

"But I want closure," Sara said.

Her friends were always talking about closure as if it was something that was given to you. Why didn't they realise that you could just take it? Closure was yours. You only had to step out of the door.

Women should always be prepared to leave – quickly, Naomi thought. She remembered the Auschwitz survivor she'd seen on television, her face remarkably open after the horrors that she'd been through. She'd spent her last days at Auschwitz hiding under a mound of corpses, so frozen they were as hard as firewood. She'd burrow underneath them in the day then sneak out at night so she wouldn't be discovered and gassed. She'd said that after Auschwitz, when people talked about their problems, she always thought: *You have no idea.* What she valued most now was a large overcoat and a sturdy pair of shoes which she kept at her front door - ready. It's what she'd dreamed about owning in the camps when shoes and a coat had meant the difference between living and dying.

When Naomi's friends complained about their problems with men. Some man they should have waved goodbye to long ago - she'd summon up that survivor's words. *You have no idea.* She'd found a comfort in that mantra that

271

intimated how the depths of real suffering could never be explained - a nonsense poem if you tried to put it into words.

She'd found it increasingly easy to leave men. Terrible at first, she did remember that first pain. She'd cut her wrists over the first. Not too deep, but deep enough to still see the silver traces where she'd cut in with the blade. She remembered the bed she'd been kneeling on, the window and the light that was coming in. She remembered very distinctly the quality of it, the hardness of it - there was nothing soft in that light. She remembered the dress. Kingfisher blue. Shimmering. Backless. A dramatic dress for a dramatic act. Very Madame Butterfly. She remembered the pain, so relentless that she'd tried to stop it with a knife. The physical pain was much better. Cutting. Scorching. Burning. A hot iron on the inner arm, held on the blue beating veins underneath. The pain refined to something indescribable. Bright extinction. Blessed release.

Blessed are those who are lost in burning. There is nothing like burning, the perfect point, the triangle - the hot tip of metal on skin. A dead give-a-way if someone saw it. She'd hidden it - hidden it all - hidden everything.

And then men and more men. It had become easier as she'd learnt she could take the pain. There came a point in a relationship where the balance tipped and it was time to sever it. It was a natural thing if only people could see it. She knew it was no use longing that anything could be different - that things might change miraculously by themselves. She would never waste her life on wishful thinking. She got out quick - jettisoned everything. She admired herself for her ability to leave. That's what they'd done in the camps, those who'd had to leave everything.

Better to have the shoes and overcoat hanging by the door - waiting.

She knew her friends might have enjoyed pitying her, as one pities a cynic or the bitter wallflower at the edges of a room. But she was never on the edges of any room, she was always in the middle. All bells ringing. She'd never had any trouble attracting men. Men were easy - easy to love, easy to leave. Women were harder to fathom. She'd had the same female friends for years against all odds - against her wishes. Sometimes she would have liked to be able to jettison them like men, to say brutally and abruptly - *it's over*. But you couldn't do that with a woman. You couldn't end things with a woman, even if you did you never really ended it, they were lodged within you. They'd eat you out like a larva laid within the unsuspecting victim of a caterpillar wasp.

You could never get away from a woman.

When she watched Sara closely, as she sat across from her through the many lunches that they'd shared together, she'd see her take a deep breath as if she had to prepare herself for something terrible she imagined was about to happen. As if she had to discipline herself just to be with her. It looked hard, like it took a great deal of effort. She wanted to slap her. Shout that she could see what she was doing. But it remained a thing unspoken. She didn't want to know why Sara felt like that about her. She didn't want to see the whole of the body dragged up from the murk - a pale taloned finger, the slim slip of a wrist, a nasty stone cold eye partially eaten by crabs was enough.

She didn't want to feel that dead woman start to rise here, now, in the cafe.

"Are you ok Naomi?" Sara asked.

She has had moments like this before when she could open her mouth and tell someone. Moments when she feels her mother glide near the surface. Moments where she feels that if she opens her throat and lets her out, the pain might stop. But what would she say? How could she translate?

273

She remembered - felt – her own small arms pushing her back. Struggling to keep her away, so small and helpless, the arms that had been so powerless against her. The arms that had been useless then.

But what could she tell Sara? What words would come out?

There had been a moment at a party when Naomi had been stood with a small group of people. She'd felt her just underneath her skin for hours until Naomi had finally opened her mouth. She had let a kind of freedom reign; her heart beating so loud when her mouth had opened that she didn't really hear what she had said.

She imagined she'd see something hanging in the air when she opened her eyes. A black velvet bouquet, a stinking parcel of roses, hovering like some dream symbol in a painting by Magritte. She could smell perfume in the air. A thick sweet scent that she could taste at the back of her throat.

And something was there when she had opened her eyes. A strange chaos had erupted. A woman was crying and accusing Naomi of deliberately wounding her. She didn't know why she was so upset. She hadn't intended to hurt anyone. But earlier, she had noticed the woman standing next to her in the small, revolving group of people that had slipped in and out of the conversation. She had detected a brittle quality in the woman's face, a fragile, obvious vulnerability. She remembered before she had cast those words out - the words she didn't remember - that she'd deliberately turned off that warning signal flickering in her head.

Margaret's just got out of a Psyc Ward, someone had whispered.

But she hadn't known that. How could she have know that? She hadn't known her from Eve.

The women in the group had quickly moved around Margaret, shuffling her off to protect her. It was *she* who had

274

gotten all the attention. The sticky tentacles of the sea anemone had closed over her - webbed her in - because she'd cried. Naomi remembered Margaret's face staring out at her in the middle of that sickly show of compassion, she saw her smile - a triumphant smile - *I am the victim here . . . never forget that I am the victim here.*

She will not reveal herself here, now, in the cafe with Sara. She will do it later when she's alone. Better to say it with flesh. Better to sear it where it cannot be misread, where it cannot be altered. The incontrovertible voice will sing in her flesh. Speaking within her. Deep and changeless like a brand.

"Perhaps he still loves you," she says to Sara.

She will be kind because that is what is expected of her. That is what women wait for. Kind words are what they want to hear. No one wants to hear anything harsh let out into the air.

"You're so strong, like a great tree you're always there for me," Sara said as she moved her hand over the table towards her.

She almost laughed - a great tree - she knew she was talking about a redwood or a pine, something green and bountiful, something tall and hospitable; lodged in a forest of trees, in a river of trees, in a sunny glade.

If you only knew me, she thought.

A spiky desert tree with a long tap root; a fat snake in the ground searching for water - snuffling it out - twisted and gnarled and able to survive anything. A tree that will grin into the dark, into the night, into the relentless heat of day. A changeless grin ringing out through silence, through hunger, through famine, through the cold - *You don't know me.*

But I know *you,* she thought.

You say you love me but you don't love me.

Beginnings and Endings

by Anne Ayres

Nobody saw how it began, but in the heavy December sky the first snowflakes formed and started their journey towards the grimy northern town. In the church the mourners weren't thinking of the weather, although Harold, standing in the front pew, was conscious of the cold. It seeped from the stones and penetrated the soles of his polished black shoes. He was conscious too of the funeral smell; lily-laden air tinged with mothballs from black woollen coats.

His eyes slid away from the coffin to the stained glass window. He remembered the anguished face of Christ on the Cross from their wedding forty years ago. Their mothers had decreed the marriage and he and Edith had acquiesced. They had rubbed along together. They expected little and they were not disappointed.

The organist was executing a subdued drone now and the vicar was gathering his notes for the eulogy. Harold turned in the pew to look back over the sparse congregation, searching the faces. In the pew behind him, crouched like a pair of ravens, sat his daughters. They watched his every movement and exchanged meaningful glances.

His daughters were a mystery to him. Emily and Pat, named for their interfering grandmothers. The quiet and unemotional union had produced offspring spiked with jealousy. Their home had become a battleground and he was glad when they married and left. Now he had only to suffer the occasional skirmishes of their visits.

The vicar had taken his place in the pulpit when the door of the church opened and everyone felt obliged to turn to stare at the latecomers. The two women, one grey and one blond, ducked their heads and smiled apologetically before slipping into the back pew. Harold turned to face the altar again. He hadn't realised that he had been holding his breath but now it drained from his body. Behind him Emily and Pat mouthed barbed comments.

For Harold there was a feeling of unreality about the service. He could not bring himself to believe that Edith was lying in the coffin on the chancel steps. It was impossible not to think of her clattering the pans on the stove or wielding a duster. His mind wandered unbidden to the last months. No one had seen it coming. Edith had always been a spare and angular woman, but imperceptibly she acquired the translucence of the terminally ill. His daughters had swooped down on them stirring the house with their anxieties, but nothing could be done.

Dr Ferguson had been sympathetic. It was he who had recommended The Willows Nursing Home where Edith could be cared for in those last few weeks when Harold couldn't cope. Harold hated it. All those relatives slipping in and out of the front door with sympathetic eyes and brave smiles. He wanted it to be over. Edith had led a quiet life and they wanted no drama at the end.

Harold's thoughts turned to Ludmilla and he remembered their first meeting. It was she who had brought him a cup of tea in the Resident's Lounge. When her shift ended the Ukrainian girl sat and talked to him. The Ukrainian girl held his hand. Hers was a nice soft plump hand, not like Edith's skeletal fingers. Ludmilla had a bright smile and hair as yellow as buttercups. The smell of the sickroom didn't cling to her skin as it did to his. He spoke little about Edith; she talked a lot about her son Mikhail. He didn't mention his daughters; she didn't mention her husband. Mikhail was a gifted child. At thirteen he spoke English and German as well as Russian. Ludmilla voiced her hopes that Mikhail would become a lawyer. Pride oozed from every pore in her body.

277

"And this is why I work here at The Willows," she said. "Momma looks after Mikhail while I am in England and I send back lots of money to look after them both."

Harold shut Edith out of his mind and spent a lot of time thinking about Ludmilla. There was so much he could do for her if they married. He was thirty years older than her but that wouldn't be a problem. She was used to old people and their ways. Mikhail could come to England and go to a good school. He wondered if his pension would stretch to law school but a talented boy like that would win a scholarship. Harold forgot about the present and his future blossomed. He hugged the dream to himself protecting it from his daughters' radar, but they found out anyway.

The service ended and the vicar led the procession down the aisle. Harold shuffled forward but already his eyes were searching out Ludmilla. It did not escape Emily and Pat that he didn't spare a glance for them. They bristled and pushed forward to form a barrier around their father as they passed the back pew. Their eyes were focussed on their mother's coffin while acid words squeezed through their tight lips.

"Blond tart. She's after his money!"

"He can't see it's the passport she wants!"

"She's not getting her hands on mother's jewellery, she meant it for me!"

This pulled Pat up short and she gave Emily a long calculating look.

Harold stood at the graveside while the vicar continued with the final acts of the service with painful deliberation. The undertakers gathered like crows around the coffin and lowered it into the grave. The vicar solemnly shook each of them by the hand and all the time the snow flurries were thickening but Ludmilla's hair still shone out across the

278

cemetery. Harold waved a hand to her indicating he would be over as soon as he could extricate himself.

Ludmilla's companion turned to her. "Well, we'd better get back to work, they'll be needing a hand with Mrs Jackson."

"I'm glad we came," Ludmilla said "Poor Mr Cooper, he is such a lonely man."

"You're too kind hearted you are," her companion pushed her gently. "You want to watch these old men. They'll think you fancy them!"

"What, Mr Cooper?" Ludmilla laughed. "Never! He is like my grandfather."

Across the graveyard she could see him and his family isolated like figures in a plastic snow dome. Together the women turned and slipped through the lych gate, their exit veiled by the swirling snow.

The Luthier's Granddaughter

by Natalie Donbavand

I have sexual problems. Well, I think I do anyway. When Eddie and I first got together I couldn't get enough of him. We used to fuck everywhere. Now I don't want him anywhere near me. I haven't grown tired of him, it was more sudden than that, everything seemed to change in a moment. One night, we were having drunken sex. I looked at him bending over me, pink-cheeked and breathless, and I felt disgusted. I pushed him from me.

'What's wrong?' he asked panting.

'I just don't think I want to have sex with you any more.'

That was it. Just saying it created a truth. Of course, I repented in the morning.

For a year I have been walking a fine line, avoiding sex where possible, giving Eddie just enough to keep him here. At the moment Eddie is trying to rehabilitate me. He has devised a seven step programme; it begins with kissing and ends in full sex. This evening we are at step six. I think it involves groping and masturbation. I lie between cool sheets and wait for him. I don't think I have ever liked sex.

He slides silently in beside me. I pretend to sleep.

'Claires,' he whispers in my ear, his lips grazing my skin. On the affectionate 's' he traces his tongue lightly against my flesh. I cannot ignore this gesture. I make a moan as if stirring in heavy sleep.

'Come on, Claire, you promised.'

'Ok, but just the next step.'

'Alright,' an impatient sigh escapes.

Eddie tugs at my pink pyjama top until it's up round my collar bone exposing my breasts. I make no move to help.

280

Damp unwanted kisses are daubed on every inch of my cheeks. He breathes heavily against my neck and his breath is warm and bitter with beer. I feel hands on my breasts. He squeezes them together, holding them with one fist before smearing them from one side of my rib cage to the other. It hurts me, but I make no sound. In the darkness I see his head travel downwards and his mouth clamps my right breast, tongue flickering over the nipple while he plucks at the left one with thumb and forefinger. I feel them grow erect from irritation rather than arousal. I turn my head to the pillow and tears escape. He cannot see me crying in the darkness, but surely he can sense my distress. If he does he chooses to ignore it.

'Ah fuck! It feels so good to be touching my fucking sexy girlfriend.'

I stay mute.

'Can I?'

'Ok.'

With my consent he straddles me, his erection pointing in accusation. He begins to touch himself, throwing his head back in excitement. I watch, feeling the itch of drying tears and wonder at my own detachment.

'Fuck, where can I cum?'

'Where ever you want.'

'All over your fucking tits.'

It is over. He kisses my forehead.

'Well done, Claire. I'll get some tissue.'

Satisfied buttocks sidle into the bathroom leaving me to look at the semen spread out across my chest.   There is saliva drying in sticky patches all over my face and neck, the sweat from his thighs forms a film round my stomach – I am covered in him.

I am sitting in the back seat of a small red car, my parents are in the front. We are parked in the centre of a

281

deserted car park. The grey of the tarmac meets the grey of the sky. Something feels threatening but we are unable to leave. Around the car circle two enormous eagles. My disquiet grows as I watch them. They are mating in mid air. The smaller male rests on top of the female. My eyes meet hers and she gives me a knowing stare.

I wake tangled in sheets. The smell of sex is everywhere.

I am off work. There is nothing wrong with me, but I can't function. I fight to think, but the effort is too great and I lapse back into something else. I have convinced the doctor, my colleagues, Eddie, that I have been bleeding for three weeks. The doctor has signed me off work with suspected anaemia. I have a week before the blood tests will come back showing nothing. The pain in my stomach feels real enough, but I recognise it as fear. I have a hospital appointment for an internal ultrasound. I am avoiding step seven. There is room for lies. I lie on the sofa and watch a continuous run of talk shows; Sally Jesse Raphael, Dr Phil, Montel Williams, Ricki Lake, Oprah Winfrey. I find something in common with every guest.

I am heavy with guilt and marking when I get in from work. A week's absence has created chaos with kids and supply teachers. It wasn't really worth being off. The worst thing was the sympathy.

'Hi Eddie.'
'Hi, Claire, how was your day?'
He is marking in the spare room.
'Fine.'
'The kitchen was a bit of a mess when I got in Claire.'
'Oh.'

282

'I had to tidy it before I started work.' He sounds waspish.

I seem to suffer from blindness with regard to household mess. From a seemingly spotless table Eddie can conjure forth an accusatory black hair, a pile of crumbs, drips of tea. I used to call him anal. Now I rarely object. I used to rage about feeling comfortable in my own home. Two years on I am meek. The reprimand has become a release. During my teacher training I was advised that prevention was better than a cure. Over the years since qualifying this has become my mantra. It seems to have seeped into every aspect of my life. I have been working harder and harder at becoming tidier. Each time Eddie raises the standard. His obsession has become mine, but for me it sits heavy, a toad in my psyche. I am so very tired.

I go to the bedroom to change my clothes.

The flat feels cool in the way that only newly built flats do in summer. I peel off my layers, lingering in various states of undress as the heat leaves my body. The inside of my wardrobe looks inviting and on an impulse I slip between the hanging clothes enjoying the textures against my skin. A polyester suit sends shooting pains through the roots of my teeth, I shimmy backwards until I touch cold satin. I rub it against my torso wondering at the smoothness.

'Claire? Claire where are you?'

'Coming, I'm here, I won't be a sec,' but moving quickly through coat hangers is impossible.

'What are you doing?'

As I reach the light Eddie's bemused face is waiting.

'Don't know.'

'You're a loony.'

I loose myself from the last coat hanger, grab a T shirt and jeans and try to move past him. He catches my elbow to pull me back. I recognise that staring, open mouth look as lust.

283

Too late, I guess his next move; his fingers are inside me and his palm cups my pubic hair.

'You're wet,' he challenges.

I lift myself from his fingers.

'I'm sweaty, I've been in a fucking suit all day, in a fucking hot classroom with no fucking blinds! Haven't you had a sweaty cock before?'

'You said you were going to try, Claire,'

'I am, but I'm tired and thirsty and disgusting.'

'Well tonight then, step seven?'

It feels like a quiet threat.

'Yes fine.'

I would promise him the world to be alone.

'When's tea?'

''bout an hour,'

'Ok, I'm off to finish those tests.'

He leaves.

I shove a lasagne in the oven and empty a bag of Caesar salad into a bowl. I sip my wine, allowing myself to feel the exhaustion. When I first started working, the frenetic teaching activity had impressed me. It made me feel like a real adult. For the first few weeks of 'living together' I was charmed by the necessity of household chores and of sharing a meal every night. Now it feels endless. Sometimes I have this fantasy; I am floating in the middle of miles of calm ocean, when I am struck with a compulsion to thrash. I thrash for a few minutes feeling complete abandon and then, slowly, I allow myself to sink. I invite the water into my open mouth. I feel guilty.

Eddie is still in the spare room. He is so disciplined. He can teach Maths all day, leave school at three, step through the door, open his brief case and *bang*, he is marking tests. My marking piles up until it seems insurmountable.

'Ed, dinner's ready. Do you want it in the study?'

'No. I'll eat with you.'

I want to watch Eastenders, but I can see from Eddie's agitated entrance that he wants to talk.

'I think I might have got another fucking three points today on the ring road.'

'What?'

'On my licence,'

'Oh dear,'

'Speed camera. Another three and I'll be banned.'

'Oh.'

'Eight miles over the speed limit and they are going to fuck me over for it.'

He is winding himself up.

'It's all money making, Claire. The government want to penalise the motorist all the time.'

'Calm down Ed.'

'I may as well just murder some one, then I'll get out after a few years – another eight miles an hour and I'll be banned from driving.'

'Did it definitely get you?'

'I'm not sure, but if I get banned I'm going to go on driving, fuck it! Everyone else does it.'

He rants on. I know better than to pacify when he starts on the state of the country. It is best to wait until he exhausts himself. Finally he picks up his plate.

'I'm off to finish those tests.'

Eastenders is over. I look around our flat and think about what to do. I am too tired to invite a friend over. I don't really like friends coming over any more. Eddie is so competitive with them. He draws them into debate and argues with public school boy aggression. They feel insulted and he acts bemused. I try to patch things over, but I know what they are thinking; *why is she going out with him?* I feel embarrassed. Of course they never say it to my face, when we

285

are out alone they hint around it. I could say he isn't like that with me, but it just seems so weak. For some reason I think of playing the guitar, but it disturbs Eddie when he is working. The spare room is full of guitars that I don't play; I rarely have the time now. They were part of my single life. Eddie wants me to sell them so we can afford blinds. A desire to play has been growing in me for weeks. I doubt I will be any good any more. I have been watching Aquilina Ramillos play at The Fleece. She is amazing. Her grandfather was a master luthier. How I would love to play Flamenco guitar in a Spanish square saturated with heat, music, shouting and laughter. The flat is silent. My own marking sits untouched. I go to bed, hoping to be asleep before Eddie wants to climb more steps.

I am on the outside of a large iron case. My best friend from school is inside. I can hear her screaming. Someone is hurting her. I Claw frantically at the box to get in. My hands are bleeding.

The dream is just another in a long line of disturbing nocturnal meanderings, but it has done its job; I can't sleep. I can't lie next to Eddie. I leave his side to pace the flat. Round and round. This time I know that I can't face the morning. I can't meet the needs of the children I teach. I can't meet the needs of my colleagues. I can't meet the needs of my home and most of all I can't meet Eddie's needs. There is not enough of me. I am patchy, insubstantial, and so tired. I stop pacing as the darkness begins to fade to grey. Exhausted, I sit on the floor of the spare room, its half-light filled with the curvy shadows of guitars. If only their sexy curves could take some pressure off me. I wrap myself around one, tracing my fingers over the tuning pegs, treble strings, base strings and finally I circle the sound hole, my fingers sending particles of pungent cedar out into the air. The smell is fresh – comforting, and I wish to be held secure in this heavy dawn forever.

286

'Claire? Claire? Where are you?'

The sound is muffled but it is enough to rouse me.

'Claire? For fuck's sake!'

There is a note of worry is Eddie's voice which forces my eyes to open. I am met by complete darkness. Confused, I attempt to move – my head, arms, knees, are pressed firm against something solid. Panic begins to engulf me. All I can do is wriggle. There is no light. I scrabble and scrape until I have turned ninety degrees. My back is forced into an aching arch. I can discern nothing. I muster all the effort I can and manage another ninety. Now I am met by a weak yellow light streaming through a port hole. I push my face towards the light until my cheek bones hit cold wire and a vibration shakes my body. I am inside a guitar.

The noise of the strings brings Eddie into the room.

'Eddie I'm here, here in the guitar.'

'Jesus Christ, this can't be happening.'

'Well it is.'

'How the fuck did you get in there?'

'Don't shout.'

'What the fuck would you do? How did you get in?'

'I don't know. I think I kind of wished it.'

'You think you kind of wished it? Why the fuck would you wish to be inside a guitar?'

'I don't know, just stuff.'

'Stuff, fucking stuff! It isn't physically possible,' he is sounding manic. 'You've gone insane haven't you? I could see this coming you know - I could. You have gone fucking insane and you're taking me with you. It isn't real, it isn't real.'

'It is real.'

He straightens up and begins pacing.

'I'm late. I'm going to be late.'

I want him to leave.

'Go to work, I'll be ok.'

'What about your work Claire? Did you forget about that while you were making your wishes?'

'Can you ring in sick for me?'

'What? Again? That will make me even fucking later.'

'Well so will arguing.'

'Oh, fine.'

He goes to leave and then turns.

'Surely, you can just wish yourself out of there then?'

'I'm not sure I want to.'

'I'm not sure I want you to either,' is his cold reply.

He storms out and I feel hot wet tears fall down my cheeks. I take deep breaths and will the cedar to lull me back to dreamless sleep.

'Claire, Claire.'

Eddie's face is pressed against the sound hole. He pushes a daisy between the strings looking sad. I take it.

'Thanks.'

'I'm sorry. I do want you to come out.'

'I know.'

'What do you think happened?'

I don't know – I think I just wanted to escape.'

'From what?'

I fall silent. What can I say? I can't say 'from you – from sex.'

'That's ridiculous! You know we have a lovely life here. How many twenty five year olds in Bath own a flat like this? I'll tell you what it is. It's depression. You let the kids get you down too easily. The mind is a powerful thing Claire. It's all chemicals. I'll call your mother.'

'Not my mother.'

My mother sits for an hour with her face pressed up against the strings. She tells me that she understands the pressures of keeping a house, of keeping a man happy. She

288

understands that my job is demanding. She tells me in great detail about a bout of depression she had at my age. At last she asks me to come out. I don't want to. She tells me that she cannot cope with me. She tells me that I have always been difficult. She tells me I am not the only person with problems. At last she leaves; angry red string prints mark her skin like war paint.

My mother's exit ushers Eddie into the room.

'What's doing this?' He rattles the strings in frustration until they hurt my ears.

'I don't know! Me - I don't know!'

'Think Claire! - Is there something special about this guitar?'

'Which one am I in?'

'Fuck. I don't know.'

'Describe it.'

'Well it's smaller and plainer than the others.'

'The Ramillos.' My mind whirls.

'Who's that?'

'A Spanish luthier from Andalusia. He's famous. Remember I told you I bought it in a second hand shop with Penny.'

'No.'

'Oh.'

'So what does that mean?'

'I don't know, nothing – maybe – I go to see his granddaughter play in The Fleece.'

'Right! How can we contact her?'

'You can't contact her. What has it got to do with her? I saw her play. I've spoken to her a few times. That's it. You're panicking.'

'How can I contact her?'

'There's a flyer in my bag.'

'Right.'

'This is silly, Eddie.'

He gets up.

'Where are you going?'

'To get the granddaughter.'

I wait anxiously in the gathering dark.

A light switch sounds and fake light streams in through the sound hole. A sharp set of features meet mine. My stomach aches with need or fear or both.

'Hello.'

Red lips look faintly amused.

'Aquilina – I'm sorry, this has nothing to do with you.'

On the contrary, my grandfather's guitars are known for their magical qualities.'

She winks at me and I can't tell if she is joking or not.

'How did you get in there?'

'I think I wished for it.'

'Why?'

'I don't know.'

'It must have been quite a powerful wish for my grandfather to help you.'

I glance away.

'I think you probably know very well Claire.'

Her eyes stare and I feel like she is seeing inside me.

'Tell me.'

I tell her everything. I surprise myself. I talk about work, my mother, the flat, Eddie and our sex life. She doesn't stop me. I talk for hours until eventually there is no more.

'You are tired, Claire.'

'I am.'

'Let me tell you a story. A fairy tale. One my mother used to tell me when I was sad. Maybe afterwards you might be able to get out of there.'

290

She begins;

Once upon a time there were two young lovers named Clamencia and Jose. When they asked for her parent's permission to marry, her mother, who was a witch, denied it.

One day when Jose was in the corral caring for the mules, the mother decided to kill him, thus ending the love affair. The witch went in search of her husband and said to him, "Old man, tell Jose to go to the pasture and bring back the black mule."

When Clamencia heard this, she guessed that the witch was trying to kill her lover. She explained to Jose, "Shortly my father will come and tell you to bring a black mule from the pasture. The mule is my mother. If you ride her she will buck you and kill you. When you mount the mule make sure you bend over and bite her ear, she will be powerless then."

Everything happened as planned and that night Clamencia and Jose decided that they would elope. Before leaving, Clamencia was careful to spit on her bed.
Soon after the witch awoke and began calling Clamencia. The spittle that had been left on the bed answered "Mother?"

The witch went back to bed. It was not until morning that she discovered that she had been tricked. She was so angry that she turned herself into an eagle and flew in search of the couple.

Later that morning Clamencia saw an eagle in the sky and recognised it to be her mother. She dropped a comb on the ground, which sprang up into a huge forest. The eagle could not fly over it, so she landed on the earth and turned back into a witch. She made the forest disappear and then resumed her disguise as the eagle.

When Clamencia saw that her mother was still after them, she threw a mirror down, which became a lake so wide that the eagle could not fly over it. The eagle landed, and the

291

witch got rid of the lake before transforming herself back again.

In a final attempt to stop her mother Clemencia threw a handful of ashes into the air. The ashes turned into a dense fog which the eagle could not cross. As it was getting dark, the witch could not follow the lovers anymore.

Before flying home, the witch cursed the lovers saying, "Bad daughter, remember that your lover will leave you as soon as you arrive at the first village."

Aquilina stops abruptly and looks round, as if noticing, for the first time, the darkness of the room.

'What happens? Does he leave her?'

'Hmm, maybe I will leave the ending up to you. Do you think you could come out now?'

The cedar has become overpowering. Her eyes are dark and concerned. She does not want anything from me. I begin to make my way out.

Eddie and I follow her down the tiny hallway. He is so grateful, and I want to be near her for as long as possible.

'Thanks for the story,' I manage, as she leaves.

'Remember, comb, mirror, ashes,'

'I will, thanks.'

Eddie shuts the door and then drapes his arm round me, his hand brushes backwards and forwards against my right breast.

'It's good to see you looking better, Claires.'

He plants a kiss on top of my head and I feel my stomach start to writhe.

Sitting at my dressing table I think of Aquilina's story and then of the silly thing I have done. I open my makeup draw to reveal a comb, a mirror and a tiny bag of ash scraped from Eddie's ashtray. Looking up I see Eddie watching me in the glass, his eyes are roaming my naked shoulders. With out

292

reasoning I pick up the comb and start separating knotted strands of my hair.

'What are you doing now?'

'Combing my hair.'

'You've just spent about fifteen minutes brushing it.'

'I want it in plaits, so that it'll be wavy tomorrow.'

'Well, hurry up.'

I have a sense of something. Using the teeth of the comb, I divide the layers of hair until I reveal the fleshy white line of my scalp. Slowly I twist and pull the hair into symmetrical school girl plaits. I turn the light out, and stagger through the darkness towards our bed. I pull back the sheets and slide in next to Eddie. Before he goes to reach me, I slide the comb between us and hope.

I feel it instantaneously, like the force between the north sides of two magnets. Eddie and I are moving, almost imperceptibly, but I can feel it. It is warm and firm against my belly, a hug from no one and I feel so secure, so peaceful. I look at Eddie, settled on the far side of the bed and his usually petulant face carries a contented smile. It is what I've imagined dying to feel like.

The card is black. In the centre of it is an Indian elephant, it is tiny and gold and so detailed! It is for her, to say thank you. I know it was her. It is the first real sleep I have had in months. Eddie says he didn't notice anything. She has given me presents to keep him away – to keep me going. I bought the card after work. I was there ages. The woman kept giving me funny looks. Nothing seemed right enough, good enough. This card was the best one. I am too shy to give it to her, so I am sending it to The Fleece. The landlord there will deliver it. I didn't know what to say. I sat in front of the computer intending to write a long letter, to tell her everything, but all that appeared on the screen was 'I think you are really

293

wonderful'. I tried to write something else but I kept coming back to that. Eventually I gave up; I printed it out, cut it out and stuck it on. I will not sign it. She will know who it's from.

I feel certain that when these three gifts run out she will send me more. I huddle beneath the duvet and place the mirror in the space beside me. I compare my domestic space with that of Clamencia and I feel hemmed in, embarrassed by the narrow limits this fantastic magic has to work in. I lie weeping quietly, listening to the click of keys coming from the spare room.

I am roused from sleep by an unusual warmth against my thigh, then there is a whisper in the darkness.

'Oh my God! Shit. I don't believe it.'

I am slow with sleep but I register that the voice is Eddie's. I struggle to gain full consciousness. He is out of bed leaning over the mattress.

'Ed, what's wrong?'

'Claire, I'm so embarrassed. I can't... I'm so embarrassed.'

'What? What's happened?'

'I don't know. I lay down for a second and I was wetting myself. I couldn't control it. I seriously couldn't control it. I'm sorry.'

I put my hand down to find that the warmth near my thigh is now cold and wet.

'Ed, it happens to us all sometimes.'

'Not at 29.'

'Come on, let's,'

'What if there's something wrong with me? I couldn't stop it.'

I get up and guide him into the living room. I make a makeshift bed on the sofa while he sits between remorse and panic. Stripping the bed, I feel ashamed. When I have finished

Eddie is nearly asleep on the sofa. I curl up next to him, holding him like a baby.

I sit at the back of the Fleece watching her. Her fingers create music faster than my racing thoughts. It soothes me. Eddie sits sipping rum and coke next to me. His hand on my shoulder. His hands are always on me. Occasionally I feel her gaze upon me. It rests more heavily than his fingers, but I turn away. When she dedicates a song to me, Eddie squeezes my arm. I have done well in his eyes, making friends with a famous person. I concentrate on the cluttered pattern of the carpet and let her voice transport me elsewhere.

Getting ready for bed, getting ready to sleep next to him makes me feel sick. Only the ashes remain. Instinctively I scatter them on Eddie's pillow. He will want sex. He always wants sex after drinking. Will she help me again after this? I am terrified of being without her. Eddie is in the bath room, humming, splashing. He is so self satisfied, so sure. How can he see so little? He turns off the light and gets into bed smelling of mint.

'Claire, where have you gone?'

He is reaching for me, but he cannot find me. He gets out of bed and turns on the lights. I sit up. I hear him storming round the flat. He cannot see me. I daren't test to see if he can hear me. Eddie rings my mother, the police, who tell him they can't do anything, all of my friends. I hear him go out to drive round looking for me. I pull the sheets up round my neck. I am too relieved to feel guilty. She makes me feel special.

I am off work. There is nothing wrong with me, but I cannot function. I lie on the sofa and watch a continuous run of talk shows; Sally Jesse Raphael, Dr Phil, Montel Williams, Ricki Lake, Oprah Winfrey. I find something in common with every guest. There are no more lies to be told. No more gifts from

295

Aquilina. There is only me. Eddie screamed at me this morning when he could see me. I stood mute. He left for work. I lay on the sofa and watched a continuous run of talk shows; Sally Jesse Raphael, Dr Phil, Montel Williams, Ricki Lake, Oprah Winfrey ...

'Claire I'm back.'

I say nothing. He finds me on the sofa.

'Claire, you've been home all day and you haven't even done the washing up.'

I sob shoulder shaking sobs. Eddie looks lost.

'Oh Claires,' he kneels beside me rubbing my back.

'I'm sorry I shouted. Come on we'll go to Sainsbury's and get something nice for tea.'

I follow him around Sainsbury's. He chatters brightly. I can't hear anything, can't see anything, all I can feel is an empty ache. I am scared this is all I will ever feel.

'What about a nice curry to cheer you up Claires?'

I don't say anything.

'Claire, talk to me.'

'I don't think I want to go out with you any more.'

The words hang in the air like magic.

The Crying of the Lilies

by Elaine Walker

Once there were stories and lilies. And the stories grew and the lilies grew and I grew among them all, nurtured by his green fingers. I grew and I flourished. I remember those glasshouse years that mark the roots of my own story. The sun always shone and I basked in his watchfulness, while his warm stories were all the seasons and the scent of lilies was creamy-white. I wandered through the forest of their murmuring green stems, over my head when I was small, until the days when I could see the open flowers face-to-face and I began to wonder.

Soon I could see over their heads and through the shining glass to the beyond, and when he said, 'Michael, have I told you ….?' I said, 'Yes, Dad, but have I told you….?'

And so it ended. I shattered the glass once its oppressive heat was all I could feel and the moist cling of peat around my feet made me fretful for my own ground. I broke out and the lilies withered a little for lack of me until he coaxed them back to life. But he sealed himself within the glass that cocooned them and he told no more stories.

Resentful, I tried to leave him behind, over time and distance, his hands in the earth and gentle on the flower stems but his face no longer smiling and opening like a book. I believed that all I had left was the memory of an unfinished tale and a withered blossom pressed and hidden between secret pages. But I was wrong, of course. Once the tale's begun, it has to follow its course. That's what neither of us realised. We didn't lose the story. We only lost the pleasure of sharing of it with each other. So while we shared only blame, recriminations and then silence, the flowers kept growing, blooming, but something inside us both shrivelled and died.

Now I'm afraid that I have no story of my own and that all that's left is to tell the lonely one which is his, over and over again. So, in need and fear, I go when the call comes, driving through the night, and I'm aware of them as soon as I arrive. Lilies, mourning, lamenting lilies. Their heavy scent is visible as I enter the house, filling the hallway as it snakes out around the slightly open door of the best sitting-room in a fine mist of white. I wonder if his soul is leaving in that soft thread fragranced with waxy sweetness so I close the front door carefully but quickly, not yet ready to let him leave.

'Michael! Come in, my love!' My aunt's voice is warm with concern and I am enfolded to a generous bosom and then moved along an awkward line of family members to be embraced or patted or hand-shaken until I reach the door where the sound is waiting.

It is a soft keening, soft but inconsolable and, as I push the door and enter alone, I'm surrounded by their drooping white faces and waxy petals, and their grieving voices. They are gathered in tall cool vases at the head and foot of the open coffin where my father lies very still, waiting for me to make my peace with him so he can leave. The lilies sob softly and I realise that their weeping's not for his death, but for his life. For its ending, when his heart was unshriven, our stories all untold, and the love undoubtedly between us still anguished and painful.

The grace of the flowers recalls my long-dead mother in her languid beauty and when I touch a petal, I feel the sliding of my fingers over her sleek black hair and translucent skin, white as any lily. Instantly, I return to the days when her affection and loveliness wrapped me in sweetness. She folded pale arms around me, kept me safe. She filled my eyes and my heart with herself. In the days after the stories ended, she protected me from my regrets. She was fragile and strong, like the lilies that surrounded the lonely man then and surround

298

him now, soothing guardians, keeping him company in his dreamless waiting. The long stamens of spring-tasting green echo the curve of the arching petals and as I lean over to breathe the heavy, familiar scent, I feel its white soul-thread like sweet smoke. It swirls through my head and down my throat to curl around my heart and only then can I take the step forward and look down upon the face in its last sleep.

My father's face, beloved and feared, the source of my narrative, dried up long ago and become silent for me, as much in life as now. He is unfamiliar, remote, his skin waxy like the flowers and the strange robe of white silk he's dressed in making him look like the Pope. I want to smile at the image to crack open my heart, but everything in me is atrophied like the still man, frozen by the falling tears of the weeping flowers. My words are frozen too and my mouth won't frame them into shapes. But as I struggle, a soft unfamiliar sound like a breeze brushes through the room and I hear my voice in the shimmering petals of the lilies.

'I'm not ready for you to leave,' I say, though my lips haven't moved and my voice is silent. 'I've missed you too much in life to let you leave me now.'

And like a blessing, he replies through that petalled sheen in the voice I once knew like sunshine on my childhood, 'Michael, son, I've missed you too. This was the only way we could find one another again. '

The soft sobbing of the lilies is a hum around his voice.

'I don't understand.' I say and I want to touch him, but I'm afraid to feel the truth of his absence and can't yet.

'Nothing else would have brought you here to share your voice with mine again, son. We stopped speaking the same language long ago.'

'You never wanted to hear me!' The wave of my voice rises, shimmering in the trembling flower heads, petulant as a child's and I'm ashamed of myself.

'Oh, but I did.' my father says, lying still, calm and voiceless, surrounded by the soft rippling music of silk and the compassionate flowers, 'Can you forgive me?'

I look at his serene face, the furious frown and deeply etched lines of bitterness I know so intimately now smoothed out and gone. I wish I'd seen such peace in his living face, just once, just always.

Something in my heart opens and flowers like a lily,

'There's nothing to forgive.' I say, but can't help letting the fear pour out of me too, 'I became a disappointment to you.'

There's a long silence as emotions surge and move between us, glimmering tracks of dark purple like old bruises, soothed by the white mist of the lily scent, until softly, so very softly, he says, 'I was more proud of you than I knew how to express.' There's a suggestion of pain and regret and the dark purple melts into violet and soft lilac, 'Once I fell silent, I didn't know how to recover the words.' Then he's silent again until his voice rises, deep green, 'When your mother kissed you and held you, I was jealous. I lost the use of my arms around you once you grew too old to listen to my stories.'

'But I never did!' I protest, with a misery that I didn't know was in me. The lilies seem to droop further over him, so heavy that their tears fall glistening onto his face to run over his cheekbones and down to his carved jaw. I lean over him so my own tears join them, and I feel their encouragement as they urge me on. I remember the days when we grew and thrived together, nurtured by his careful hands. My voice is incandescent, radiating through their soft light, 'I always wanted your stories. I thought you stopped telling them to punish me. I never stopped missing them.'

300

'I was afraid of you outgrowing them. I stopped telling them before you could say you didn't want them anymore, because I couldn't bear it.'

I'm sobbing like the lilies now, and I feel the surging green of my own growth begin to move. The long years wasting in the bud have made me fearful but now I'm unfolding,

'Dad, I'd never have done that. But I grew old enough to have stories to tell you, too. We could have shared them, but it's too late now.'

The fragrance of the flowers swirls around us like a spring breeze and they raise their drooping faces in hope.

'Son, it's never too late. That's why I've waited, so I could tell you this best story of all - that none of them ever end and they're all true. Tell me your stories and I'll hear, wherever I am. And if you listen, mine will reach you. You know how, don't you?'

I smile then, looking at the flowers, hearing his voice in the flowers, 'Yes, I know. I'll take care of them and while I do, I'll tell you everything and I'll listen. I'll listen always Dad.'

I feel a touch, an embrace, and as I lean down to return the kiss, the touch of my lips on his cool brow releases him. I see him leave, his glimmering soul blue like the evening, entwined with the white fragrant flower-mist. He weaves his way around me and up to fade into the shadows of the room and we're both at peace.

The door opens cautiously and my family look in, wary and careful, aunts, uncles, cousins, gathered awkwardly dutiful and truly concerned. I turn to smile at them, full of stories, as the flourishing lilies lift up their faces and begin to sing.